Amy

Linda Sole titles available from
Severn House Large Print

The Bonds That Break
Bridget
A Cornish Rose
The Hearts that Hold
Kathy
The Rose Arch
A Rose in Winter
Song for Athena
The Ties That Bind

AMY

Linda Sole

Severn House Large Print
London & New York

This first large print edition published in Great Britain 2005 by
SEVERN HOUSE LARGE PRINT BOOKS LTD of
9-15 High Street, Sutton, Surrey, SM1 1DF.
First world regular print edition published 2004 by
Severn House Publishers, London and New York.
This first large print edition published in the USA 2005 by
SEVERN HOUSE PUBLISHERS INC., of
595 Madison Avenue, New York, NY 10022.

British Library Cataloguing in Publication Data

Sole, Linda
Amy. - Large print ed.
1. East End (London, England) - Social conditions - Fiction
2. Domestic fiction
3. Large type books
I. Title
823.9'14 [F]

ISBN 0-7278-7423-3

Printed and bound in Great Britain by
MPG Books Ltd, Bodmin, Cornwall.

One

As a small child I was afraid of the man with the staring eyes. In my worst nightmares he came after me, shouting and threatening to kill me. His breath stank of strong drink and his eyes were bloodshot. In my dreams he caught me and then my father came and chased him away – but he always came back, and I knew that one day my father would not be there to save me.

Perhaps it was because of the dream that I hated living in the lanes. In the dream I was playing in the lane near my home with other children, and it was there that the man came after me. For as long as I could remember I had wanted to escape, to live somewhere different, away from the dirt and noise of the area around the London docks, and I envied my uncle Tom, who had gone away to be a doctor. I had promised myself that when I grew up I would leave, too, and my idea of heaven was probably very like the house that Matthew's parents lived in, at which I had been staying for the past few days.

Living in suburbia might not be everyone's

idea of perfect bliss, but it was certainly mine. Looking back at the Corders' house on that sunny morning in June 1923, I experienced a deep sense of loss and regret that it was time for us to leave. There was nothing remarkable about the house; it had three bedrooms and a bathroom upstairs, a sitting room, dining room and kitchen downstairs, and was furnished in a very ordinary way. Yet for me those few days had been ones of perfect contentment.

'What was that sigh for?' Matthew asked, looking at me with a little smile of amusement flickering about his mouth.

Matthew Corder was twenty-three, four years older than me, attractive rather than wildly handsome, with reddish-brown hair and dark chocolate-brown eyes. It was his smile that had made me notice him, the laughter in his eyes that saw the fun in everything that first made me fall in love with him.

We had met at Bournemouth, when Matthew was on holiday and I was taking the art classes that my mother thought were a waste of time. Although she had encouraged my brothers, Jon and Terry, to leave when they were my age, she had wanted to keep me at home. My father had persuaded her that it would do me good to see more of the world, to broaden my outlook on life, and so in the end she had agreed that I should go.

To me, my father was the most wonderful person in the whole world, and I adored him. Although even I couldn't have called him handsome, he had a kind, generous face and there was so much love in him for all of us. When I was small I loved the days best when my father took us somewhere special. It might be the seaside, or a trip to the fair or a visiting circus, or it might just be a day spent walking in the country, but whatever it was I was happy because he was with us.

In the eyes of the world, Joe Robinson had done all right for himself. He owned a lot of property and he wasn't short of a bob or two, as the people of the lanes might say. He could have lived in a house like the Corders owned, or perhaps somewhere even better, but my mother refused to move from the lane she had lived in for most of her life, and my father always gave her exactly what she wanted.

Sometimes I felt angry with my mother because she refused to let him buy us a better house, but deep down I loved her. I loved her almost as much as I loved my father, but not quite. No one could ever take my father's place in my heart – not even Matthew.

'I was just wishing we didn't have to leave,' I said and shook my head as I saw the teasing light in his eyes. 'It's all right for you – you don't have to go back to the lanes.'

'I like your parents' house,' Matthew said and looked serious. 'I know the area isn't the best, but the house is lovely inside.'

'I hate the lanes,' I said. 'I want to live in something like this one day, Matt. And I want it to be in a nice area, a place where people don't swear and drink all the time.'

'That's a bit harsh. There are some really good people in Farthing Lane. Your parents don't drink to excess and Joe doesn't swear either. I admire your parents, and particularly your mother for being proud of her roots.'

'But I can't stay in the house all the time. You haven't heard the noise they make coming out of the Feathers on a Saturday night. It's enough to waken the dead.'

'You're a snob, Amy Robinson,' Matthew said with a teasing smile. 'Your father gave you everything you ever wanted and you've been utterly spoiled.'

'Yes, I know.' I was half ashamed as I met his eyes. We'd had this conversation before and he always won, because in my heart I knew he was right. 'It isn't that I don't appreciate all they've done for me. I just don't want to live there any more.'

'Surely you can put up with it for a while?' Matthew raised his brows at me. 'We agreed that we wouldn't get married for another year or so. I can't afford to buy a house yet, and I don't want to start out living with my parents.'

'I wouldn't mind.' I gazed back longingly at the house we had just left as Matthew opened the door of his Austin saloon for me. He was the sales representative for a firm of gentlemen's tailoring and he had to travel all over London and the Home Counties with his samples, which was why he could afford to run such a nice car. 'I like your parents, Matt. And it would only be for a while.'

'No, Amy,' Matthew said and his mouth drew into a thin line. We'd had this conversation more than once, too. 'I told you it would be a while before we could marry, and you agreed you were willing to wait.'

'Of course I'll wait,' I said, sliding into the car which smelled of leather and new clothes. 'I don't have much choice, do I?'

Matthew closed the door on me. Glancing at his face as he slid into the driving seat, I saw that a little nerve was flicking at his temple and knew he was annoyed with me. I bit down on my bottom lip, stopping myself from saying all the things that were on the tip of my tongue. How could Matthew understand what I felt about going home when I had never told him?

I might have told him about the dreams if I had thought it would make a difference, but I knew he would just dismiss them as being nonsense.

'It was just a dream,' he would say.

'Besides, you're grown up now and you should have the sense to stay away from men who have been drinking.'

Matthew was very practical. Sometimes I would have liked him to be more romantic. It would have been nice to be courted with bouquets of flowers and expensive gifts, but though he bought me some good perfume on my birthday and a box of Cadbury's chocolates when we went to the pictures, he was never extravagant.

'If we want a nice home, I have to save,' he'd told me when he saw the expensive leather bag and shoes my father had given me for my birthday. 'I'll give you things like that one day, Amy – when I've climbed up the ranks a bit. I'm not going to be a sales rep all my life. I'm going to apply for a manager's job the first chance I get, and one day I'll have a shop of my own.'

I knew that my father would have lent him the money to set up his own business if he'd asked, but it would be a waste of breath to tell him that. Matthew was proud, and I admired him for his determination to get ahead by his own efforts. In fact I was pretty much head over heels in love with him, and I hated our quarrels, all of which were of my making.

Matthew was hard working, honest and decent – all the things I had been taught to admire and wanted in the man I would marry one day. Yet there were times when I wished that he would do something reckless for once. My life was pleasant and easy, but not often exciting.

Hearing me sigh, Matthew glanced my way.

'Couldn't you go and stay with your aunt again? I thought she wanted you to work for her?'

'Yes, she does.' I smiled as I thought of Aunt Lainie. She owned an expensive gown shop in the West End of London and lived in the flat above. I had stayed with her several times in the past. 'But my mother doesn't want me to live with Lainie. When I suggested it she looked hurt and I felt awful.'

'I'm sure she would understand if you explained. After all, it would be a nice place for you to work, wouldn't it?'

'Yes...' I left my thoughts unspoken. Matthew was thinking that we could save more if I was also at work, and that was true. What I didn't care to explain was that I didn't particularly want to work in my aunt's shop – or any shop. My ambition was to design clothes. At art college I had discovered that I was quite good at it, and I'd already sent out some of my designs to various commercial fashion houses. So far I hadn't received any replies. 'It's a nice shop. Aunt Lainie has made it even more exclusive now that she owns it. She says they get a really good clientele these days, so I suppose it would be all right.'

Matthew laughed. 'Lainie O'Rourke is an even bigger snob than you, Amy. To speak to her you would think she'd been born with a silver spoon in her mouth, and she couldn't be more different from your mother. No one would ever think they were sisters.'

Matthew made no secret of the fact that he adored my mother. He had told me that Bridget Robinson was one of the finest ladies he had ever met. It wasn't that he disliked Lainie, simply that he thought her a little selfish sometimes.

Of course, he didn't know Lainie as I did. She might seem selfish to people who only saw one side of her, but I knew she was very different underneath. Lainie was tough in matters of business, but she could be kind when someone was in trouble. I remembered the way she had looked after one of her girls at the shop when her father had thrown her out of her home because she was pregnant. Lainie had sent the girl away somewhere to have the baby, and afterwards she had given her a job in the back room doing alterations. Most employers would have sacked her, but Lainie had gone out of her way to help, and I admired that.

'Sally has put the baby out with a good family,' Lainie told me. 'She needs to work to support her son, but at least she wasn't forced to give him up.'

Her eyes had seemed to reflect a deep sadness as she spoke, and I'd sensed something hidden. I had always known that Lainie had a secret. As a small child I'd picked up whispers, sentences left unfinished and knowing looks between my mother and aunt. And I knew that Lainie hated the area in which she had lived as a child as much as I did.

'If it were not for Bridget I would never set foot in that street again,' she had told me once when I'd asked why she didn't visit us very often. 'I don't want to remember that part of my life, Amy. It's over and finished, and I am a different person. I've educated myself, dragged myself out of the mire and slime, and it was damned hard work. I shall never let myself be dragged back into that kind of a life, and if Bridget had any sense she would move right away from the docks. Joe wants to buy her a decent house somewhere and she's a fool not to jump at the chance.'

'I wish she would! Then I needn't go back ever again.'

'You could always live with me, Amy. You know I would love to have you.'

There was something in her eyes then that made me wonder if she was lonely. Lainie was an attractive woman, with softly waved fair hair that she kept looking immaculate, and a trim figure. In her early forties, she had never married but I didn't know why. She must surely have been asked.

I knew she had lots of friends – married couples and more than one single gentleman. Occasionally she went out to dinner with one of the gentlemen, but I didn't think that any of them were ever invited to stay over at her apartment. I certainly hadn't seen any telltale signs of a male guest when I stayed there, though I believed there must have been men in her past.

Had someone hurt her badly? I'd tried to ask my mother about it once, but she had simply changed the subject. It was a part of the secret I had always known existed.

'So what are you thinking now?' Matthew's question brought me out of my reverie.

'Nothing much. When am I going to see you again?'

'Not for a couple of weeks, Amy. I've got one of my big trips on again. The firm has a new customer from Manchester and they want me to set up the account.'

'Couldn't someone local do it?'

'It's important, Amy. If I do this right it may mean a chance for promotion.'

'Yes, I know. You told me. It's just that I shall miss you. I hate it when you go away.'

'I shall miss you too,' he said, and smiled as he pulled into the forecourt of what appeared to be a sixteenth-century inn. It was set back off the road amongst trees and had a pleasant, peaceful atmosphere, almost as if we had been whisked back in time. 'I thought we would stop here for a drink and we might have a meal. I believe they do reasonable food here and it's not too expensive.'

'That would be nice.' I leaned across to kiss him as he pulled on the handbrake, breathing in his fresh, clean smell. Matthew was wholesome and decent, and I loved him. 'And I'm sorry if I was grumpy earlier. I do understand that we have to save. I'll talk to Mum about going to work for Lainie. If I'm earning as well we can get things we want for the house that bit sooner.'

Matthew gave me an approving smile. 'A year or so will soon go round,' he promised. 'Believe me, it's even harder for me to wait than it is for you, love.'

I knew that it had sometimes been difficult for Matthew to call a halt when we had been kissing in the back seat of his car. We had reached the stage where I had allowed him to fondle my breasts, but Matthew himself had insisted that anything more was out for the moment.

'If I touched you there...' His breathing was heavy and he smiled in that self-mocking way that made me love him so much. 'I don't think I could stop myself going all the way, and we would end up having to get married. That's the last thing we need, Amy

– much as I want you.'

I didn't want to *have* to get married either. For one thing it would hurt my parents, especially my father, and I wanted a special wedding with all the trimmings and lots of presents. In April, Lady Elizabeth Bowes-Lyon had married her duke, wearing a lovely gown, and I had already planned my own, which would be quite similar to the one she had chosen. So I hadn't tried to persuade Matthew into something that we both knew was wrong.

'We'll wait,' I said as he opened the car door for me to get out. I was hit by the smell of roses and stocks from the flowerbeds, and as we walked across the moss-covered flagstones towards the inn, I was conscious of the sun shining warmly down on us. 'We'll do things properly the way you want, Matt. As you said, it won't be forever.'

'I love you, Amy,' Matthew said. 'And one day I'm going to give you all the things you want.'

'I know you will, but mostly I just want to be with you.'

I linked my arm through his, shivering slightly as we entered the cool of the inn, which smelled a little musty despite the copper bowls of dried rose petals that stood on an oak hutch just inside the door. It was foolish of me to be so impatient when I had so much.

* * *

I awoke with a start that night, shivering and slightly damp because I had been sweating. The room was in darkness and I was trembling as I reached for the switch, flooding the corners with electric light. I was so thankful that my father had had electricity installed when he did up the house. I was shaking too badly to have lit the paraffin lamps that most people in the lanes still used upstairs, though they had gas downstairs.

The dream had been so vivid this time, and it had changed. I was no longer a little girl but a woman. The man who had threatened me had had no face, but I knew exactly how his eyes would look – open and staring as if he were dead.

Getting out of bed, I pulled on my dressing gown and slippers. I would never rest unless I made myself a warm drink and waited for the dream to fade.

I was just making a mug of cocoa in the kitchen when my father came in, also dressed in pyjamas and a comfortable old robe.

'Did I wake you?'

'I wasn't asleep. Some nights I don't sleep much any more, then I come down and make myself a drink.'

I looked anxiously at him. He wasn't ill, was he?

'Have some of mine. I've made enough for

two. In the lodgings I shared in Bournemouth there was always someone to share it.'

'Are you missing that? I know there isn't much for you to do here, Amy.'

'I think I should get a job, Daddy.'

'There's no need for you to do that. Unless you want to?'

'As you said, there isn't much for me to do here.'

'Your mother thought you might like to help with the flowers for her stalls sometimes, what with you being good at artistic things. She sells quite a few of her arrangements these days. People come from all over to buy them. She has made quite a reputation for herself. I've offered to set her up in a shop but Bridget has always liked market trading.'

'Yes, I know.' I smiled at him, feeling a warm affection for this man who loved us all so much. He was so very special. 'I don't mind helping while I'm here.'

'You're thinking of going somewhere?'

'Lainie wants me to live and work with her. It's just until I get married, and the money would help Matthew buy his house. It's the sort of shop I would enjoy working in, Dad, with a good clientele, and I can work on my designs in the evenings sometimes. It would only be until Matthew can afford to get married.'

'I've told you I shall give you both a good

wedding present. Matthew could set himself up in the shop he wants now if he wasn't so stubborn. I should count it a privilege to help that young man'

'You know he won't let you. He wants to do it by himself. He's so independent!'

'Can't say I disagree with the idea, Amy. I started with nothing. It's the right way to be, but if you are unhappy...'

'I had the dream again.' I paused to sip my drink. 'It was the first time for ages. I think it's being here in the lanes.'

My father looked worried, then annoyed. 'It was Ernie Cole who frightened you, Amy. He was drunk and he shouted at you, but that's all that happened. Besides, he's dead now. He can't hurt you or your mother any more.'

Ernie Cole had tried to attack my mother some months previously, but Kathy Ryan had stopped him. He'd turned on her then, beating her senseless, and she'd been in hospital for weeks. Thankfully she had recovered and now she was married to my uncle, Tom O, and living in America. Ernie Cole had hung himself over the banisters in his home.

'I don't remember Mr Cole shouting at me, Daddy. I'm not even sure it's anything to do with that – it's just the man with the staring eyes. And it's different now.'

'In what way different?'

'I've grown up in the dream, and I don't think it's the same man. I can't see his eyes or his face now, I just know he's going to hurt me and there's nothing I can do to stop him.'

'Perhaps you should see a doctor, Amy. I mean a special one who helps people who have bad dreams.'

'I'm not ill, Dad. Most of the time I'm happy and normal. I shan't have the dream at Lainie's. I never do.'

He was silent for a while and then he nodded. 'I'll speak to your mother. She won't like it. I know she was looking forward to spending some time with you, perhaps buying a few things for your bottom drawer.'

'We can still do that, Daddy. I don't want to disappoint you or Mum. I'll visit sometimes, and she can meet me up West for a shopping trip and lunch on my half day off – but I can't live here, not all the time.'

My father sighed and finished his half of the cocoa.

'You haven't disappointed me, Amy. I want you to make something of your life, and I approve of Matthew. I just wish that he would let me help him get started. You will be safe married to that young man. I would rather you were married than living with Lainie.'

'Matthew says it will be at least another year.'

'Then I suppose I shall have to give my permission, but leave it to me, Amy. Your mother is bound to be upset, and I want to talk to her in my own way.'

'Yes, of course, Daddy. You know I love you both. I don't want to hurt either of you.'

'Leave it with me.'

I nodded and finished my cocoa in silence. My father was a man of few words but you didn't argue with him. When he said he would do something he did it, but you couldn't hurry him.

I washed the mugs, leaving them clean and dried back on the stained pine dresser where I had found them. Everything in my mother's kitchen was spotless and in its place, and she did most of the work herself. There was a woman who came in to scrub floors and clean windows, but my mother was always busy. When my father told her to rest, she laughed and shook her head.

'I like to be busy, Joe. I was brought up to it and you won't change me now.'

'I wouldn't want to change you, lass, but I don't want you wearing yourself out.'

As I went back to bed I was anxious in case I had the dream again. However, the milky drink had done its work and within a short time I was asleep. If I had a dream this time it did not disturb me.

'I don't like the idea of you living with

Lainie,' my mother said, looking at me unhappily. 'I know you'll be safe enough with her. Lainie has promised me she will take care of you, but I still wish you would stay home with us.'

'I'll come and see you every week on my day off,' I promised. 'Please don't say I can't go, Mum. Lainie is going to pay me three pounds to start and more when I know what I'm doing.'

'If it was only money...'

'You know it isn't, don't you?'

My mother sighed and looked at me sadly. 'Ernie Cole has a lot to answer for! I shall never forgive him for shouting at you that day, Amy. You were so frightened and I don't know what would have happened if your father hadn't come along when he did. It was because he hated me, of course.'

'Why should Mr Cole hate you?'

'It's a long story. He wanted to marry me once but I wouldn't look at him then. Then he got a girl into trouble and married her. I might have married him when I was ready if he hadn't.'

'I'm glad you didn't!'

'So am I,' she said and smiled. 'Very glad. Your father is the man for me. And he says we must let you go to Lainie's, so I suppose we must. Just be careful, Amy. There are a lot of people you can't trust, and they don't all live in the lanes. Some of them look respectable and talk as if they've got a plum in their mouth, but underneath they are worse than the lowest scum.'

'I'm not a little girl, Mum. I do know that some people aren't what they seem. Besides, I'm in love with Matthew. I shan't be going out with other men – respectable or not.'

'I know you're not a child, Amy.' My mother laughed. She had a wonderful smile and most people who knew her loved her. 'I expect I'm fussing too much, but you will be careful?'

'I promise,' I said and went to hug her. 'I don't want to hurt you, Mum. It's just that I can't live here, and I do need a job.'

'I understand, darling. Your father and I just want to see you happy.'

'It's only for a year or so until Matthew saves enough for the house.' I gave her a teasing look. 'What can happen in a year? I'm not likely to get abducted by a white slaver, am I?'

'Please don't joke about such things!' she said sharply. 'You are so innocent, Amy. I shall be glad when you get married.'

Her tone and her look surprised me. It was unlike my mother to be so sharp, and for a moment she had looked almost frightened.

'What have you been buying?' Maggie Ryan stopped me in the street as I made my way home that evening. 'You're looking well,

Amy. Are you home for good now?'

'I'm not sure. I may go to stay with my aunt for a while. She's offered me a job in her shop.'

'Oh well, take care of yourself, love.'

Maggie nodded and went inside her house. She lived a few doors away from my parents and had been my mother's friend for years. It was her daughter-in-law, Kathy, who had saved my mother from being attacked by Ernie Cole. Kathy's first husband, Billy, had been killed in a fight with the police on the docks some months ago now.

I heard my parents talking in the kitchen when I went in. I had been to the market to see if there were any nice pictures on a stall that sold the work of unknown artists, and I had managed to buy a pretty view of a country cottage that I thought my mother might like.

'You know why I'm worried, Joe,' my mother was saying as I paused outside the door, which was slightly open. 'Amy is so trusting. If *he* wanted to harm us...'

'You worry too much, lass. The man could have caused trouble for us years ago if he had wanted. In my opinion he has forgotten we ever existed. That business is over and done with. Put it right out of your mind.'

'I've never forgotten what he did to Lainie. If it hadn't been for that it might never have happened. I still blame myself, Joe...'

The back of my neck prickled as I listened. Who were they talking about, and why was my mother so worried?

'That was years ago. He hasn't bothered her, why should he harm Amy or us?'

'You don't know him as well as I do, Joe.'

'Amy has me to look after her. If he hurt my girl I would kill him. He knows it, Bridget. I wouldn't stand by and let him get away with it again.'

I decided it was time I went into the kitchen and made my presence known. My father smiled as he saw me, but my mother's eyes were clouded by shadows. I felt an ache somewhere in the region of my heart, and felt that I wanted to banish those shadows.

'I bought this for you, Mum. It will go in your bedroom. The artist is unknown now, but he's good. One day his work will probably be worth a lot of money.'

Her eyes filled with tears as I showed her the painting, and then she jumped up and hugged me. I hugged her back, my throat tight with emotion.'

'I love you, Amy.'

'I love you too, Mum. You don't have to worry about me. I promise you I'll be sensible.'

'Of course you will,' she said, laughed and brushed a hand across her eyes. 'I'm being silly. You're my little girl and I make too much fuss. You go to Lainie's and enjoy yourself.'

'Thanks, Mum ... Daddy.' I sent a special smile to him, knowing he had talked her round for my sake. 'I won't do anything to make you ashamed of me, I promise.'

'I never thought you would,' my father said. 'I've always trusted you completely.'

He turned away to fiddle with his wireless set, which my mother had bought him for the previous Christmas. It took a lot of skill and practice to make it work, but there were now regular broadcasts from the BBC, and my father was an enthusiastic listener.

My mother had begun to set the table for supper and I helped her, taking the blue and white plates down from the dresser and placing them on the snowy-white cloth.

'Your brother Jon is coming home for a few days next week,' my mother said as she took a pie from the oven. 'You will wait to see him before you go, won't you, Amy?'

'Yes, of course, Mum. I'm going out after supper. Matt is back from his trip and he's taking me to the pictures this evening, so I'll have to hurry and get changed...'

I emerged breathlessly from Matthew's crushing embrace.

'If that's what being away for two weeks does to you...' I murmured and laughed up at him. 'I like it. I like it a lot.'

'I missed you so much!' He touched my

cheek with his fingertips, looking serious and a little apprehensive. 'And I've got something to tell you, Amy.'

'Something I shan't like? I can see it in your face. Is it another long trip?'

'It's worse,' Matthew said. 'The firm wants me to go up to Manchester for six months. They are setting up a distribution centre for the north and they want me to run it for the first few months.'

'But you can't!' I stared at him in dismay. 'I should never see you.'

'I'll come back as often as I can at weekends. Perhaps once a fortnight if I can manage it.'

'Once a fortnight!' I couldn't believe what he was telling me. 'It was bad enough when you had the long trips, but this is impossible, Matt. Please tell them you can't do it.'

'This is very important to me, Amy. It is a step up the ladder to promotion. They've promised me another ten pounds a month, and perhaps more if I show them I can do it.'

He was prepared to desert me for ten pounds a month! I felt terribly hurt, even though I knew it was a lot of money to Matthew. But my father could give him the sixty pounds he would gain and never miss it.

'Daddy will lend you the money for a house,' I said sulkily. 'He will give us a good wedding present and you could open your own shop. You wouldn't have to go away and leave me all the time.'

'That isn't the way I do things, Amy.' His mouth had pulled into a grim line and I knew he was angry. 'I've told you before, I want to stand on my own feet. Ten pounds a month may not sound a lot to you, but the extra will make a difference when it's added to what I've already saved.'

'But I don't want you to go!' I drew back, looking at him unhappily. 'If you loved me you wouldn't leave me, Matt.'

'Whether you believe it or not, I do love you, Amy. But I have to do this for us.'

My eyes filled with tears I was too proud to shed. He was cruel to hurt me like this and I wanted to hurt him back.

'If you go there might not be any more us.'

The moment I had said it, I wished the words unspoken. Matthew's eyes were icy cold, his expression disapproving.

'If I thought you meant that I would take you home right now, Amy Robinson, but I know you don't. You're hurt and angry, and you've been spoiled. I'm afraid it isn't always possible to get what you want in life, and you are just going to have to take no for an answer for once.'

His words struck deep. How could he say such a thing to me? I wasn't spoiled, just indulged by loving parents.

'Sometimes I don't like you very much.'

'Believe me, there are times when I don't

like you, Amy.'

'Take me home! You don't care about me a bit.'

'Don't be a fool!' Matthew reached out for me, pulling me roughly into his arms. For a moment I fought him, but then I gave a sob of despair. 'It's only six months, my darling. I'll telephone you at Lainie's and I'll come and visit as often as I can.'

'You promise?'

He nodded, and then he was kissing me, his mouth taking hungry possession of mine, his tongue flicking inside my mouth as I opened to him. I clung to him desperately, feeling that I never wanted him to let me go. I was heedless, ready to do whatever he asked, needing this moment to last forever.

'Oh, Amy,' he croaked as he let me go. 'Perhaps it's as well that I'm going away. I'm not sure how much longer I can hold out. I want you so much...'

'I want you, Matt. Make love to me ... Everything.'

He shook his head and looked rueful. 'That isn't going to work, Amy. I'm not irresponsible and I don't want to run any risks now. It would be awful for you if you fell for a baby and I was away. You would feel guilty and upset and I wouldn't be here to comfort you. No, my darling, much as you tempt me, I'm going to wait.'

I knew there was no persuading him.

Matthew had a will of iron. Besides, he was right. If we went all the way now I might fall for a baby before we could get married and my father would be disappointed in me. He trusted me and loved me. I didn't want to see hurt or shame in his eyes.

'Perhaps it is best if you go for a while,' I said huskily. 'But it's going to seem such a long time...'

Two

'I've changed the single wardrobe in your room for a double one,' Lainie said as she helped me carry my cases up the back stairs. 'You'll need more space now that you've come for a longer stay.'

The new wardrobe wasn't the only change she'd made. As we went into the bedroom I saw that she had hung pretty cream lace curtains at the windows and the bed was covered in a quilt edged with the same lace. Lainie had cleaned the dark walnut furniture with lavender-scented polish, and there were lace mats under the rose-patterned china pots on the dressing table. A vase of roses had been placed on a table by the window.

'It looks lovely,' I told her. 'You've been to

so much trouble for my sake.'

'It wasn't any trouble,' she assured me. 'I'm pleased you've come, Amy. One of my best girls is leaving to get married soon and I need someone I can trust.'

'I don't know much about the business, Aunt Lainie.'

'You will soon learn. Just watch the other girls for a start. I'll show you how to pack a gown myself – there's an art to getting it right so that it doesn't crease during delivery – and the till is simple to work. If a customer wants to pay by account come and ask me first. Quite a few of my better-class ladies ask for the account to be sent to their husband, but there are one or two with outstanding accounts to be settled. In that case I shall deal with it myself.'

'That must be a little embarrassing for you – if you have to say no.'

'Not at all. It just means that I promise to deliver as soon as a payment is made. I keep the gown for a week and then it goes back on sale if the account isn't paid. Business is business, Amy. If you let people get away with things they walk right over you.'

It was when she spoke in that tone of voice that people thought she was hard. Lainie could be tough when she needed to, and I suspected that life had taught her to look out for herself. I was certain now that something unpleasant had happened to her when she was younger, and that it had been something to do with the mysterious man my mother seemed to fear.

'So will you be able to settle here?' Lainie was looking at me anxiously.

'Yes, of course, it's lovely.' I smiled at her. 'I'm looking forward to starting work.'

'Well, that won't be until tomorrow. We've got the afternoon to ourselves, Amy, which is why I suggested you come on a Sunday. I thought we might have tea somewhere and listen to a concert in the park. Or we could go to the pictures?'

'There's a new Valentino film on at the Regal Cinema,' I said. 'Or have you seen it already?'

'Yes, I did go with a friend,' Lainie said, and I thought I detected a faint flush in her cheeks. 'But I wouldn't mind seeing it again with you.'

'He's so good, isn't he?' We laughed together, feeling a little silly but sharing our enthusiasm for the film star who had had women swooning ever since his first picture was released. 'Mum said she wouldn't cross the road to see him, but I think he's wonderful.'

'Bridget always was sensible,' Lainie said and then pulled a wry face. 'It's a pity I wasn't more like her ... But that's water under the bridge. I'm going to put the kettle on now and make us a cup of tea. You unpack your things, Amy. I'll call you when it's ready.'

'Thanks, Lainie.'

I hung my clothes in the spacious wardrobe, packing my underwear and three brand new packets of Red Seal silk stockings into the chest of drawers. The stockings had been a gift from Matthew before he left for Manchester.

'Think about me when you're wearing them,' he'd said with a naughty look and then kissed me. 'I shall lie in bed and imagine you putting them on. You have the most fabulous legs, Amy, especially when you wear that French outfit.'

My father had bought me a little suit in the new style made fashionable by the French designer, Coco Chanel. It had a very short skirt, which finished only just below my knees, and a jacket that was soft and looked like a tailored cardigan. The style was so much more relaxed than the fashions women had worn before the war, and my mother had been slightly shocked when she saw me wearing it for the first time.

'It's hardly decent, Amy!'

'Everyone is wearing short skirts now, Mum.'

'I'm not – at least, not that short.'

'Daddy bought it for me.'

'Sometimes I wonder if your father has the sense he was born with, so I do.'

She always resorted to her Irishness when she was losing an argument, but I could see she was laughing inside.

'You're teasing me, Mum!'

'O' course I am, Amy. You look very pretty, so you do – a young lady of the twenties, very modern and stylish. I'm glad you haven't had your hair cut short, though. It's so pretty as it is.'

My hair was dark brown and hung in soft waves to my shoulders. Matthew liked it that way, and begged me not to when I had thought of having it cut into a fashionable bob. He said my eyes were green when I was angry, but I thought they were really more of a hazel colour. My mother and Matthew both said I was beautiful, but they were biased in my favour. The truth was probably that I was an attractive, modern young woman who liked to look nice.

I hung up the outfit Matthew liked so much. Lainie had provided me with more than enough space for my clothes, and I left the bottom drawer of the chest empty. I would buy something every week for my new home, such as pillowcases or towels – just little things we would need when we got married.

'Oh, Matt,' I sighed as I glanced at myself in the wardrobe mirror. 'It's going to be such a long, long time without you.'

Picking up my folder of designs, I flicked

through them, quickly becoming absorbed as I thought about some new ideas I wanted to work on. If I couldn't see Matthew, I would just have to spend more time on my work.

I had been staying with Lainie for a week when I found the gun in the top right-hand drawer of the bureau in her sitting room. She had run out of postage stamps when writing out accounts in her office downstairs, but remembered having put some in her personal writing bureau.

'Would you pop up and fetch them for me, Amy?' she asked.

'Of course.'

'I think I left them in the top drawer, the one on the left.'

I nodded and went through the door at the back of the office to the stairs leading to her private apartments. Running up the stairs, I opened the drawer to the left first, but after hunting for a few seconds I discovered the stamps were not there. So I opened the drawer to the right, and there, lying on top of what looked like some old letters, was the gun.

The shock of seeing it there made me go cold all over and I shut the drawer quickly. Why did Lainie keep a pistol in her desk? Could she use it? I suspected she could or she would not have bought it. When my aunt made up her mind to do something, she did it properly.

'I came to tell you the stamps are in the silver box.' I turned to find Lainie watching me. 'You found the gun, of course. I keep it for protection, Amy. A woman living alone can't be too careful.'

'Would you use it?' I was fascinated; a little shocked at this revelation.

Something flickered in her eyes. 'If it came to the point where I was desperate – yes. Yes, I would, Amy. There are certain circumstances when self-defence is not only permissible, it is vital.'

'If you were being threatened by an intruder?'

'Yes, exactly. I knew you would find the gun when you couldn't find the stamps. That's why I came after you. I wanted to explain.'

'You don't have to tell me anything.'

'I was hurt badly once. I don't intend anything like that to happen again, either to me or to you.'

'Do you want to tell me what happened?'

'No. I don't think you need to know that, Amy. It wasn't very pleasant and it was a long time ago. Besides, I'm over it now. I just wanted you to understand why I keep a gun. I've never had to use it, but it's there just in case.'

'I hope you will *never* have to use it!'

Lainie smiled. 'I don't expect I shall. I'm going out for a while now. Don't forget about the account customers. Just look in my black book if you're not sure. If they are blacklisted they will be in it; if not it's safe to let them take what they want. Ruth will know if they're regular customers anyway.'

'I'm sure we can manage for a while.'

Lainie nodded her encouragement. 'You're doing very well, Amy. You have a talent for picking exactly what will suit someone. Within a few weeks you'll be capable of running this place single-handed.'

'I think it's going to take a bit longer than that,' I said and laughed.

I was pleased by her praise. Going back down to the shop I forgot about the discovery I had made. Lainie had explained that the gun was just in case, and I didn't think it very important. We were never likely to need it.

There were four customers being served when I went into the showroom and only two girls to cope with the sudden rush. Ruth shot me a look of relief as I went to assist her.

'Mrs Holland has brought her niece in to buy an evening dress, Amy. It is for a very special dance. I've shown them several gowns but none of them were quite right. Could you suggest something?'

I glanced at the young lady sitting with the

rather severe-looking matron. She was pretty with soft brown hair and a gentle, sweet face. She seemed unsure of herself and was clearly at a loss as to what to choose.

'Did you show them the cream satin?'

'Yes, but Mrs Holland said the neckline was too low. I think her niece liked it, though.'

'Let me see if I can persuade her to try it on.'

I took the dress from the rail and approached Mrs Holland, who had bought a dress the previous day for herself.

'Ah, there you are, Amy. I wondered where you had got to. Can you find a pretty dress for Mary? She wants something that isn't too sophisticated.'

'I thought this might suit her?' I offered the cream satin dress.

'The neckline is much too low!'

'But we could alter that quite easily. The ruching could be eased at the neck here, and a silk flower placed at the point where it dips. That would give it a more youthful style and the colour would be good on Mary.'

'It's just right for me if the neckline were different,' Mary said. 'And it's the only dress we've seen all afternoon that I like, Aunt.'

'You are so difficult to please.' Mrs Holland sighed. 'I had hoped we wouldn't have to have all your clothes made, Mary. It would be so much easier if we could buy at least some of them off the peg. Otherwise we shall be spending weeks on the fittings.'

'Why don't you let Mary try the dress on?' I suggested. 'I could have the alterations done by tomorrow – and if you don't approve, Mrs Holland, we can return it to the rail.'

'Would Miss O'Rourke be prepared to do that?' Her eyes narrowed intently.

'I think my suggestions will make the dress look perfect on Mary.'

'Very well, you may try it on, Mary – but I want to see what it looks like before the alterations are done.'

I followed Mary into the changing rooms. She gave me a shy but grateful smile as I helped her slip the gown over her head.

'Thank you for persuading my aunt into letting me try this,' she said in a soft, nervous voice. 'I loved it when the other girl showed it to us, but Aunt Emily said it was too sophisticated.'

'Let me fasten the back for you ... There. Now look at yourself.'

Mary twirled in front of the mirror. 'It is beautiful, but I suppose the neckline is a bit low. I couldn't wear it like that. My father wouldn't approve. He likes young ladies to look modest.'

'That's easy to sort out.' I took a pair of scissors and snipped through some stitching at the back of the heavily ruched neck. 'We'll make this much softer here and put a silk flower just there so that you can't see it has been altered – do you see?'

'Oh yes, that looks much better. You can't see so much of me, can you?' Mary looked pleased with the result of my work. 'May I show my aunt?'

'Let me just pin a flower. This isn't the one we'll use, but it gives you more idea of what it will look like.'

'That's even better. You are so clever, Amy.'

'It's what I should like to do – design gowns for people like you.'

'You should do it,' Mary said. 'Let's show Aunt Emily.'

We went out to the showroom where Mrs Holland was waiting. Her eyes went over Mary critically and then she nodded her approval.

'That was very clever of you, Amy. How did you know what to do? Most shop girls wouldn't have the first idea.'

'I took a course in dress designing at art college,' I replied. 'It's what I'd like to be doing – if I could get someone to buy my designs.'

'Have you done many designs of your own?'

'I have a folder of them upstairs. I draw them to amuse myself in the evenings.'

'I would have thought an attractive young woman like yourself would be courting?'

‘Aunt Emily! That is so personal.’ Mary blushed and looked at me awkwardly.

‘I don’t mind. My young man is working in Manchester for six months. He has to save for another year or so before we can get married.’

‘He sounds like a thoroughly sensible young man.’ Mrs Holland looked thoughtful. ‘Will the alterations be done in your own workrooms?’

‘Yes, we do everything ourselves. Sally and Margaret are very good.’

‘The proof of that will be in the finished article. We shall see what you have made of this gown tomorrow. Come along, Mary. We still have to find you some shoes.’

Mary pulled a face at me as her aunt swept from the shop. I smiled at her but I was thoughtful as I took the gown into the workroom and explained what I wanted done.

Margaret smiled as I entered. She was a pretty girl with soft fair hair and a sweet face. She was a year older than me, but had been at work since she left school at fifteen.

She looked at what I’d done and then nodded her understanding.

‘Yes, I can see what you want, Amy. It gives a much nicer, softer effect for a young girl.’

‘Mrs Holland took some persuading, but I think I talked her round in the end. Make a really good job of it for me, won’t you? I think we might get several orders if they like the result.'

'I shall do my best,' Margaret said. 'But it doesn't look too difficult.'

'If this works out for us it could mean a lot of extra work for you and Sally, and a lot more customers for the shop if my aunt likes my ideas.'

Margaret looked curious but I shook my head. I had to talk to Lainie first before I told anyone else.

Lainie stared at me as I finished showing her the designs in my folder that evening.

'I'm not sure, Amy,' she said. 'I've always stuck to ready-made with a few simple alterations when necessary. Making individual gowns for customers would be a huge step to take.'

'Yes, if we did it all the time, but we could try one or two of our own designs in the shop. If people liked them we could make them to order for special customers.'

'But what about the cutting? That takes skill. I'm not sure my girls are up to it.'

'I was taught to cut patterns at college, and Margaret told me she worked for a tailor for two years, though I'm not sure where she learned to cut. It's a while since she did any, of course, because she hasn't needed it here, but I am sure we could do it together.'

'Margaret has never mentioned her extra skills to me.' Lainie was thoughtful. 'If I agree, you would like to show some of your designs to Mrs Holland tomorrow?'

'Just those four dresses – two for evening and two for afternoon occasions. Nothing else I've done would be suitable for Mary, but if they liked the idea I could come up with more in a week or so.'

'You know she will want to pay less than she would at any established couturier, don't you? I've known Mrs Holland for years and she will never pay sixpence if a penny will do.'

'I can work out the costs on these dresses and add on some profit for you, Lainie.'

'And something for yourself. Don't work for nothing, Amy. I know these people. They have more money than we could ever dream of, but they are as mean as can be. Some of them will do anything to avoid paying their bill.'

I laughed as she screwed up her mouth in disgust. 'I'll put an extra ten-per cent on top so that you can give her a discount if she asks. Besides, I think Mary usually gets her own way in the end.'

Lainie smiled at that. 'I shall make a business woman of you yet.'

'It's my father coming out in me.'

'Yes,' she agreed. 'It probably is. Joe Robinson knows a thing or two about making money. I've always admired him for that. It's a good thing Bridget married him and not that Ernie Cole she was sweet on for a while.'

'Did Mum really consider marrying that awful man?'

Lainie laughed. 'He wasn't so very awful then. Ernie was what we called a looker when he was young. It was a bad marriage that turned him sour, and then he had an accident and couldn't do his proper work with the horses any more – and he was jealous of your father, of course. All that was a long time ago. We've put it behind us and moved on. You don't need to bother your head about any of it, Amy.'

It was on the tip of my tongue to ask her what she meant, but I decided against it. The past was over and gone, and I was more interested in the future.

'So what do you think?' I asked eagerly. 'Should I show Mrs Holland my designs or not?'

'See what she thinks of the dress we're altering when it's finished, and then we'll see how we go from there...'

Mrs Holland looked at Mary for what seemed like an age before she spoke, her expression giving nothing away until she finally nodded her approval.

'Yes, that looks very professional, and much nicer for Mary now that the neckline is softer. Will you put it on my account, please, and send it to the usual address.'

'Yes, of course, Mrs Holland. Is there anything else I can help you with?'

'Mary will be having several social engagements over the next month or so, though she won't be presented to Their Majesties as such. Her father was against that and he has the last say, though I would have arranged it all, of course. However, she has been invited to several more dances, afternoon parties and lunches, and she will have her own dance in September. Will you have anything suitable in stock before then?'

'I wondered if you might like to look at one or two of the designs I told you about? There are a few that might suit Mary.'

She stared at me in silence for a moment. 'Are you suggesting that the gowns could be made here for Mary?'

'Yes, if you approved.'

'They would need to be top quality.'

'Of course. Would you care to see the designs?'

'I would,' Mary said. 'Please may we, Amy?'

'It won't take a moment to fetch them. I left them in Miss O'Rourke's office.'

My heart was racing as I walked into the office. I thought all four gowns would look well on Mary, who was a slender, fragile girl and could wear simple elegant styles with the softer look that Paul Poiret had first brought to the attention of fashionable women in the early years of the twentieth century. My own designs were similar, but with a more modern style and hemline; I had included a swatch of materials to show what I had in mind.

I handed two drawings to Mary and two to her aunt, feeling nervous. Would they like them or turn them down instantly? I held my breath as they examined each drawing in turn, exchanging them back and forwards more than once before Mary gave her verdict.

'I like all of them, but I would prefer the blue evening gown in emerald-green.'

'They look very stylish on paper,' Mrs Holland said. 'How long would it take to make one of these evening gowns?'

'The blue one that Mary would prefer in green should take two weeks, because there is only one panel of beading on the back of the bodice. She would need to come for a preliminary fitting in a few days' time, but the beading on the back should only take me a day or so. If I work at it I might have it done in ten days.'

'And how much exactly would that gown cost?'

'You will have to ask Miss O'Rourke about that, but I think around twenty pounds.'

'That's ridiculous! The gown you just sold us was only fifteen pounds, and that was more than enough.'

'Miss O'Rourke might be able to give you a discount, but you must ask her about that. I merely work here.'

'It would be perfect for the Marlborough ball,' Mary said. 'I am sure Daddy wouldn't think it too much. He said I was to have the best available and the gowns at Worth's were far more expensive. Besides, I like this better than those we saw there – it's simpler, with less frills and furbelows.'

'You have no idea what constitutes value for money. Wait here, Mary. I shall speak to Miss O'Rourke and see what she has to say. If she is prepared to be sensible we might order more than one gown.'

Mary pulled a face at me as her aunt went off to speak to Lainie. 'Aunt Emily makes such a fuss about money. Anyone would think it was her own money she was spending. Daddy gave me two thousand pounds for my clothes and I've hardly spent anything yet. I couldn't find anything I liked.'

'That was very generous of your father.'

'Oh, Daddy has lots of money. He doesn't care what I spend as long as I stay out of his way and don't bother him when he has his business friends to the house.'

'What does your mother say about your clothes?'

'She died when I was quite small,' Mary said. 'Aunt Emily was her closest friend, and she has been very good, taking me about with her since I left school at Christmas – but she is rather strict.'

'I am sorry you lost your mother when you were small. Was she very ill?'

'I'm not sure. I think she was unhappy. She used to cry a lot and hug me – and I think she drank too much alcohol.'

'Oh...' I wasn't quite sure what to say. 'I'm sorry, Mary. I shouldn't have asked such a personal question.'

'It doesn't matter. I cried a lot when Mummy died, but then Eleanor came and took me home to stay with her and I felt better. Eleanor was Mummy's sister's daughter. I felt better when I stayed with them. Eleanor was good to me but she died during the war. She was a nurse in France and the ambulance she was travelling in was blown up while on a rescue mission to bring injured men back to the hospital. It was terrible.'

'That was very sad. You must have been very upset.'

'Yes, I was. Very upset. Eleanor was my best friend. I loved her very much, and I still miss her. If she had been alive she would have come with me to choose my clothes and it would have been so much more fun...' She sighed deeply. 'You can't imagine how many establishments we've been to, trying to find the right clothes, Amy.'

'I know a lot of the styles this season are very sophisticated.'

'Some of them are so fussy. I like simple things like these designs of yours. Paul likes me in green best, that is why I chose green for that evening dress.' She smiled to herself. 'He has been in France, taking part in the first twenty-four-hour race at Le Mans...'

She broke off and glanced towards Mrs Holland as she came back to join us, looking pleased with herself. I guessed that Lainie had given her a generous discount, which we had allowed for in the costing, knowing that she would not be satisfied with just a few pounds off the asking price.

'I have ordered the green gown,' she said. 'We shall see how that looks for a start. Miss O'Rourke has told me she has a new line of ready-made afternoon dresses coming in soon, and we shall look at those before we make any further decisions.'

Mary pulled a face at me as she followed her aunt from the shop.

'When shall I come for my fitting?'

'On Tuesday afternoon at half past two – if that suits you?'

She nodded and smiled, then disappeared out into the bright sunshine.

I waited until they had gone and then went into the office, where Lainie was looking at some patterns of silk and satin materials.

'She insisted on the best material, Amy,'

Lainie said. 'I told her that would be another five pounds, and she haggled so we ended up at fifteen pounds and ten shillings – will that cover your costs?'

'Yes, quite easily with some to spare,' I said. 'But I had quoted for the best quality material, Lainie.'

'I know, but Mrs Holland likes to think she is getting the best of the deal so I put the price up and then came down more than I could have done if I'd stuck to your original quote.'

'I shall have to remember that in future.'

Lainie nodded, looking at me thoughtfully. 'Yes, I think she will order several more gowns if she is satisfied with the first ... I wonder if you know what you've started, Amy?'

'What do you mean?'

'Mrs Holland is the sort of woman who likes to talk when she has discovered something she considers above average. We shall probably have other customers asking us to make things for them before long.'

'Would that be a problem?'

'I might have to take another girl on in the sewing room if we can't cope, but if we were making money out of the work ... I suppose it might be worth it.'

'Well, let's see how it goes,' I said. 'They may not be satisfied with the dress when we've finished it.'

'I don't see why they shouldn't be,' Lainie said. 'That dress you made for your eighteenth birthday party was rather lovely, Amy. I didn't realize you had made it yourself until you told me last night.'

'I think Margaret should do most of the sewing on Mary's gown, and I shall do the beading myself, of course. That will leave Sally free to carry on with the alterations as usual, and I don't mind working in the evenings to finish it on time.'

'Well, you mustn't work all the time,' Lainie said with a smile. 'How would you like to go out this evening? I thought we might go to the theatre to see Noel Coward's play.'

'Yes, I should enjoy that,' I told her with a smile. 'And I shall go to see my parents this weekend. After that I can really get down to work on Mary's new gown.'

'Did she give you permission to call her Mary?' Lainie asked with a little frown. 'Some of the customers do, I know, but it is a little familiar.'

'I don't even know her second name,' I said. 'She talked about her father a lot but neither she or Mrs Holland mentioned her surname.'

'Well, I suppose it's all right then. As long as you remain respectful, Amy. You have to be careful with customers, especially people like Mrs Holland.'

'Yes, of course,' I replied. 'But Mary is so friendly, and I know how to treat Mrs Holland.'

I was a little resentful that Lainie should have thought it necessary to warn me to keep my place with the customers. I wouldn't have dreamed of addressing most of them by their first names, but Mary was different.

'How exciting for you,' said my mother when I told her we were making up one of my designs for a customer of Lainie's. 'You draw some beautiful things, Amy. I think they are quite as good as any of the expensive designers I see the quality wearing at their social events.'

'And when do you see them all dressed up then, Bridget?' my father quizzed her with a wicked twinkle in his eyes. 'I didn't know you'd been invited to dinner at Buckingham Palace!'

'Go on with you, Joe Robinson!' My mother pulled a face at him. 'You know very well that the papers are full of pictures of the royal family and other members of the aristocracy.'

'I didn't know you were wasting your time looking at them.'

'It's little enough time I spend sitting down, but I do like to read the papers, and I have a magazine now and then as a treat.'

'Now the secrets are coming out!'

'Oh, do stop teasing her,' I said and shook my head at him. 'Lainie says she might have to take on another seamstress in the workrooms if my idea catches on.'

'I hope she's paying you extra,' my father said. 'You will be doing a lot more work, Amy.'

'We've written my fees into the costing,' I told him. 'If I had sold my designs to one of the big stores I approached I would have received a fee, and Lainie insisted I include something for my time.'

'So I should think,' he said, but again there was a twinkle in his eye. 'When are you expecting to see Matthew next?'

'He wrote in his letter that he hopes to come up on Saturday and go back after tea on Sunday.'

'You can bring him here for Sunday lunch if you like,' my mother said. 'But perhaps you would rather go somewhere on your own?'

'Matthew talked about taking a picnic out to Epping Forest,' I said. 'But it all depends on the weather.'

'Your mother always cooks far too much anyway. I expect there will be enough if you decide you want to come, Amy.'

I smiled at them. It was good to hear their friendly banter, and I liked being at home for a few hours, as long as I didn't have to live there.

'Are you sleeping well?' My mother looked at me anxiously. 'I must say you look very well, Amy.'

'I feel fine,' I told her. 'We went to the theatre the other evening. It was a play by Noel Coward and it was really amusing.'

'A play is it? You'll be getting too grand for the likes of us soon, Amy Robinson.'

'Don't tease her, Joe,' my mother said. 'Haven't you got anything better to do than sit around here with us?'

'Now I've got my orders I'd better go and do some work,' he said and grinned at us good-naturedly. 'It was nice seeing you, Amy love. Be good – and I won't say the rest or your mother will have my guts for garters!'

'I should think not either!' Mum shook her head at him, then smiled as he went out. 'Now we can have a good chat by ourselves. You are happy at Lainie's? She treats you well?'

'Of course she does,' I said. 'She was a little bit doubtful at first about my designs, but then I showed her the dress I made for my eighteenth birthday party and she was impressed.'

Mum looked thoughtful, then nodded. 'I was anxious about you going there to live, Amy, but I can see it suits you. I'm glad you're happy.'

'It's good fun. I get on well with the other

girls, especially Margaret. She's very clever at what she does, and I enjoy talking to her – and I've been out with Lainie in the evenings a few times.'

'Well, living up there you've got all the best theatres and cinemas to choose from,' she said. 'But you ought to have some friends of your own age, Amy.'

'I don't mind things the way they are for the moment. I've got plenty to do to amuse myself, and there are always Matt's visits to look forward to. I like Mary though...'

'She is the customer you are making the dress for, isn't she?'

'Yes, and she's really nice, Mum. You would like her. She has lovely manners and she speaks softly, and she's a little shy. And she talked to me about her mother and cousin. She loved her cousin but she was killed in France during the war.'

'A lot of good people died during the war.' My mother shivered suddenly. 'What is Mary's other name?'

'She hasn't told me,' I said. 'It doesn't matter, does it?'

'I shouldn't think so, if she's as nice as you say. It's a pity you can't make friends with her – but I expect that's out of the question. A girl from that sort of family isn't likely to mix with someone who works in a shop.'

'Oh, that's so old-fashioned, Mum. I know it used to be that way, but attitudes are changing a lot. Besides, I've been to college and I'm as good as anyone else.'

'Possibly better,' my mother agreed with a loving smile. 'But be prepared for Mary's friendliness to wane, Amy. I've met people like that before and they can be as nice as pie one minute and the very opposite the next.'

'You're as bad as Lainie, Mum. I think Mary is really nice, and I wouldn't hesitate to be her friend if she asked me.'

'The thing is, she probably won't, and I shouldn't like you to be hurt, love.'

'Mary isn't a snob,' I said. 'Besides, I'm not sure she's out of the top drawer as they say. I think her mother was from a good family, but I think her father might not be quite the thing.'

'What makes you say that?'

'I'm not sure. It's just a look in Mrs Holland's eyes when Mary mentions her father. I don't think she really approves of him, though she is fond of Mary.'

'Mary's mother must have married for money. He's probably trade or something. Well, I'm not telling you that you mustn't be friends with her, Amy. Just don't expect too much, that's all.'

'I'm not expecting anything, Mum,' I said honestly. 'It's just a commission for a few dresses, that's all.'

Three

'But you promised, Matt,' I said into the receiver of Lainie's private telephone. 'You said you were coming on Saturday afternoon and staying over until Sunday after tea. I've been looking forward to it so much – and now you say you can't come.'

'I didn't promise, Amy. I said I hoped I would be able to come, but things have changed since I spoke to you. I've been told there's a big consignment due from the factory on Saturday morning, which means I shall have to stocktake all afternoon – and Sunday too, if necessary. I want to get the new lines out to the salesmen by Monday.'

'But that's not fair! Why should you have to work all the time? Surely the new line could wait a day or so?'

'Business isn't like that,' Matthew said and I heard the note of impatience in his voice. 'I'm sorry, Amy. I'll come next week if I can.'

'I suppose that means you'll change your mind again at the last minute. You're not being fair. It's ages since I saw you.'

'Not that long,' he replied. 'You don't

suppose I like having to work when I was hoping to see you?'

'I don't know what you like any more.'

'Please don't be upset, Amy. I'll make it up to you when I come.'

'*If* you come!'

'I'll come as soon as I can, I promise.'

'I've got to go now. I think you are being unkind. Your work seems to mean more to you these days than I do.'

I hung the earpiece back in its place, holding my tears inside. I was upset but I was angry too. It was Friday morning and I had been looking forward to his visit so much.

'Is something wrong, Amy?'

Lainie had come into the parlour behind me. I turned to greet her with a sigh.

'Matthew isn't coming. He has to work.'

'That's a shame, but I suppose he can't refuse.'

'I don't see why he has to work all weekend.'

'You would if I asked you. He's just trying to impress his employer.'

'Well, I wish he wouldn't!'

Lainie smiled and shook her head at me. 'You're so impatient, Amy. I was just the same at your age. I wanted everything now, at once, but I've learned to be more sensible. Sometimes you have to wait for the good things in life. Anyway, I came to tell you that Mary has arrived for her fitting.'

'She's early. It wasn't supposed to be for another half an hour.'

'I suppose it suited her to come sooner. She is on her own today.'

'On her own?' I was surprised. 'I wonder why.'

'Perhaps Mrs Holland had another appointment.'

'Or Mary escaped?'

'Amy!' Lainie laughed. 'I hope you won't say anything of the sort to Mary?'

'No, of course I shan't. I'll go down now.'

'That's right. You can have your break later.'

Mary was looking through the rails of afternoon dresses when I went into the showroom. Her face lit up with pleasure when she saw me.

'I'm sorry if I came too early.'

'Of course you're not too early. I am sorry to keep you waiting. I was taking a private phone call just now or I would have been here when you came in.'

'Not bad news, I hope?'

'In a way...' I screwed up my mouth. 'Matthew can't come up to town this weekend because he has to work. We were going out and I was looking forward to seeing him.'

'How disappointing for you,' she said. 'It must be nice having a proper boyfriend. I haven't met anyone I should like to marry so far; at least no one my father approves of. A lot of Daddy's friends are older, though of course I do meet people of my own age.' She sighed. 'I don't like many of them. Aunt Emily's friends are so ... snobbish.' She glanced over her shoulder guiltily. 'It's a good thing she can't hear me!'

'Mrs Holland didn't come with you today?'

'She is lying down with a bad headache. She wanted me to cancel my appointment, but I told her I should be perfectly safe to come here alone, and she was feeling too ill to argue.'

'I see.' I smiled at her. 'Shall we see how they are getting on with your dress?'

'Yes, please. I feel quite excited.'

I took Mary into the dressing room I had reserved for her. The skirt and bodice were cut and tacked together but not yet sewn into place, so that we could make adjustments if necessary.

'It is beginning to look like a dress.'

'Yes – and the best thing is that we can alter anything you don't quite like at this stage.'

'Everyone wanted to know where the cream satin gown came from,' Mary confided, looking shy as I helped her into the half-finished gown. 'Aunt Emily went around looking like the cat that had gobbled up all the cream. I expect you will soon have more customers asking for you, Amy.'

'We were very busy yesterday. I sold two afternoon dresses myself, one of which we are altering for a titled lady. It is the first time she has been to us. Lainie was very pleased to have her custom.'

I fastened the bodice at the back with pins, fitting it to Mary's slender waist. She gave a cry of pleasure as she saw herself in the mirror.

'Oh, it is beautiful, Amy. The colour is wonderful, and I love the way the neck sits and the flow of the skirt. It almost looks medieval.'

'It's the cutting that gives it that effect,' I explained. 'You get a flowing line, and the waist hasn't got all those tucks and gathers you dislike, Mary.'

'You are so clever!'

'Margaret did the cutting for me – or most of it.'

'But it was your design. I know it's going to be marvellous when it's finished.'

'The beading is very simple, but it will set the whole thing off,' I said, feeling pleased as I helped her out of the gown. 'I'm glad you like what we've done so far.'

'Very much.' Mary was fastening the tiny pearl buttons at the cuffs of her white linen blouse. She gave me a speculative look. 'I don't suppose you would like to come for lunch with me on Sunday, as you aren't going out with your young man?'

For a moment I wasn't sure that I had heard her correctly. 'Did you just ask me to lunch?'

'Yes. Would you come? My aunt is going away for a day or two and I shall be alone. But perhaps it would be too boring for you?'

'It wouldn't be boring at all. I should love to come – but are you sure you want me to?'

'Why shouldn't I?'

'I work in a shop, Mary, and I don't usually visit people like you, though at college we all mixed in together.'

'Don't be a snob, Amy,' Mary said and laughed. 'I like you better than any of the girls Aunt Emily thinks I should know. Besides, this is 1923. We women have to stick together. An actress has just been elected as our third female Member of Parliament, did you know that? I think women should always be the equal of men, don't you?'

I laughed as I saw the militant expression in her eyes. On the surface Mary appeared to be a shy, gentle girl, but she knew her own mind and I suspected she could be stubborn when she chose.

'Oh, I do so agree!' I said. 'Thank you for inviting me, Mary. It will be lovely.'

'I'll give you my address,' she said and took out a little silver card case from her bag. She wrote her address on a plain card and gave it to me. 'I prefer these to those printed things.

I only give my address to people I really like. Will you be able to get there all right – or shall I send the car for you? I can have a car if I ask for one.'

I saw that the address she had given me was in Hampstead.

'Yes, I can find this. I can come on the tube and if need be I'll get a cab from there.'

'See how you get on this time. If it is too much trouble I'll make sure one of Daddy's drivers brings you home.'

'I'm sure I can manage, Mary. I shall look forward to it.'

'I had better go home and enquire if my aunt is better. I hope she is feeling well enough to go away as she intends.'

'Would she be cross with you for inviting me to lunch?'

'Aunt Emily receives a commission for looking after me,' Mary said. 'She cannot dictate what I do in my own home, Amy.'

I was silent. It sounded odd to me that Mrs Holland should take money for being her niece's chaperone, but it was not for me to question Mary. Besides, I very much wanted to visit her on Sunday.

'She invited you to lunch?' Lainie looked surprised and then a little anxious. 'Are you sure you should go, Amy?'

'Why ever not? Mary knows her own mind. Besides, she will be alone. Mrs Holland is going away for a few days.'

'What about her family?'

'Her mother died when she was young and I think her father is often away or out on business. I don't think he bothers with Mary much. He gives her money but he is too busy working to spend time with her.'

'Poor little rich girl,' Lainie said with a wry twist of her mouth. 'She's probably lonely, Amy.'

'Yes, I am certain of it. She says her aunt's friends are boring and she likes me better than other girls she has met.'

'It's up to you, of course. I just hope you won't be hurt if she suddenly drops you, Amy.'

'Mary isn't like that.'

'She still hasn't told you her second name then?'

'It hasn't been necessary. It doesn't matter ... Does it?'

'I shouldn't think so.' Lainie smiled. 'You're a sensible girl, Amy. All I'm going to say is that you should be careful of any men you might meet at Mary's. Don't trust them until you get to know them – and then be careful.'

'You don't have to warn me, Lainie. I'm in love with Matthew. I'm not interested in other men.'

'I thought you had quarrelled with him.'

'I have – but I'm going to telephone this

evening and apologize.'

'Good. He's decent and honest, Amy. If he has decided to do this extra work it's only so that he can save more.'

'Yes, I know. I was upset because he could not get home, but I don't mind so much now.'

I was secretly rather pleased that Matthew hadn't been able to get home for the weekend. I missed him terribly, of course I did, but I was excited at the prospect of going to Mary's house.

I was a little overawed as the cab stopped outside the huge red-bricked house situated close to Hampstead Heath. There were a lot of impressive houses in the area, but Mary's was by far the biggest and I double-checked the address on her card before paying my taxi and letting it go.

Feeling nervous, I opened the gate and went inside, walking up the tree-lined drive towards the house. A dog was barking and it suddenly came round the corner of the building, rushing towards me in a fierce manner and snarling. I stood absolutely still, wondering what to do and not daring to move. Then a man came round the corner and called to it.

'Here, Brutus! Come here, boy.'

The dog gave me another menacing look, then went bounding off to meet the man who continued to walk towards me as I stood unmoving, still afraid of being attacked.

'Hello,' he said, smiling at me. 'I'm sorry if you were frightened. He is a bit of a brute if you don't know him.'

'It was just the shock,' I replied, managing to breathe at last.

He offered his hand, his clasp firm and cool.

'I'm Paul Ross by the way. Mary's cousin. It was my fault about the dog. Mary warned me not to let it out because you were coming, but the poor thing needed some exercise. I'm afraid they get neglected at times, that's why I come round as often as I can to keep an eye on them.'

'It's all right now you're here. I was afraid the dog might bite me, but you seem to have him under control.'

'Oh yes, he does what he's told.'

Paul Ross was perhaps in his early thirties. He was extremely handsome, with aristocratic features, dark honey-blond hair and blue eyes, and he had a lovely smile. Dressed in a smart navy-blue blazer, white open-necked shirt and grey flannels, he was quite obviously a gentleman – out of the top drawer, as my aunt would say.

'Do let me take you in. Mary is waiting for you and I was about to leave.'

'You're not staying to lunch with us?'

'No, unfortunately I can't,' he said, looking regretful. 'I wish I could, Amy. Forgive me, I only know you as Amy. Mary didn't tell me your surname.'

'It's Robinson. Mary probably doesn't know it.'

'Amy Robinson. Very pretty, like it's owner.' He gave a soft chuckle as he saw my blush. 'No, I didn't mean to embarrass you, Amy. Mary told me you were pretty and the words were in my mind. Forgive me for being familiar.'

I wasn't sure how to respond, and felt flustered.

'It was a compliment, so naturally I forgive you,' I said.

'I am so glad. Let me take you to my cousin, and then I must go.'

I felt a little shy as I glanced at him. He was very different to anyone I had ever met before. His face was thin and he had a sensitive, artistic look about him, and his hair was perhaps a little too long. But he was very charming and his smile lit up his face as well as his eyes, though when he wasn't smiling there was something oddly sad about him – almost haunted. But no, that was silly!

Mary was at the back of the house. The long glass doors were opened and she was sitting in a cane chair on the lawn, which had been set with various chairs and small tables. There was a huge oak tree some distance from the house and beyond that lay a tennis court set behind a formal rose garden and an old stone sundial. The atmosphere was peaceful and welcoming, and some of my nervousness fell away.

'Oh, there you are!' Mary cried with a look of relief. 'I was afraid that the dog would frighten you off. It scares me half the time, but my father says it helps to keep intruders away. He has three more like it shut up somewhere. I never go near them.'

'Brutus isn't so bad,' Paul Ross said. 'Anyway, I didn't let anything happen to your friend, Mary.'

'Just make sure it's safely locked up before you go.'

'Your wish is my command, my lady.'

Mary stuck her tongue out at him in a most unladylike way and he went off laughing, with the dog trotting at his heels.

'I'm so glad you're here,' she said and came to kiss me on the cheek. 'We'll have drinks on the lawn and then go inside for lunch. It's impossible to eat out here when it's so hot. I thought we might play tennis, but it is much too warm.'

'I do play a little,' I said. 'They taught us at school, but I'm not terribly good.'

'Nor am I,' Mary confessed. 'Paul is marvellous, of course. Eleanor was too ... Did you like my cousin? He can be rather a tease but he isn't too bad – at least not with me. My father doesn't care for him much. They don't get on, but they are always polite to each other for the sake of appearances.'

'He seemed very pleasant,' I said, letting the comment about her father pass.

'Paul is charming when he wants to be, though he isn't as nice as he was before the war. That changed him, I suppose. He hated every minute of it, but his father insisted he join up. He was in the Royal Flying Corps as a pilot. A lot of his friends were killed, but Paul was wounded and discharged a year or so before the end. He had a nervous breakdown and spent some months in hospital. I think Eleanor's death had something to do with his illness lasting as long as it did.'

'He was her brother?'

'Yes, of course. And he absolutely adored her. I'm fond of Paul, but I don't trust him as much as I did Eleanor. He ... Well, he can be a bit odd at times.'

'What do you mean, odd?'

Mary shrugged. 'I'm not sure. Changeable might be a better word. I suppose he's moody. Eleanor said it was because he is such a gifted pianist. Did you notice his hands?'

'No, not particularly. Should I?'

'He has beautiful hands, long fingers.' She splayed her own. 'I play the piano but not like Paul. I could listen to him for hours, but he is very private about his music. If he knows I'm listening without his permission he will stop.'

'That is strange. Has he always been like that?'

'No, not before the war. He used to play all the time then. Now he only opens the piano if he thinks he is alone.'

'Have you ever asked him why he doesn't want you to listen?'

'No. Paul won't answer questions like that these days. Eleanor knew how to coax him, but he just sulks if I try. Sometimes he sulks and I don't see him for days.'

'I shouldn't like him much if he was like that with me.'

'You probably would,' Mary said with a sigh. 'I like Paul despite his moods. I feel sorry for him because he is so unhappy. He hates his father. He never says as much, but I know. I understand him because...' She broke off and frowned as if fearing she had said too much. 'We *are* friends, even if it doesn't sound like it.'

'He is a complex character,' I said. 'I don't think I've ever met anyone like that. My father and brothers are very straightforward and uncomplicated.'

'How many brothers have you got?' She looked at me curiously.

'Jon and Terry,' I replied. 'Jon was a pilot in the war, like your cousin. He joined as soon as he was old enough, but Terry is still at medical school. He is very clever and he's going to be a doctor.'

'It must be nice to have brothers. Do you have a sister?'

'No. My father said three children to plague him were more than enough, but he's always teasing us so it may just be that no more children came along.'

'My mother had two miscarriages after me,' Mary said. 'Then I think they gave up trying. She slept alone. I don't think she liked my father very much.'

'Mary!' I was shocked. 'Surely that can't be true?'

'Yes, it is. He wasn't always very nice to her, Amy, though he could be charming if he chose. I don't know for certain, but I think...' She broke off as a maid came out of the house carrying a tray. 'Ah, here comes our iced lemon barley water. We'll have some wine with our lunch, but this is nice on a hot day – don't you think so?'

'Yes, lovely.'

I sipped my drink and waited for Mary to continue what she'd been saying before the maid came out, but she didn't. Instead, she started to talk about various functions she had been to and the people she had met. It was so peaceful, the only sound that of a blackbird trilling from the branches of a cherry tree.

'We're going to a performance by the

Ballet Russe next week. They are performing the first showing of Stravinsky's *Les Noces*. I don't much want to go. Do you like the ballet, Amy?'

'I've only been once with my school to see *Swan Lake*, but I enjoyed it – why don't you want to go?'

'We're going with the Bradwells. Aunt Emily thinks the Bradwells are marvellous,' she said and pulled a wry face. 'That's because Mr Bradwell was an equerry to the King before he retired. Their son is a major in the regular army. He must be forty or more, but she thinks he would be a perfect husband for me.'

'You wouldn't marry a man so much older than you, would you?'

'No, certainly not. I wouldn't have Major Bradwell whatever age he was. Besides...' She wrinkled her nose in concentration. 'I am not sure I want to marry anyone, Amy. My father and Aunt Emily both say I should marry into a good family but I don't think I could unless I was in love. I'm not sure I'd want to, even then.'

'I think it will be nice to be married, to the right man, of course.'

'It might be worth trying if he was like Paul...' She sighed. '*That* would never be allowed, of course.'

I thought I understood what she meant.

'Cousins are allowed to marry, aren't they?'

'Not in my family. Aunt Emily certainly wouldn't approve. She says there's bad blood in the Ross side of the family and my father wants more than that for me. I think he hopes I'll marry a viscount or something – and he doesn't get on with Paul's father. They had a huge row years ago.'

'You wouldn't really want to marry Paul – would you? Not if he's so moody.'

'Perhaps not.' Mary looked thoughtful, unsure. 'I'd rather marry Paul than most of the men I know, but it won't happen. Daddy would do something to stop us.' She shivered despite the heat of the sun, and once again I sensed something hidden – something that bothered her deeply. 'No, I mustn't even think of it.'

'You might meet someone wonderful at a dance, Mary.'

'I might,' she agreed. 'If I don't I can always go off and become a nun or something.'

I laughed because there was mischief in her eyes and I believed she was joking.

'Make the most of your Season first then, Mary.'

'I intend to,' she said and giggled. 'My father is giving an evening party for my friends next Friday. Would you come, Amy? He phoned me and told me to ask whomever I want.'

'He probably didn't mean a shop girl,

Mary.'

'Daddy owns shops...' She frowned, again seeming uncertain. It was becoming clear to me that Mary's feelings about her father were very mixed. At times she seemed almost to fear him, at others to accord him a reluctant respect. 'At least, I think he does. He owns all kinds of things. He won't even ask who you are. I shall tell him I like you and he won't care about anything else.'

'Well...' I hesitated and was lost as I saw the eagerness in her eyes. 'I should like to come, Mary. What do I wear?'

'A long dress of some kind. It doesn't have to be extravagant, just fairly formal. Daddy doesn't like short dresses, especially in the evening. He says decent women shouldn't show too much of their legs.'

'I had better not wear my best suit then. Don't worry, Mary. I'm sure I can find something suitable.'

I decided I would wear the dress I'd made for my eighteenth birthday party. It was the only formal evening gown I possessed.

'If not, I could lend you something. You could soon alter it to fit you.'

'Not if I'm going to have your gown ready on schedule.'

'I'm looking forward to wearing that,' Mary said. 'How is it coming along? Have you done any more designs that might suit me?'

'Yes, one or two. I'll show them to you when you come for the final fitting.'

Since the subject had turned to fashion, we talked about various ideas. Mary had heard of Coco Chanel, of course, but her aunt did not approve of the French designer's casual style.

'I'm sure Aunt Emily would have me wearing whalebone corsets if she could,' Mary said and laughed.

'My mother thought my Chanel-style suit was too short at first, but my father bought it for me so she couldn't forbid me to wear it.'

We talked about clothes until lunch, and then Mary took me inside. The house seemed dark and cold after the warmth of the sun, but despite the formality I could see that it was the home of a very wealthy man. There were antiques, silver and what I presumed were valuable paintings and huge mirrors in each of the rooms we passed through, and the dining table was set with beautiful crystal, china and silver.

The meal itself was very nice. We had iced soup with watercress to start, followed by fresh salmon poached in white wine with tiny new potatoes, minted peas and green beans. For dessert there was a choice of lemon meringue pie or chocolate cake and coffee. The white wine was chilled and delicious. I was careful to drink only one glass, because I was afraid it might make me giggle. I wasn't used to drinking wine in the middle of the day, or at any time really.

After lunch, Mary put some jazz records on the gramophone and we practised a new dance that had just come from America.

'Did you know there's a craze for marathon dancing out there?' she said. 'They just go on and on for hours at a time.'

'Yes, I know. I read about a new record for the amount of hours danced in the paper. It's absolutely mad, isn't it?'

'My father goes to America sometimes,' Mary said. 'I went with him once on a huge liner. It was quite exciting. They have some marvellous shops in New York, and the women have fabulous furs and jewels. Daddy says he may retire there one day. I hope he doesn't make me go with him; I don't think I would like it.'

'Oh, my uncle has gone out there to live with his new wife. Why didn't you like it, Mary?'

'It was nice for a holiday but I prefer the country. We have a lovely house in Hampshire, much nicer than this. You must come and stay with me for the whole weekend, Amy. We could go down in one of Daddy's cars and stay there – just you and me.'

'Would your father allow that?'

'Oh yes, he scarcely ever goes there himself. It was my mother's house really, left her by her grandmother. She lived there most of the time after ... after she couldn't have more children.'

'It sounds nice, Mary, but I would have to have time off. I usually work on Saturday mornings.'

'Miss O'Rourke would let you off for once,' Mary said. 'Especially if you were working on dresses for me.' She gave me a wicked smile. 'I could order several if I wanted – and tell all my acquaintances where I bought them.'

'That's blackmail, Mary.' I was both amused and shocked by this revelation of another side of her character.

'Well, why not? I'm not above using a little persuasion if it gets me what I want. Other people do it all the time.'

I wondered what kind of people she knew, but didn't comment. I wasn't sure I liked this side of Mary. I preferred the shy, gentle girl she seemed to be most of the time. But there appeared to be two sides to her, and I thought she was probably more like her cousin than she knew or admitted.

'Matthew is coming next Saturday, and there's your own party on Friday...'

'We'll go the week after,' she said. 'You speak to Miss O'Rourke and I'll ask her very nicely when I come in for my final fitting.'

Mary looked at me with such appeal in her eyes that I gave in, and one part of me was very willing to go along with all she said. Mary's friendship was opening up a new way of life for me, and I wanted it to continue for a while.

Lainie took me to see Lillian Gish in her latest film and we both wept all the way through the second half.

'She certainly is the queen of tragedy,' Lainie said afterwards. 'I don't know why I enjoy films like that, they always make me cry.'

'Perhaps we should have gone to see Charlie Chaplin,' I said, teasing her. She didn't answer and I saw that she had gone quite pale, her eyes concentrated in a fixed stare as she looked across the road to the theatre that was hosting a new musical starring Fred and Adele Astaire. People were coming out at the end of the show, and many of them looked wealthy and richly dressed.

'What's wrong, Lainie? You look as if you've seen a ghost.'

She closed her eyes for a moment, then looked at me and gave a little shake of the head as if trying to dismiss her thoughts. 'In a way I have – a ghost from the past. Just someone I thought I had forgotten, that's all.'

I was concerned for her. 'Do you feel unwell? You looked as if you might faint for a moment.'

'It was a bit of a shock,' Lainie admitted. 'Shall we have a drink before we go home? There's something I want to tell you, Amy.'

'Yes, of course.' I took her arm, steering her towards a rather attractive-looking public house. 'You should sit down for a few minutes. Give yourself time to recover.'

We went into the bar and found a table. Lainie sat down while I fetched us a drink – a small brandy for my aunt and a lemonade for me. A few eyebrows were raised as I was served; it was still frowned upon by some for ladies to enter a public house without a male escort. I reminded myself that this was 1923 and ignored the implied criticism in their looks as I carried the drinks back to Lainie.

'I should have done that,' she said. 'People were staring because you're so young to be in a public bar without an escort, Amy.'

'Let them.' I was defiant. 'At art college we often went out as a crowd of girls. We didn't need a male escort.'

'That was different,' Lainie said and smiled. 'You went to places where you were known. Somewhere like this ... Well, we'd better finish our drinks and leave.'

'When you're feeling better.'

She drank her brandy and stood up. I had hardly touched my lemonade. I followed her, feeling slightly annoyed that we were being driven out by unwarranted prejudice.

'I don't see why we had to leave so soon.'

Lainie hailed a taxi. She didn't speak until we were safely inside.

'A pub like that – in the centre of Theatreland – you could be taken for something you're not, Amy.' She pulled a rueful face as she saw I didn't understand. 'A prostitute. No, don't look so shocked. It happens. And that is why you were stared at.'

'I don't look like a tart!'

'No, of course you don't look like a streetwalker, but there are high-class call girls, Amy. They dress well, speak well, and sell themselves only to wealthy clients.'

'But that's horrible,' I said and a little shiver went down my spine. 'Just because I bought a drink, it doesn't give people the right to think I'm like that!'

'No, it doesn't, but too often people jump to conclusions. Or maybe it was just me ... seeing...' Lainie broke off. 'Forget it, Amy. I shouldn't have suggested having a drink. Let's change the subject. I wanted to tell you that I have a friend coming to stay – not this weekend but next.'

'That's when Mary wants me to go down to the country with her.'

'Yes, I know. It will suit me if you go, Amy. My friend will use your room. You won't mind, will you?'

'No, of course not.' I looked at her curiously. 'Is this the first time she has stayed with you?'

'For a while.' There was a faint blush in her cheeks. 'Harold lives in the country. We met three years ago. He asked me to marry him last year but I said I wasn't ready to think about it yet. He hasn't visited me since.'

'I expect he was disappointed.'

'Yes, he was very upset.' Lainie wrinkled her forehead in thought. 'I am fond of him, Amy. Harold Brompton is a good man – a nice man. If he lived in town I think I might have said yes, but I can't see myself being happy in the country for long. I should be bored within a month.'

'There's so much going on here,' I agreed. 'Cinemas, theatres, shops – and your business, Lainie. You wouldn't want to give that up.'

'Harold thinks I could have a shop in Cambridge. There's a good train service from where he lives, and he says he will teach me to drive a car. I suppose it might be a good idea.'

'He sounds nice. I should like to meet him.'

'Perhaps another time...' Lainie looked oddly nervous. 'Harold has something important to tell me – not about us getting married, something else.'

I looked at her curiously but she shook her head.

'I'm not sure yet, Amy. I may have some news for you – and Bridget. Bridget will want to hear it if this turns out well. It was because of her that I started this and the reason I met Harold...' She laughed as she saw my expression. 'Yes, I know I'm being mysterious, but I really can't tell you more just yet, Amy. I don't know myself. Harold just said it was important.'

'You don't have to tell me anything you don't want to,' I said and smiled at her. 'And thank you for letting me go to stay with Mary next weekend. You do realize it means I won't be able to work on Saturday?'

'Yes, of course. I don't mind that. You've worked hard since you've been with me, Amy. You deserve a bit of fun. You ought just to ask your parents if they agree, of course – but as far as I am concerned, it's fine with me.'

'I'll let Mum know I'm going to Mary's for the weekend,' I promised. 'But I know she won't mind. She knows I'm not going to do anything silly.'

'Of course you won't,' Lainie said. 'You're a sensible girl, Amy – and Mary is decent and looks like becoming a good customer, thanks to you. If you hadn't designed that first dress for her, I doubt we should have seen her again. You are an asset to the business and you deserve your fun.'

Four

I was nervous of attending Mary's party. I wasn't sure my best dress would be smart enough, even though Lainie told me I looked very pretty.

'Don't let them upset you,' she told me. 'Keep your head up and keep smiling whatever they say. Remember you are as good as any of them, even if you do work in a shop.'

As I was driven in a taxi to Mary's house that evening I had an attack of nerves and wondered what on earth I was doing. I must have been mad to agree. I didn't belong in this world and I could only blame myself if Mary's friends looked down their noses at me.

There was music playing loudly as I rang the front doorbell and I guessed that the party was being held on the back lawn. However, I wasn't prepared for the huge marquee outside or the board laid on the grass for dancing. There were at least fifty people standing around talking and more couples dancing. All of them looked wealthy and well dressed, their jewels flashing like fireflies in the light of the lanterns strung from the trees.

I noticed that several of the ladies were wearing dresses with an Egyptian inspiration. Vionnet had brought out some wonderful designs after the opening of Tutankhamen's tomb the previous year and I could see that they were still popular. It was not a fashion I particularly admired, preferring the simpler styles of Poiret.

'I didn't invite half of these people,' Mary whispered as she greeted me with a kiss on the cheek. 'Most of them are Aunt Emily's friends – or my father's.'

'I thought it was your party?'

'So did I,' she said and pulled a wry face. 'This isn't what I wanted, believe me. Apart from you, there's only Jane Adams and Millicent Fairchild that I like. Come and meet them. They are just like you and me, Amy. Most of the others are awful snobs.'

I was pleased to discover that both Jane and Millie were pleasant and very like some of the girls I'd known at art college. We talked about the clothes we liked, music and art, and then Jane was approached by a young man who asked her to dance. Moments later, Mary and then Millie were claimed by partners.

I stood awkwardly for a few minutes wondering what to do. Not having met any of the other guests, I was uncomfortable. I knew there was a buffet in the conservatory and was considering whether I should go and find something to eat when someone spoke to me.

'It was thoughtless of Mary to leave you alone, Amy.'

Turning, I saw Paul Ross and smiled.

'Hello. I didn't know you were coming this evening.'

'Mary begged me to. I don't like these things much, because I'm not very good at dancing these days. I might manage a slow waltz – if you would like to dance?'

'Don't if you would rather not,' I said and blushed because he was being kind to me.

'Oh, I can manage a couple during the evening.'

Paul took me out on to the floor, placing his hand lightly at my waist. I let myself move with the music, following Paul's lead. He was a good dancer and after my initial hesitation I was soon enjoying myself.

When the music ceased he led me back to Mary, but when the band started to play one of the modern dances that was taking the country by storm, he shook his head.

'Perhaps later,' he told Mary when she invited him to dance with her. He walked towards the house and disappeared inside.

I was anxious in case all the girls would be asked to dance and leave me on my own again. However, the young man who had danced with Mary introduced himself as Alan Bell and asked if I would like to try.

I looked at him shyly. 'I haven't done this one before, but I wouldn't mind having a go.'

'It's great fun.' Alan smiled his approval. 'We all look silly so it doesn't matter if you make a mistake, no one will notice.'

The dance called the Charleston involved a lot of rather peculiar steps, arm waving and leg crossing, and it was gradually becoming all the rage at private parties after a film featuring it had been shown in America earlier that year. It was yet to be accepted by everyone, but it was a lot of fun – and so was the evening for me, after my initial awkwardness. Mary's friends rallied round me and the only dances I sat out were when I was eating some of the delicious food the caterer's had provided. More than an hour passed before I at last met my host. Looking rather sheepish, Mary brought him up to me as I was sipping a glass of cool lemonade, momentarily alone.

'Daddy wanted to meet you, Amy.'

'My daughter has rather unfortunate manners at times, Miss Robinson,' he said and smiled at me. 'It would have been nice had she introduced you at the start, but better late than never.'

'It's nice to meet you, sir,' I said looking at him rather uncertainly.

'Maitland – Philip Maitland,' he said,

offering his hand. 'I believe you have designed a rather lovely gown for my daughter. How clever you must be.'

His smile was charming; his manner seemed warm and friendly – a perfect gentleman. I had expected Mary's father to be a bit of an ogre and I wondered at the faint hostility I glimpsed in her eyes.

Why didn't Mary like her father? She seemed nervous, almost frightened of him, and yet he appeared to be a kind, generous and indulgent father.

'Amy is going to be a famous designer one day,' she said. 'I'm lucky to be her first client. Now go away and talk to your own friends, Daddy. Amy and I want to have fun.'

'I beg your pardon, Miss Robinson,' Mr Maitland smiled oddly. 'Perhaps we may meet again. I should like to hear more of your ambitions. I might be able to help.'

'Do go away, Daddy!'

His eyes narrowed for a moment and I sensed he was angry with her, which was hardly surprising considering Mary's behaviour.

'I didn't want to bring him over,' she confessed as she hurried me away, back to the dancing. 'He always spoils things.'

'Your father didn't spoil anything,' I said. 'He seems nice, Mary.'

He was in fact an attractive man, sophisticated and self-assured, but interesting despite the age gap. I had quite liked him and would not have minded talking to him a little longer.

'You don't know him as well as I do,' Mary said. 'Besides, you're my friend, not his. He knows my friends are out of bounds as far as he is concerned.'

I wondered what she meant but I didn't ask. Mary's relationship with her father was obviously a complicated one.

Mr Maitland made no further attempt to speak to me that evening, but I noticed him looking at me rather intently once, so I smiled. He smiled back, a flicker of amusement in his eyes that made me look away quickly. Of course, he would think that I was just a foolish little shop girl his daughter had chosen to add to her circle of friends.

Paul Ross danced with me again before the end of the party. He asked how I was getting home and offered to take me. I told him there was a taxi arranged but thanked him, feeling disappointed. I liked Paul and I would have been happy for him to drive me home, but perhaps it was best this way.

I was in love with Matthew and we were engaged. I must remember not to get too involved with my new friends. They were exciting and fun, but I had to remember that my life was meant to be a very different way. I was a working girl and I did not really belong in Mary's set.

* * *

Matthew's visit that weekend was all too brief for my liking. On the Saturday evening he took me to see a show at the Haymarket Theatre, and afterwards we went out for supper. I clung to him as he kissed me good-night.

'I've missed you so much, Matt.'

'I've missed you just as much. And I'm really sorry about last week.'

'I shouldn't have made such a fuss.'

'I can't blame you. I did let you down.'

'You didn't have much choice. I know your work is important to you.'

'You are just as important, Amy. Don't think I enjoy being away all the time.'

'The months will soon pass and then you can come home and we can get married.'

'The sooner the better as far as I am concerned.'

Matthew's kiss was hungry and it felt so good in his arms that I knew nothing else mattered but this feeling between us. I knew we must get through the period until our marriage as best we could.

On Sunday we visited my parents, who were delighted to see Matthew and made a big fuss of him. Later we went walking in the park, lingering to listen to an open-air concert for a while. Several families were taking the air but we saw more than one man begging for money because he was out of work.

Times were difficult and there had been a few strikes since the end of the war due to the general dissatisfaction many people felt.

It had been promised that working and living conditions would improve after the war, but so far nothing much had been done. I had only to think of the way people lived in the lanes to know that there was a huge void between them and Mary's friends. There was so much unemployment that it was hardly surprising that people were saying there needed to be a change in the government, and that left-wing speakers attracted great crowds in the industrial areas of the country.

Matthew didn't talk about things like that often, but I knew he felt fortunate to have a job that paid well, and it made me realize that I must try harder to understand his point of view. I had to be patient and wait for things to come to me, instead of expecting them immediately.

'If I can earn promotion it means a decent home and a good life for our children. A little patience now could make all the difference to our future, Amy. I don't want you to struggle to make ends meet like so many women have to all their lives. I want to give you everything you need.'

I didn't tell him that my father would see we never went short, because it would only have made him angry. Matthew was determined to do things his way, and if I wanted him I had to go along with his wishes.

Besides, for the moment I was having fun staying with my aunt, and my friendship with Mary was exciting. I had enjoyed her party after my initial nervousness, and I was looking forward to staying with her in the country the following weekend.

I told Matthew she had invited me to stay, but I didn't mention the party I'd been to at her house. Somehow I didn't think he would be pleased to hear that I had been dancing with other young men, some of whom had been outrageous flirts.

He wasn't too keen on the idea of my going to her country house, but accepted it when I said it was really a working trip.

'I'm going to be showing her designs and working on a few patterns,' I said, not looking him in the eyes. I felt a bit deceitful for not telling him everything, but he would have been annoyed and I didn't want to spoil the short time we had together. After all, I hadn't known Mary's party would turn out to be a dance. 'Don't be cross with me, Matt. I have to do something with my time while you are away.'

His eyes were serious as he looked at me, vaguely disappointed, as if he was hurt that I could just go off and enjoy myself while he was working all hours for our future.

'Just don't get too involved with this girl, Amy,' he said. 'I don't want to stop you having fun, but I'm not sure she is the right sort for you. Some of these rich girls can be very spoiled. You see pictures of them at Ascot in the paper, and coming out of night-clubs at all hours in the morning. Some of them seem to have forgotten how to behave like decent young ladies. You don't want to get mixed up with that crowd.'

'And you called me a snob!' I cried. 'You haven't even met her, Matt. Mum and Lainie both hinted that she might drop me when she's tired of my company, but Mary isn't like that. She's really nice, and a bit shy sometimes – and I like her. I don't think Mary goes to nightclubs, her aunt wouldn't allow it – and if she did I shouldn't go with her.'

'And I'm being selfish,' he said. 'I can't expect you to sit alone all the time – and as you say, it is work. So I don't really have a leg to stand on, do I?'

'Don't let's quarrel,' I begged. 'I've looked forward to this for so long.'

'So have I,' he said and put his arms about me, kissing me softly on the lips. 'I apologize for doubting your friend. Go to the country with her and have a good time.'

Later, when I was alone, I thought about my own behaviour and felt the shame wash over me. Matt was working all hours so that we could be married sooner and I was keeping things from him. He wouldn't have liked me to visit Mary if he'd known about the party and some of her friends, who I was quite sure did all the things he thought unladylike. I'd seen some of them smoking in public, and at Mary's party a few of the guests had been drinking more than they ought to. And then there was Paul, whose lean, rather haunted features were beginning to play on my mind, making me think of him all too often.

Perhaps I should draw back now, before I got in too deep.

But Mary's other friends wouldn't be there at the weekend. She had said it was going to be just her and me.

'I've persuaded Paul to come down with us,' Mary told me when she called for me in her father's car that Saturday morning. It was a large, luxurious saloon with leather upholstery. 'I was sure you would be pleased. Paul is no trouble. He will just mooch about on his own most of the time, and he'll be there if we want him to take us on the river in a boat.'

'I don't mind Paul coming,' I said immediately. 'Will there be anyone else, Mary?'

'Oh, I shouldn't think so for a moment,' she said a trifle airily. 'Jane and Millie know we are going down, but I doubt they will want to leave town. It depends on the weather of course.'

I wasn't sure how to take Mary's remarks. She had been certain we were going to be alone in the country at the start, and now she wasn't so sure. And the dinner party had turned out to be more of a dance than a dinner. I hoped the weekend wouldn't turn out to be something similar.

Paul had driven himself down to Grayling, which was the name of Mr Maitland's house. He was waiting for us when we arrived and looked very attractive in his pale fawn slacks, open-necked shirt and striped blazer.

We had lunch in the conservatory, which was rather grand with lots of long arched windows, greenery, fancy wrought-iron tables and basketwork chairs. Afterwards, we debated whether to go on the river or sit in chairs out on the lawn.

'It will be cooler on the river,' Mary said. 'It's so hot in the gardens today.'

'Cooler for you, perhaps,' Paul replied with a wry smile. 'You don't have to row.'

'I'll help with the rowing,' I offered. 'At college some of the girls used to take a boat on the river and I went with them. We all had to share the rowing. Mary is right, it will be nicer on the river.'

'It looks as if I'm outnumbered,' Paul said. 'I may as well give in or Mary will sulk for hours.'

'Sometimes I hate you, Paul.'

'I know you do, my darling – but I still love you.'

Paul was only teasing. He didn't really mind taking us out on the river, which passed the house just beyond the garden wall. A wooden gate led to a jetty with a rowing boat moored ready for use.

Mary's suggestion proved a success. It was much cooler on the river and a pleasant way to spend the afternoon. We talked and laughed, Paul going out of his way to entertain us. I could see why Mary loved him when he was in this mood, and I rather liked him too.

I was sorry when it was decided that we should go back to the house for tea. I had enjoyed myself a lot and was glad that Paul had come down for the weekend.

However, when we returned to the house we discovered that several others had arrived. Jane Adams, her brother Harry, who was several years older than her, Millicent Fairchild and Alan Bell were sitting on the lawn, and tea was already being served to them. Jane greeted Mary with an exaggerated cry of relief.

'We were beginning to think you'd got lost,' Jane said and I could see she wasn't pleased that no one had been here to greet her when she arrived.

'Sorry,' Mary apologized. 'I wasn't sure you and Millie were coming.'

She flopped down into one of the chairs. Paul, who had said he was dying for a cup of tea, stood looking at the others in a brooding manner for a few moments before walking into the house. I thought he was not best pleased by the unexpected arrival of Mary's friends.

After a slight hesitation, I sat down and allowed the maid to serve me tea and a jam scone with thick cream on top.

'I don't know how you dare eat that,' Jane cried. 'If I ate even half I should put on a pound in weight.'

'I never do, whatever I eat.'

'Lucky thing,' Millie said. 'I have to watch my weight too.'

I thought of all the hours I spent on my feet at the shop. These girls had probably never worked in their lives, but instead of telling them they needed to exercise more I smiled and sympathized. I couldn't afford to antagonize either of them.

Millicent Fairchild seemed happy to accept me as one of the group, but I didn't think Jane liked me much. She made a couple of remarks that might have been meant to put me in my place, but I ignored them and kept on smiling. This was Mary's house, not Jane's, and I had been invited.

The afternoon did not end as perfectly as it had begun because Jane had a tiff with her brother, who went storming into the house.

'Harry is such a bore,' Jane muttered. 'He didn't want to come at all. He never leaves town unless forced.'

I wondered why she had bothered to persuade her brother to leave his beloved London. She looked bored and directed several sulky looks towards the house. It was only later that evening that I discovered the reason for her moodiness.

As I was leaving my bedroom to go downstairs I happened to meet Paul coming along the landing. He smiled as I waited for him to catch up to me.

'You look pretty, Amy.'

'Thank you.' I blushed. 'You look nice too.'

'Do I?' He laughed. 'Not many girls would tell me that, Amy. You're very different from most of Mary's friends.'

'That's because I work in a shop and my parents live near the docks.'

'Perhaps that is why I like you, because you're so honest and open. And you don't make eyes at me all the time – like some I could name. I would never have come this weekend if I'd known Jane Adams and her prig of a brother would be here!'

'You're scowling,' I said. 'Don't you like Jane? She's rather pretty.'

'And she knows it! I'm not interested. Between us, I'm not looking for a wife, and it certainly wouldn't be Jane if I were.'

'Perhaps you ought not to have told me that.'

'Probably not, but I can't take it back, can I? Besides, I think you can keep a secret, Amy.'

'Oh yes, close as the grave, that's me.'

We were laughing as we walked down the wide, very grand staircase together. It was a beautiful house, old and graceful, furnished with exquisite antiques, which I guessed were valuable.

Jane, her brother and Alan Bell were already gathered in the large drawing room, which was gracious in crimson and dusty gold. The look Jane flashed at me as I walked in with Paul was so full of malice that I caught my breath. Why had she suddenly turned against me?

As the evening progressed I realized that Jane was jealous because I'd been laughing with Paul. She followed him like a shadow all night and I understood why he had told me he wasn't interested. Her smiles were so false, her manner so shallow, her laugh so irritating. I could see that it was taking him all his time to be civil to her.

I felt sympathy for her despite her growing hostility towards me. It must be awful to want someone that badly and know he was indifferent. She must sense his rejection, I thought. Why didn't she just ignore him and talk to someone else? Why pursue him when he simply didn't want to know?

After dinner, Jane played the piano for us. Paul walked out instantly, a pained expression in his eyes.

'Let's put a record on,' Millie said when Jane had finished her piece. 'You've got some new jazz records, Mary. I just love Bessie Smith singing the blues, don't you? We could dance if Paul came back.'

'You and Mary can dance,' Jane said sulkily. 'I'm going for a walk in the garden.'

I thought she was probably going in search of Paul so I didn't offer to go with her. Feeling that I was a little in the way, I walked through the long dining room and into the conservatory.

Paul was standing at the far end, the door open. He was smoking a cigarette and something warned me he had come here to be alone. I hesitated, about to turn away when he spoke, his back still towards me.

'Don't go, Amy.'

'Are you sure? I didn't know you were here or I wouldn't have intruded. I thought you might have gone into the garden.'

'That's how I knew it was you; the others wouldn't have hesitated to make themselves known. I was going to rejoin you all in a moment.' He looked round and grinned wickedly. 'I just couldn't stand to hear that particular piece of music being murdered. It used to be a favourite.'

I couldn't help laughing, though I knew he was being very unkind.

'I expect Jane was doing her best.'

'If that is her best she should stay well away from a piano.'

'You are very cruel, Paul.'

'Am I?' He was silent for a moment. 'I suppose I am, but Jane makes me angry. I can't stand women who run after me. She is so thick-skinned. She just doesn't seem to realize that I'm not interested in her and never will be.'

Looking beyond Paul to the garden I noticed someone in the shadows just outside and knew instantly who it must be. Jane must have seen Paul standing there and been on her way to join him. For a moment the shadowy figure stood as if turned to stone, then suddenly whirled around and ran away into the shrubbery.

She must have heard what Paul was saying! I felt dreadful. If I'd realized she was there earlier I would have stopped him.

'What's wrong?' he asked, eyes narrowing.

'I think Jane heard what you were saying just now.'

'Damn!' He stubbed his cigarette out in a plant pot. 'I had no idea she was there.'

'Nor had I until she ran away. I'm almost sure she heard.'

'Well, if she did it may stop her making a nuisance of herself in future.'

'I don't think that's very nice.'

'That's because I'm not nice,' he said and walked towards me.

'I don't think I like you much when you're in this mood.'

'That's a pity, because I like you.'

As I turned to leave, he caught my arm, swinging me back to face him. I noticed his hands then. His fingers were long and sensitive, the hands of an artist just as Mary had told me. Fascinated, I didn't immediately try to move away, and then, before I guessed what he meant to do, he caught me to him and kissed me. It wasn't gentle and sweet the way Matthew's kisses were, but hard and demanding. Suddenly brought to my senses, I struggled to break free and after a moment he let me go.

'How dare you?'

'I dare many things,' Paul muttered. 'But I probably shouldn't have done it. You are such a bright, clever little thing. You go to a man's head, Amy – but as I told you earlier, I'm not interested in marriage.'

He walked past me and into the dining room. For a moment I stood without moving, my cheeks warm. Then as I turned, about to join the others, a man entered the conservatory through the garden door.

'You should have struck him, Miss Robinson. Would you like me to make him come back and apologize?'

'Mr Maitland...' I was shocked as I saw Mary's father. He was dressed in a black evening suit and looked as if he had just come from a formal occasion. 'I–I didn't know you were here.'

'I wasn't expecting to be here. It was so hot in London that I decided on the spur of the moment to drive down and join you all.'

'Did you know Mary had friends staying?'

'Others besides you and Paul?'

'Yes.' I named them and he swore softly, apparently no more pleased to discover they were here than Paul had been.

'I was hoping for a quiet weekend.'

'Mary didn't think you ever came here.'

'I never do as a rule. I knew you were coming with her. I was hoping for a quiet chat with you, Miss Robinson. Mrs Holland told me that Mary insists on having several of her dresses designed by you and made by your aunt's workrooms.'

'I ... Yes,' I said, my breathing a little faster than usual. 'Mary has talked of ordering more gowns if she likes my designs.'

'Have you many to show her? Mary can be very difficult to please. My wife was just the same.'

'We shall probably look through what I've done in the morning. At least, that is what we had planned to do before the others arrived.'

'Miss Adams and Miss Fairchild will not appear much before noon,' he said with a faint smile. 'I should be interested to see your designs, Miss Robinson. Will Miss O'Rourke's workroom be able to cope if Mary orders several gowns from you?'

'Oh, yes. My aunt said that she would take on an extra seamstress if need be.'

'How very obliging of her.' His mouth curved in an odd smile and I could see that he was amused by something, though I did not know what it could be. 'I should be pleased if every effort could be made to accommodate Mary.'

'Of course. My aunt always tries to please her clients.'

'And you, Miss Robinson – do you always try to please? My daughter can be very demanding.'

'I like Mary.' I blushed as his gaze narrowed intently, sensing something hidden behind his words, as if they had a second meaning I did not understand. 'She has been nice to me, inviting me to her home and down here.'

'Ah yes,' he murmured. 'Please remember that I would like to see your portfolio, Miss Robinson.'

'Yes, sir.'

I felt I had been dismissed and was a little disappointed. He was not an easy person to understand. I wasn't sure whether he approved of me or not.

Returning to the drawing room, where Mary was dancing with Paul, I soon forgot my brief conversation with her father. Harry Adams was dancing with Millie and Alan Bell came up to me as I entered.

'I wondered where you had got to, Amy. Jane disappeared ages ago.'

'I think she went for a walk.'

'She's probably sulking,' he said. 'I think she is rather keen on Paul, but he has other ideas.'

'What do you mean – other ideas?'

'Paul has expensive tastes. He'll settle for money when he gets round to finding a wife.'

'That's a bit harsh, isn't it?'

'Yes, but it's perfectly true.'

'He told me he wasn't interested in getting married for a while.'

'Moody chap. Forget him and dance with me, Amy.' He smiled at me. 'I must say you look awfully pretty this evening. That dress suits you.'

It was my only evening dress but I didn't tell Alan that. If Mary continued to invite me to her parties I should have to buy myself another gown.

Paul came up to me when the dance ended. He looked a bit sheepish as he asked if I would dance with him.

'I owe you an apology,' he said when I hesitated.

'Yes, you do – but I might forgive you if you promise not to do it again.'

'Next time I'll make sure you want to be kissed,' he said and grinned in the way that made him so attractive. 'I'm a moody devil, Amy, but pretty harmless. I might snatch a kiss from you, but I wouldn't hurt you. I give you my word.'

'I didn't think you would. I wasn't frightened of you, Paul – but I'm not free to carry on a flirtation. I haven't got a ring because my boyfriend is saving for our house, but I am more or less engaged. We are going to marry as soon as he can afford it.'

'Yes, Mary told me.' He sighed deeply. 'Your fiancé is a lucky chap, Amy. Had things been different I might have tried to cut him out, but...'

'Is something bothering you, Paul?' I saw the way his eyes had clouded. Once again I sensed that something was haunting him, never letting him be entirely free.

'Nothing that either you or I can cure.' He smiled oddly. 'Let's enjoy ourselves, shall we? Seize the day, as they say – or evening, rather.'

The shadows in Paul's eyes made me wonder what secret caused him such pain, but in another moment the thought was lost as Jane walked in. She was soaked to the skin, her hair and clothes streaked with mud, and her face scratched. She looked as if she might have been attacked and Millie screamed at the sight of her.

'Jane! What happened?'

Everyone stopped dancing and looked at her.

'Good God!' Harry exclaimed. 'What happened to you?

'I went for a walk by the river and fell in. Not that you would care. None of you would have turned a hair if I had drowned.'

A shocked silence followed her bitter words, and then her brother caught her by the arm and marched her from the room. We could hear them arguing as they went upstairs.

'Do you think we should send for a doctor?' Mary asked no one in particular.

'I doubt she needs one,' Paul said. 'I imagine that was another of Jane's attempts to draw attention to herself. She probably threw herself in deliberately.'

'Paul!' Mary cried. 'Don't be so mean about poor Jane. I'll go upstairs and see how she is.'

'Trust Jane to do something silly,' Alan said. 'I suppose that puts paid to the evening. Anyone fancy a nightcap? What about you, Paul? I think there's a billiards table somewhere.'

'Yes, I'll show you. Excuse us, ladies.'

Millie looked at me as they went out.

'What a fright Jane must have had. Shall

we go up now? Or do you want to watch the men play? They would probably rather we didn't.'

'Then we shan't,' I said. 'If you don't mind, I think I shall go up. I have something I need to do before I go to bed.'

We parted at the top of the stairs. I wasn't in the least tired, even though it had been a long and eventful day.

Getting out my book of sketches, I looked through it with a critical eye. Why did Mary's father want to see my designs? Would he insist on approving them before she ordered anything else?

I was just putting my folder away when Mary knocked and then entered my room.

'Jane is in a dreadful mood, but I don't think she's really hurt. Fortunately she can swim and the river is shallow where she slipped in. I suppose it was an awful shock for her, falling in the water like that. I can't imagine why she wanted to walk by the river alone.'

'She was upset. She heard something Paul said about her.'

'Oh...' Mary looked as if she understood. 'Paul doesn't much like her, does he?'

'Not very much. She was in the garden and the conservatory door was wide open. I think she heard, though I'm not sure how much. He was rather rude about her playing the piano.'

'He would be. Paul is a perfectionist himself.'

'And cruel. He doesn't seem to care what he says.'

'Paul can be very sharp – but he's usually sorry afterwards. He didn't mean Jane to hear.'

'No, I am sure he didn't – but he still shouldn't have said what he did about her. It wasn't nice.'

'Paul isn't nice.' Mary gave me a teasing smile. 'I think Alan is getting a crush on you.'

'Surely not! He is just being friendly.'

'Don't say I didn't warn you. He's not as wealthy as my father, but he's quite a good catch.'

'I'm more or less engaged. Besides, my father has money. I don't need a rich husband.'

'I didn't realize that.' Mary looked curious. 'You've never mentioned it before, Amy.'

'Well, there wasn't any reason to. Dad isn't as rich as your father, but he has enough. He owns quite a bit of property and various businesses.'

'You've got two brothers, haven't you?' Mary looked thoughtful. 'You're not an heiress or anything?'

'No, of course not. I shall get a good wedding present, but that's all.'

'Paul has expensive tastes. I don't suppose you'll get enough to make it worth his while to marry you.'

'Mary!'

She laughed at my shocked expression. 'I'm thinking like Aunt Emily. Money is everything in some circles. Paul won't marry without money, Amy.'

'Paul can do whatever he likes. I'm going to marry Matthew.'

'Jane thinks you want Paul.'

'Then Jane is wrong.'

'Good.' Mary had a look of her father about her at that moment. 'Paul is mine. We might not get married, but he's mine until I let him go.'

'He certainly isn't mine. Much too moody!'

Mary laughed. 'That's all right then.'

'Did you know your father is here?'

'Yes. I've been told.' Her smile vanished. 'I wish he hadn't come. I shall tell him to stay out of our way.'

'He wants to see my designs.'

'I hope he isn't going to interfere.'

'We shall have to show him.'

'I suppose so,' she said sulkily. 'But he has no idea of what I like and I shall tell him to leave us alone.'

It was a while before I could sleep that evening. I went to sit on the window seat, looking out at the gardens. The moon was quite bright, turning everything it touched to silver. I saw a man leave the house and begin to walk across the lawns.

I knew at once that it was Paul. Obviously he could not sleep either. I believed he was deeply disturbed about something; it haunted him and was responsible for his moods. Mary had thought it was the war that had made him this way, and perhaps that was true. I knew that a lot of men had been scarred by the terrible things they had seen during the war. And yet I felt it was something else, something more personal that made Paul want to be alone so often.

I had particularly noticed his hands that evening. There were no scars, nothing to prevent him from playing the piano if he wished. If he had scars they must be inside, where no one could see them.

I got up from the window seat and went to bed. I must not let Paul and his secrets turn into an obsession.

Mary and I had breakfast together in the conservatory. No one else had appeared yet and we were able to spread out the designs at one end of the table, passing them back and forth as we discussed the ones that Mary liked best.

'This would be lovely in pale blue,' she said. 'And this is beautiful, Amy. I should like both of them – and that afternoon dress you showed me earlier.'

In all she picked six gowns; two for evening, two for afternoons, one for an informal party and one for mornings. Several of them were the more relaxed style I favoured, simple and elegant with just a touch of embroidery to make them individual.

'I think that should keep your aunt's people busy for a while,' she said with a satisfied smile.

'May I have a look now?'

We turned as Mr Maitland entered, Mary's smile fading as she saw him. My heart raced. Would he say that his daughter could not buy so many gowns from us?

'Of course, sir,' I replied, and passed the folder to him. I had marked the gowns Mary had chosen so it was easy for him to pick them out. He studied them carefully, then went on to the others. At last he closed the folder and returned it to me.

'You have talent, Miss Robinson. I congratulate you – and you, Mary, for having the eye to see what you've found here. These are original and exciting.' He turned his gaze on me. 'You are wasting your time working as a shop girl, Miss Robinson. You should be designing gowns for discerning clients full-time.'

'I don't think my aunt would want to go into anything like that.'

'There are other ways. The right backer could set you on the path to fame and fortune. I am sure I know someone who could help.'

'Daddy!' Mary's voice was sharp, angry. 'Leave Amy alone. I found her. She's mine, not yours.'

I wasn't sure I liked being claimed as anyone's property, but I was fascinated by the clash of wills between father and daughter. I had always thought of Mary as being shy and a little unsure of herself, but at this moment she might have been a tigress defending her young. Her eyes flashed with anger and her father was clearly influenced by her show of spirit.

'Of course, Mary. Your friend is perfectly safe. I was merely thinking that such talent should not go to waste.'

'Amy's talent isn't wasted. She hasn't time to make gowns for anyone but me – have you, Amy?'

'No,' I said. I certainly didn't have time to work on gowns for anyone else, but Mr Maitland's encouragement had started me dreaming. 'Not as things are...'

Was that a gleam in Mr Maitland's eyes? I couldn't be sure, because Mary jumped up and grabbed my arm, hurrying me out into the early-morning air.

'What's wrong?' I asked as I saw how pale she was.

'You mustn't trust him,' she said. 'Promise me you won't listen to anything he says,

Amy.'

'Why don't you like your father?'

'Because ... because he wasn't kind to Mummy.' Her eyes filled with tears, which she dashed away with the back of her hand. 'Don't listen to him. You can't be his friend *and* mine. I want you to be my friend, Amy.'

'Of course I am your friend. Anyway, in a few months Matthew will come home and I shall get married. I couldn't do what your father suggested. I might design a gown sometimes for a friend, but I expect we'll have children.'

'Good.' She smiled at me, her humour restored. 'That's best. You marry your Matthew and make me a dress now and then – and forget all Daddy's silly ideas.'

I hadn't realized how selfish Mary could be. If I had been free to follow a career, Mr Maitland's suggestion would have been the first step on the ladder. But it was better to be less ambitious. If I was lucky I might sell one of my designs to a fashion house sometimes.

Matthew and our marriage had to come first.

Five

Jane, her brother and the others left immediately after lunch. Millie and Alan said goodbye to me and said they looked forward to seeing me again soon. Jane and her brother totally ignored me. Clearly, Jane had decided that the conversation she had overheard was my fault, and her brother simply thought I was beneath his notice.

Mary didn't want to leave at once. She would have liked to remain in the country a few more days if I was free to stay with her, but I told her firmly that I could not.

'My aunt let me have Saturday off as it was, Mary. I can't expect anything more.'

'I shall stay,' she said. 'You'll stay with me, won't you, Paul?'

'I'm sorry. I have appointments in town. Besides, you can't just send Amy off on her own. If you're not going back to town I'll drive her myself.'

'Oh, there's no point in staying here alone,' Mary said and pulled a face. 'If you're both going back I might as well take Daddy's car and go too.'

Paul made a wry face at me. He was obviously aware that Mary could be a selfish brat, but he was fond of her and put up with her ways.

I decided that I would take the same attitude as Paul. He treated her sulks as if they meant nothing, and eventually she came round to his way of thinking. I made up my mind then that I wouldn't run after Mary, but I wouldn't take offence either.

She apologized to me on the way home.

'I know I'm rotten sometimes,' she said. 'I don't mean to be, but it's something inside me – something I can't help. Paul says I've got the same bad blood as him, and he tells me to relax and be calm and I'll feel better, but there are times when I just want to scream and scream.'

'It can't be very nice to feel like that,' I said. 'What does Paul mean exactly by bad blood?'

Mary shrugged. 'I think some of the older generation were a bit wild or something. No one ever tells me in what way, though I believe Paul has gone into it a bit more since he came back from the war. It's the reason he says we can't marry – because we're too close and it would make the bad streak come out in our children.'

'I don't suppose it is good for close cousins to marry,' I agreed. 'I've heard that in some cases there can be problems with the children of such a marriage.'

'Paul says he wouldn't marry me even if my father agreed,' Mary said, frowning. 'So I suppose we shan't, but he still belongs to me. He always will, even if he marries someone else.'

'He told me he wasn't thinking of taking a wife, so perhaps he won't.'

'Good. That way I can keep him all for myself.'

Mary's love for her cousin seemed slightly obsessive to me, but I didn't comment on her remarks. After all, it wasn't my affair. I liked Paul but I wasn't in love with him, and I was going to marry Matthew. After that my friendship with Mary would probably fade into the background.

I didn't mind that, though I was enjoying myself now. I wanted it to continue for a while.

I could tell that a man had been staying in my room, though it had been tidied and polished. There was a faint, lingering smell of tobacco and a different feel to things. I found a stray cufflink in the top drawer that I had cleared for his things, and a shirt button on the floor. I put them to one side for Lainie to send on, then opened the window a little and went through to my aunt's parlour.

'Did you have a good weekend?'

We both asked the same question at once and laughed.

'You first,' Lainie said and so I told her about going on the river, about one of the girls falling in, and about Mary's father showing an interest in my designs.

'You next,' I said, because I could tell from her manner that she was trying to keep her feelings under control. 'Something happened this weekend, didn't it?

'Yes...' She took a deep breath. 'I'm going to tell you something that may shock you, Amy. When I was not much older than you are now I had ... an unfortunate affair that left me pregnant. I wasn't married, and had no hope of getting married.'

'I'm so sorry,' I said at once. 'That must have been terrible for you.'

'It was frightening at first,' she said. 'I was very unhappy – the affair ended badly, and there was no money. Bridget and I quarrelled a lot and I felt I was in the way. She had enough to do at home without looking after another baby, and I didn't want my child – at least, I didn't want him then.'

'Poor you. It must have been an awful time for you.'

'It was. I can't tell you how bad but I hope you never experience anything like it, Amy. I was wretched for months – years. I had my baby in a home for unmarried girls and they gave him away for adoption. I had to sign a form agreeing to that before they would take me in. At the time I thought it would be best for everyone, but afterwards...' She paused and I could see that she was greatly affected by her memories. 'I began to feel guilty and to worry about what had happened to my son. As the years went on and I became settled in my work, finally inheriting this business and property, I knew I wanted to find him.'

'Is that where Harold Brompton comes into it?'

'I knew you would guess, Amy,' she said and smiled. 'He owns and runs an agency that traces lost people. He did a lot for women who had lost touch with husbands or lovers through the war, and I heard about him from a friend. After we'd met a few times I told him about my son and he said he would try to find him, though he didn't hold out much hope at the time. These things were arranged to prevent that happening.' She paused breathlessly and I could see the gleam of excitement in her eyes.

'But now he has found your son?'

'Yes. He gave me the name of the family who adopted him, their address and the place where my son works. Their name is Fisher and they called him John. It's up to me now what I do about it.'

'Does your son know he was adopted?'

'Yes, he is aware of that. Harold was able to

find that much out without alerting him to the fact that I was trying to find him...' She looked and sounded nervous. 'I'm not sure what to do next, Amy.'

'You want to get in touch, don't you? You must do or you wouldn't have had him traced.'

'I needed to be sure he was all right, but I don't want to interfere in his life. He might not want to know me. He might hate me. After all, I did give him away.'

'You didn't have much choice, from what I've heard.'

'Bridget would have helped me if I'd stayed with her. She was upset because I didn't keep my baby – but there were reasons, Amy. I can't tell you, but believe me I had reason enough not to want my child then.'

'You've regretted it so much, haven't you?'

I understood the underlying sadness and the loneliness now. I had guessed there was a tragedy in my aunt's past, and even now I believed there was a lot more she wasn't telling me.

'I'm sorry something bad happened to you,' I told her. 'You've got to make up your own mind, of course, but I think you should see John and tell him the truth.'

'Perhaps...' She smiled and I could see she wanted to change the subject. 'Harold asked me to marry him again. He refuses to give up and says he's going to ask me every couple of months until I say yes.'

'I would really like to meet him.'

'Perhaps next time. Anyway, I'm pleased things went well for you this weekend. You are certainly going to have a lot of work in the next few weeks, Amy.'

'The most intricate work is on the evening dresses, the others are fairly straightforward. If Margaret could be persuaded to do a few hours overtime it shouldn't be a problem.'

'I should imagine she would be glad of the money.' Lainie looked at me thoughtfully. 'It's really you who should benefit from this, Amy. Your friendship with Mary seems to have brought in quite a lot more custom, and I think the made-to-order clothes should be entirely your department.'

'Have you had other clients asking about my designs?'

'Yes, this weekend. A woman came in on Saturday. She was obviously wealthy and she asked specifically for you. I told her you would be in the showroom this morning and she said she would call in again.'

'If I take on more work it means you will have to get that extra seamstress you were thinking about.'

'Yes, well, it might be worth it if trade builds up.' Lainie was thoughtful. 'If I wanted to get married – and I'm not saying I've made up my mind yet – do you think you could manage the shop? You would need to employ more staff, but you and Matthew could live in the rooms over the shop if you wanted. It would give him longer to save for the house and business he wants and I would feel happier about leaving this in your hands.'

'Do you think I could manage it?' I stared at her excitedly.

'I don't see why not,' she said and smiled as she saw that I was pleased with her idea. 'I've been thinking about this for a long time, Amy. I wasn't sure it would work out, but you're so good with the customers, and this design business is exactly what you need. You are wasted as a shop girl.'

She was echoing Mr Maitland's words, but I didn't tell her so. For some reason I was wary of mentioning Mary's father too often, though I couldn't have explained why. I suppose I was afraid that if my aunt or my parents thought he might be a bad influence on me they might try to stop me visiting Mary.

I wasn't a foolish girl, whatever they might think, and I knew that it wasn't usual for an older man to show a particular interest in a young girl – unless he had something particular in mind. From Mary's protective attitude towards me I had gathered that any attention her father paid me might not be in my own interests. I was a shop girl, not one of Mary's well-bred friends, and I supposed as such I might be considered fair game. If I wanted to continue visiting Mary as a friend, I should have to stay well clear of her father.

She had warned me that I couldn't be both her friend and his, and after thinking about it for a while, I believed I had found an explanation for her cryptic statement.

I thought that perhaps Mr Maitland liked to have affairs with pretty young women. He was an attractive man, and his wealth must appeal to many girls in the same kind of situation as myself. I could imagine that a lot of girls would leap at the chances he had offered, but I wasn't one of them.

I was a marriage or nothing sort of girl. And I was going to marry Matthew.

Mary didn't invite me to her house for a couple of weeks, though I saw her at least twice a week during that period for fittings. I couldn't have gone anyway, because I was working all the time, on her gowns and on one for another lady who had asked me to make her a simple afternoon dress.

Mrs Simpson had come into the shop on the Monday morning and had spent half an hour persuading me to show her my designs. I did so reluctantly, remembering that Mary had wanted me to work exclusively for her, but in the end I was persuaded.

'Yes, I would like that in the dark-blue material,' Mrs Simpson said when I finally gave in. 'You will do that for me, won't you, Amy?'

'Yes, but you may have to wait for a couple of weeks. We have a big order on at the moment.'

'Good things are always worth waiting for,' she said, smiling mysteriously. 'As perhaps you may discover one day.'

I wondered what she meant, but I was too busy to dwell on it. Mary's clothes were taking up all my time and I was working nearly every evening to catch up – though I did take one off to go to the cinema with Lainie to see Gloria Swanson in a new film directed by Cecile B. DeMille. To me this actress symbolized the new era of freedom that modern women were enjoying, her sensual performances on screen matching the scandal that characterized the real lives of many Hollywood celebrities.

In the past year or so, Fatty Arbuckle, the popular comedian, had been charged with causing the death of a starlet at a wild party, and a director had been murdered. Two actresses had been suspected of being involved, but though they were not charged, their careers were ruined. Fatty Arbuckle's films were removed from cinemas across America, despite his being acquitted. And there was talk of another popular actor having died in a sanatorium from taking drugs.

When Mary came into the shop at the end of that week she apologized for not having asked me over for a while.

'I have so many prior engagements,' she told me with a sigh. 'Most of it is such boring stuff, Amy. I wish I could take you with me, but they are not the sort of people you would want to know – Aunt Emily's friends. It's all visits to the opera or the ballet, and some very stuffy evening parties. It bores me to death and I'm sure it would you, Amy.'

'I wouldn't expect to be invited to the houses of your friends, Mary.'

'Paul is giving an afternoon party soon. He told me that he is going to invite you. I'll have one of Daddy's cars pick you up – it's on Sunday next. I think he chose that day especially so that you could come.'

'That is very kind of him,' I said. 'But I'm not sure I shall be able to come. Matthew is telephoning this evening. He may be coming up this weekend.'

'Can't you put him off?'

'No, not if he wants to come. We don't see each other very often as it is, Mary.'

'Oh well, if you would rather be with him...'

I could see she was annoyed but I wasn't going to put Matthew off for Paul's sake.

'I'd like to come and see you another time, Mary. I'm your friend, not Paul's.'

'Yes, I suppose you are. It's just that he asked specially, and I wanted you there.' She pulled a wry face. 'It doesn't matter. I shall probably have a party myself the following week. Daddy is going away so it will be safe to have my friends round.'

'I would like to come then if I can,' I said, but as she frowned, I said, 'No, I shall come, Mary. Matthew won't come two weeks running.'

'Will this afternoon dress be finished by tomorrow?'

'Yes. I'll work extra hours on it to make sure it is.'

'Thank you. You are so nice to me, Amy.' She smiled, her good humour restored. 'Have you heard about Jane?'

'No – what about her?'

'She's engaged to Sir Andrew Barclay. He's fifty if he's a day, but very rich. He gave her a huge emerald and diamond ring, which she is flashing under all our noses. She's acting like the cat that got the cream – but I'm sure she only took him because she heard what Paul said that night. She isn't in love with him. She can't be – he's so stuffy and boring.'

'That was foolish of her,' I said. 'She can't really want to marry him, can she?'

'Oh, I don't know, he's got pots of money. If she can't have Paul, she might as well take the money.'

'I feel sorry for her. I think she's making a terrible mistake.'

Mary shrugged. 'Perhaps – but it's what most of the girls do in the end. All the attractive men are looking for heiresses, and there aren't enough to go round. I think Millie will probably settle for Alan, unless she can find someone with more money.'

'At least Alan is young and attractive.'

'I told you he likes you, didn't I? He keeps asking me when you are coming to a party again.' Mary's eyes sparkled with mischief. 'He would be a much better catch than your Matthew.'

'I'm in love with Matt.'

'Oh well, you know your own mind,' she said, dismissing the subject. 'I'll be in for my fitting again tomorrow.'

I finished making the adjustments after she had gone, then took the dress through to Margaret in the workrooms.

'Can you get this done this afternoon?'

'Yes, I think so,' she said, then hesitated. 'I was wondering ... A few friends are having a little do this Sunday afternoon. Would you like to come?'

'Matthew is probably coming for the weekend.'

'You could bring him too if you like ... Unless you have something else lined up?'

'No, I shouldn't think we have,' I said. 'We shall visit my parents in the morning, but we usually just go for a walk in the afternoon.'

'Come and have tea with us then,' she said. 'It's a bring and buy sale for the church, and then a lovely cream tea. Outside if it's fine and in the tent if not. You would both be very welcome.'

'Yes, we'd like that – thank you for asking us.'

'I would have asked you to come out with us before,' she said, looking a bit shy. 'But you're always so busy, Amy – and of course you're friendly with that customer. Mary ... What's her other name?'

'Maitland,' I said. 'I am friendly with Mary, but I wouldn't mind going out with you and your friends sometimes in the evenings – but not until I get most of this work finished. How is Mrs Simpson's dress coming on by the way?'

'I've cut it out,' Margaret replied. 'But the bias is difficult and it will need time to get the hang right. Give me a couple more days before you make an appointment for her fitting – especially if you want Miss Maitland's dress ready for this weekend.'

'Yes, Mary's must come first,' I said. 'I've promised it will be ready, and I'm going to do the embroidery on the cuffs this evening.'

'She's lucky you put all that work in for nothing,' Margaret said. 'I saw a dress of this quality in a magazine the other day and it cost twice as much as you're charging. You don't want to let her get away with it too cheap, Amy. She'll take advantage of you if you do.'

'We've had a lot of trade through Mary and Mrs Holland,' I said. 'It's worth giving some customers a good deal. Besides, I don't mind doing the embroidery in my own time.'

'Well, you know best,' Margaret said. 'But I shall look forward to seeing you and Matthew this weekend.'

'I just hope he doesn't have to cancel at the last moment.'

'Keep your fingers crossed!'

'And your legs,' Sally chirped from her corner.

The new girl smiled but said nothing. Her name was Peggy and she was good at plain hemming and buttonholes, but very quiet and reserved. I had spoken to her a few times, but she wouldn't talk about herself.

'Peggy has had a hard life,' Lainie told me when she took her on. 'Some wouldn't employ her, but as long as she does her work and keeps her opinions to herself, that's fine by me.'

It was Margaret who had told me that Peggy had a baby. She wasn't married, and she had been forced to do all kinds of piece-work, for which she received a pittance, until Lainie gave her the job. She sat over her work all day, scarcely looking up, and was worth every penny my aunt paid her.

I understood now why Lainie was so good to girls like Peggy. She had been through the same experience, and she gave them a chance – though they would have been out on their ear if they had bad-mouthed a customer or slacked over their work.

I sometimes wondered what Lainie's more snooty customers would think if they knew that two of our workforce had had illegitimate children. They would certainly turn their noses in the air, but would they withdraw their custom? Lainie was taking a risk, but it was all right as long as no one knew.

Matthew rang that evening to confirm that he would be coming up on Saturday. He said that he was looking forward to seeing me.

'I've had a rise,' he told me proudly. 'My boss is so pleased with the way things are going that he gave me another ten shillings a week.'

'That's good, Matt. I've got something to tell you – but it will keep until the weekend.'

'You are being very mysterious.'

'Well, it isn't certain yet. It's just something that might happen.'

'Oh, well, in that case it will keep. I like certainties.'

'Yes, I know, but it might work out for us,' I said. 'And we've been invited out on Sunday afternoon. It's a bring and buy sale for Margaret's church – and a cream tea. I said we would go, is that all right?'

'Yes, why not? I would much prefer you to make friends with Margaret than Mary Maitland.'

'Mary is all right. She gave us a really good order.'

'But Lainie had to give her a big discount. You could design dresses and put them in the shop if you really wanted to, Amy – or send your designs out as you were doing.'

'We've got another customer who wanted us to make a dress for her. I suppose we might get more if we advertised the fact, but Mary wants me to design just for her.'

'If you ask me, that young lady wants too much of her own way. Besides, when we get married you won't have time to run after her.'

I didn't reply. There was no sense in arguing with Matt. I loved him but I didn't want to give up my friendship with Mary just yet. It was for this reason that I didn't mention the party the following week, or the one Paul was giving that I had refused to attend.

Matthew took me to the cinema on Saturday. It was an old-fashioned comedy with the Keystone Cops and we laughed all the way through, even though we had seen it before. Afterwards we walked home because it was a lovely evening, Matt's arm about my waist.

'I shall be glad when I can come back to London,' Matthew said. 'But it won't be so much longer. I was thinking that we might manage to get married by next spring, Amy.'

'That would be lovely,' I said, clinging to his arm and smiling up at him. 'But if Lainie gets married we might manage it before that.' I explained about the offer she had made me and he frowned over it for a few minutes. 'Don't look like that, Matt. It was only a suggestion.'

'I want us to have our own house,' he said. 'But it might be a way of bringing the wedding forward if the rent isn't too much – I don't want to use money I've put aside for our house.'

'You mean you will think about it?'

'Yes – if Lainie gets married. But don't get your hopes too high, darling. She obviously hasn't made up her mind yet.'

'I think she may; she just isn't quite ready.'

I didn't tell Matthew about Lainie's son, that wasn't my secret. If she wanted him to know she would tell him herself.

As we joined a queue at the hot pie shop to buy our supper, a man tipped his hat to me as he walked by.

'Good evening, Miss Robinson. It is a pleasant evening, is it not?'

'Yes, sir,' I replied. 'Very pleasant.'

He walked on past, then hailed a taxi. Matthew looked at me.

'Who was that?'

'Mary's father. I met him at her home. He approved of my designs – told me I should be working for a fashion house.'

'For goodness' sake, don't listen to him!' Matthew said. 'I didn't like the way he looked at you, Amy. Just be careful of him. Men like that are dangerous.'

'I'm not a silly child, Matt. I do know what goes on – and I shall be careful. I told him I wasn't interested, and that I was going to get married soon.'

Matthew nodded, but I could see that he was controlling his annoyance with difficulty. He hadn't liked my seeing Mary before and he certainly wouldn't be happy about it in future. I should just have to keep my visits to Mary's home to myself.

The next day was just as warm, perfect for the church sale. We had lunch with my parents, and then left to join Margaret and the others. The sale was held in a large field at the back of the church, and there were lots of stalls selling needlework, cakes and sweets made by the ladies who ran the stalls. There was also a white elephant stall, which had all kinds of second-hand items for sale, including a rather pretty pair of brass candlesticks, which I decided to buy for my bottom drawer.

As well as the stalls, there were games

going on for the children – the sack race and the three-legged race being open to all. Matthew and I joined in the fun. He came second in the sack race, but we were a poor third from last in the three-legged event.

'Never mind,' Margaret said afterwards. 'You've done your bit by the look of things, Amy. Now you can come and have your tea.'

The scones were delicious and had been made by the ladies who helped out at the church. We ate them with lashings of cream and jam, laughing as we got the cream on our noses. I recalled the last time I had eaten scones and realized that this was a much nicer event, the people more friendly than Jane Adams and her brother.

All in all it was a pleasant afternoon and we both enjoyed ourselves. We were tired and happy as Matthew took me home later.

Lainie was out so we had the parlour to ourselves. Matthew drew me to him as we sat on the sofa and his kisses were so passionate that they made me tremble with anticipation.

'I love you so much,' he murmured throatily. 'I think about being with you all the time, Amy. If your aunt gets married we'll do what she suggested. It won't be for long – just until I can get us our own home.'

'Oh, Matt,' I said and sighed. 'I do love you...'

He tore himself away with reluctance. We

had gone further in our loving than ever before, only just stopping short of consummation because we both wanted to wait for our wedding. But it was certainly getting more difficult each time.

After Matthew had gone, I lay in bed alone, dreaming and thinking about the future. It was all so exciting. I couldn't help hoping that Lainie would make up her mind to get married.

She told me the next day that she had written to her son.

'I've told him that I was unmarried and forced to give him up. He must decide if he wants to see me or not.'

'I'm sure he will,' I told her. 'Why shouldn't he?'

'He might hate me. I couldn't blame him if he did.'

'I can't see why he should hate you. He might feel upset because you gave him away, but he will understand if you tell him what happened to you.'

'Perhaps.' She looked doubtful. 'I don't want to hurt John more than he has already been hurt. We'll see what comes from the letter. I've sent it now, so all I can do is wait.'

Mrs Simpson came for her first fitting the next day. She looked at the dress with a critical eye as I made one or two small adjustments on her.

'It will be finished properly inside, won't it? I do like good finishing.'

'Margaret's work is very good,' I replied. 'We've never had any complaints.'

'Then I'm sure I shall be satisfied.'

'If you are dissatisfied with the finished article you don't have to buy.'

'Oh, I am sure I shall be. I love the way the dress hangs. That was a clever idea of yours, Miss Robinson. When would you like me to come for my next fitting?'

'On Friday afternoon. I have someone coming in the morning, so shall we say three o'clock?'

'Yes, that's perfect. I like the drape across the front. Who did the cutting for you?'

'Margaret and I usually do it together.'

Margaret had done this one herself, but if there were complaints I would take the blame.

'You are both talented young ladies, especially you, Amy. You should be working for a fashion house as a designer. You are wasted here.'

'I've offered some of my designs to various houses. So far no one has been interested.'

'That's a pity,' she said. 'But it takes time for talent to be recognized. Perhaps you will sell something one day.'

'Yes, perhaps I shall.'

After she had gone I tidied up the dressing

room. As I returned to the shop I heard a woman speaking. She was actually laughing in a rather shrill manner and I recognized that laugh at once.

Jane turned just as I was wondering whether I could make my escape before being noticed. As her eyes gleamed I knew it was too late, and that she had come in with a purpose.

'Ah, there you are, Amy. I was afraid you were hiding away from me.'

'Why should I do that, Jane?'

'You didn't come to Paul's party on Sunday. I was so looking forward to seeing you. Poor Paul was devastated. He held the party on a Sunday especially so that you could attend. Everyone was so disappointed.'

Why was she being so friendly to me? I might have been her best friend. I could hardly believe my ears, but I knew she was playing a part. She had revealed too much of herself that weekend at Mary's country house, and now she wanted to pretend that it had never happened.

'I had a prior engagement.'

Her eyebrows went up. I could tell she thought I was lying; though why she thought I should do that, I didn't know.

'My cousin and I are both looking for evening dresses,' Jane said after a moment's silence. 'Sylvia liked the one Mary was wearing recently. She said it came from here.'

'Yes, it did – but not from the rails. We made it especially for Mary.'

Jane frowned. She obviously hadn't been told that part and I knew Mary wouldn't want Jane to pick out one of my designs for herself.

'However, we can show you what we have in stock, and we're always happy to make alterations.'

I signalled to one of the other girls and she went to fetch the gowns I thought Jane's cousin might like. She returned with three, which she displayed for Sylvia.

'Oh, I like that green silk,' she said immediately. 'May I try this on, please – and the cream one you have in the window?'

'Certainly. Ruth will fetch it for you in a moment. She will be able to take care of you and if you need a minor alteration I shall see to it myself.' I turned to Jane as her cousin went off. 'I can show you two gowns you might like, but neither of them are as individual as Mary's.'

'Show me what you have. Mary said the clothes here were reasonably priced and I've overspent my allowance this quarter.'

'Of course. Please sit down while I fetch them.'

I selected a very simple plain grey gown with loose sleeves that I thought would make Jane look slimmer, a dark-brown satin and, at the last moment, I picked up a frilly yellow silk gown with tiny cap sleeves. It wasn't really suitable for her but I thought I ought to show her more than two.

She discarded the brown satin at once, which was a pity because the thin shoulder straps and draped neckline made it particularly stylish and sophisticated, and the colour would have complemented her eyes.

'I hate dark colours,' she said. 'That grey is so plain. I could try the yellow, I suppose.'

'The grey would look wonderful on you, Jane. It's elegant and beautifully cut.'

'I'll try the yellow.'

She obviously wasn't going to be guided by me. I didn't argue but let her try the yellow dress. It looked pretty on her but it was too girlish and sweet.

'No, I don't like it,' she said. 'Haven't you anything else?'

I brought three more gowns for her to see. She tried them all and rejected each in turn. I fetched another three. The same thing happened every time. I thought perhaps she was being deliberately difficult because it was me, but I kept on smiling. We had been through all the gowns in her size, apart from the brown and the grey.

'Couldn't you make me something? There's nothing put out of the way anywhere?'

'I'm sorry. We have everything on show. Our order books are full at the moment. It would be a month before we could start to make anything for you.'

'I want a dress for tomorrow.'

Jane went back to the two dresses I had not yet replaced on the rail. She stared at the grey for several seconds.

'I had better try this.'

It fitted her perfectly, making her appear slimmer and enhancing her English-rose colouring. She was looking at herself in the mirror when her cousin walked in.

'Oh, that is perfect, Jane!' she cried. 'You've been ages trying things on. I bought the first one I tried.'

'I suppose it will do,' Jane said grudgingly. She gave me a sullen look. 'You're sure you haven't anything else?'

'Not at the moment, though we are expecting some new gowns next week.'

'I'll have this,' she said. 'I suppose you know I'm getting married at the end of September?'

'I knew you were engaged.'

'I shall want a trousseau. I might buy some things here – if you were to show me your designs.'

'I'm afraid I couldn't promise you very much by then. But we could alter anything you bought from the rails. I could embroider a plain gown, for instance.'

'Could you embroider this one?' Jane asked and I groaned inwardly.

'I could do a small design on this shoulder by tomorrow morning – if that would help?'

'Yes, please.' She smiled for the first time. 'It was the embroidery that I particularly liked on Mary's gown.'

'It will be just a simple design – a flower stem or something, so that it looks rather like a corsage. I haven't time to do anything more elaborate.'

'I'll leave it to you. Mary's dress was gorgeous. Everyone was raving over it.'

'Come in tomorrow at about eleven and it will be ready for you.'

'I'll put it on account if you don't mind. My father settles all my accounts at the end of the quarter – which is next month.'

'I'll speak to Miss O'Rourke.'

Lainie listened as I told her what Jane wanted to do.

'I expect it's all right. I know of the family. They aren't rich but very respectable – and that ring she is wearing must be worth a fortune.'

'It is. I'll tell you about it later.'

Jane was pleased when I told her my aunt had agreed.

'I'll definitely be back,' she said as she left. 'And I shall bring my friends.'

'You are certainly an asset to the business,' Lainie told me after they had gone. 'You must have wanted to scream, but you kept your patience, and in the end it paid off.'

'Jane needed a new dress. I would be willing to bet that she had been everywhere else first. Besides, if I don't please her with the embroidery she might change her mind.'

Six

Jane didn't change her mind; she was delighted when I showed her the dress.

'But that makes all the difference!' she cried. 'It looks like something from an exclusive fashion house now. No wonder Mary wanted to keep you a secret. Millie wormed it out of Mrs Holland. She will be green with envy when she sees my dress.'

'I am glad you are pleased, Jane.'

'Yes, I am. I didn't think we would find anything when we first came in, but now I am pleased that we did.'

'I hope you enjoy wearing your dress this evening.'

'Yes, I shall. Thank you.' Jane hesitated as though she wanted to say more but changed her mind. 'I may see you at Mary's this weekend. Everyone has gone tennis mad this last week or so. Have you been to Wimbledon at all?'

'No, I've been working.'

'Oh, of course.' She blushed. 'Well, thank you again.'

It surprised me that Jane had been so nice. I wondered what she had been on the verge of telling me, and I was lost in thought as I went back into the showroom.

'You look as if you've lost a shilling and found sixpence.'

I whirled round as I heard the voice I knew so well.

'Terry!' I cried as I saw my brother grinning from ear to ear. 'What are you doing here?'

'I'm on holiday,' he said. 'It's the end of term and I've been staying with friends, but now I've come home – so I thought I would pop over and see you, Amy. You're all grown up. I hardly knew you.'

'You haven't changed,' I said and smiled at him affectionately. 'Have you seen Mum and Dad?'

'They told me where to find you,' he said. 'I wanted to talk to you, Amy. Can I take you out to dinner this evening?'

'Of course you can. I would love it.'

'We'll go somewhere special. Put your glad rags on, Amy.'

'Have you come into a fortune?'

Terry laughed. 'Dad told me I can have a job with him until I go back to college. I might as well spend some of my wages on my pretty sister.'

'You're making me blush!'

'I don't see why. That was a pretty girl I saw leaving just now. A pity she's engaged.'

'That would be Jane Adams. She is pretty. I understand her fiancé is very rich.'

'He must be to afford a ring like that one.' He pulled a face.

'It looks as if we're going to be busy,' I said as the doorbell went and several customers came in at once. 'What time will you pick me up this evening?' One of the new influx was Mary. She came up to me immediately. 'Hello, Mary. This is my brother, Terry. I told you about him – he is going to be a doctor.'

'How clever you must be,' Mary said, fluttering her eyelashes at him. 'What are you doing here?'

'I've come to invite Amy out to dinner this evening.'

'Lucky Amy.' Mary smiled at me. 'Why don't you bring your brother to my party this weekend?'

'I'm not sure – it's a party on Sunday.' I looked at Terry. 'I don't know if you will still be here?'

'Yes, of course,' he said. 'I'd like to come to your party, Miss...?'

'Mary, call me Mary. All my friends do.'

'A lovely name,' he said. 'I shall look forward to the party. I'll pick you up at seven this evening, Amy.'

Mary watched him leave the shop.

'I like your brother. He's nice – rather attractive, too.'

'Yes, he is nice.'

It occurred to me that he was too nice for Mary and her friends, but I didn't say anything. I wasn't sure why I didn't want Terry to become involved with Mary, but for some reason I was uneasy in my mind about it.

I enjoyed having dinner with my brother that evening. Terry took me to a smart restaurant up West and I was shocked by the prices on the fancy menu.

'You shouldn't have brought me here. It will cost you a fortune.'

'It will be worth it to take my sister out.' He looked thoughtful for a moment. 'Tell me something about your friend, Mary. She speaks like a girl from a good family.'

'She is, I suppose. Her aunt is very upper class. I'm not sure about her father, though. Mary doesn't like him much.'

'Do you know why?'

'No. He has been pleasant to me, and he's always polite. He seems to care for Mary, even though she is sometimes rude to him. I'm not sure I trust him, though. I wouldn't go into a dark corner with him, if you see what I mean.'

'Yes, I think so. Be careful of him, Amy.'

'He isn't often around. Besides, Mary is very protective of me. She told him I was her friend and not his – and he seems to do whatever she wants.'

'That sounds as if she knows something about him and doesn't approve.' Terry looked thoughtful again. 'I liked her, though. Is she courting?'

'No – although there is someone she is fond of. She can't marry him because they are cousins and Paul thinks it isn't a good idea.'

'It can be tricky if the relationship is too close,' Terry said. 'Most of the time it's all right – unless there's already some kind of problem in the family.'

I didn't tell him that I suspected there might be. Perhaps I should have said something, but I let the chance go and then Terry said something that drove Mary and her family right out of my mind.

'Have you seen Dad recently?'

'Yes. I was there for lunch on Sunday with Matthew. Why?'

'I'm a bit worried about him, Amy. He wouldn't tell me what's wrong, but I think he may be ill.'

A cold chill went down my spine. My father, ill! I couldn't believe it and my stomach clenched with fear. He was still a young man; he couldn't be ill, not really ill.

'What's wrong with him?'

'I'm not sure. It may be nothing or something.'

'You wouldn't have said if it was nothing.'

'He doesn't sleep, and I think he has pain in his chest.' He reached across to touch my hand. 'Don't look so worried, love. It doesn't mean it's serious. I'll try to persuade him to see a doctor. It might be just indigestion or something.'

Or something! I knew that Terry was worried or he wouldn't have mentioned it to me. It made me feel sick. I didn't want my father to be ill.

'I'll go over on Saturday afternoon when I finish work.'

'Don't make a fuss, Amy. You know he would hate that.'

'I shan't say anything. Do you think we should let Jon know?'

'Not yet. It would be silly to panic. I just wondered if you had noticed anything.'

'He did tell me he wasn't sleeping well, but he seemed all right. I didn't notice he was in pain.'

'He wouldn't want you to. I suppose I'm more aware of these things.'

It hurt me to think that I hadn't noticed my father was unwell, and I decided that I would go to see him as soon as I could.

We were sitting in a corner of the restaurant by a window. Glancing up at that moment I happened to see a man passing by with a woman on his arm. The woman was Mrs Simpson and the man with her was

Mary's father. He tipped his hat to me and smiled.

'Who was that?' Terry asked.

'Mary's father.'

'Why are you frowning?'

'I knew the lady with him. She is a customer at the shop.'

'Why should that make you frown?'

'No reason. I was just surprised I suppose.'

It was more than that but I didn't want to go into involved explanations at that moment. Besides, I wasn't sure why seeing Mrs Simpson with Mary's father had disturbed me. I was more concerned about my father.

'You will let me know how Dad is? If you can persuade him to see a doctor, that is.'

'I'll make him see sense somehow.'

Terry changed the subject again, almost as if he felt that perhaps he shouldn't have said anything to worry me too soon, but I couldn't think of much else and the evening had lost its sparkle.

My father had always been there for me. Even a faint possibility that he was ill was enough to distress me.

It wasn't until long afterwards, just as I was about to fall asleep, that a thought came to my mind that made me uneasy in another way.

Why had Mrs Simpson been with Mary's father? There was no reason why she shouldn't be, of course, but it bothered me. I had thought the recommendation about my designs had come from Mary or Mrs Holland – not from Mr Maitland.

I wasn't sure why that should worry me, but it did.

'How are you, Mum?' I kissed her cheek when I visited her on Saturday and gave her the box of Fry's chocolates I had bought. Then I looked at my father. 'Are you all right, Dad? Up to your usual tricks I suppose?'

I kept my voice light and teasing, because Terry had warned me not to make a fuss.

'I'm fine,' my father said. 'Your mother has been overdoing things as usual, but I'm as fit as a fiddle.'

I looked at him without appearing to be concerned, but I could see he had shadows beneath his eyes. He was probably tired if he wasn't sleeping well, but if he had any pain he was hiding it well.

'So how are you getting on with Mary's dresses?' my mother asked. 'Lainie told me she had taken on a new girl to help her out in the workroom.'

'Yes. Peggy is very good at plain sewing but Margaret is the one who helps me most. I wouldn't be able to manage without her.'

'You look after her then,' my father advised. 'Good workers are worth their weight in gold.'

'Terry said you had given him a job for his holiday break.'

'He wanted to earn some extra money. I'd have given it to him, but he says I've given him enough and he wants to earn it – stubborn lad.'

'Just like his father then,' my mother said.

'Now who's calling the kettle black?' He arched his brows at her and grinned.

'Haven't you got something better to do than sit around here, Joe Robinson?'

'Got my marching orders.' He winked at me. 'Your mother means she wants to talk to you – but you'll stay for supper, Amy? I can run you back in the car afterwards.'

'Yes, of course I'll stay, though I can get a cab.'

'I shall take you myself.' He smiled at me and went out.

'Your father isn't too well,' my mother said as soon as she was sure he couldn't hear her. 'I've wondered for a while, but he never complains. I caught him rubbing his chest last night and he said he had a bit of indigestion. I want him to see a doctor. Terry thinks it may be a problem with his heart.'

'Oh, Mum...' I looked at her in dismay. 'I hope it isn't serious. You must persuade him to see someone.'

'He might let Terry have a look at him for a start, but he thinks I'm making a fuss.'

'And of course he hates that.'

'Don't worry, Amy. I'll make him see sense eventually.' She smiled at me. 'So have you been anywhere exciting this week?'

'I've been working hard to finish one of Mary's dresses. But I'm going to her house tomorrow afternoon.'

'Terry told me your friend had invited him to go with you. That was nice of her, Amy.'

'Yes, I suppose it was. As long as he doesn't fall for her.'

'What do you mean? I thought you liked Mary.'

'Yes, I do, but she isn't always nice. I don't think Terry would be the kind of husband her family is looking for.'

'Are you saying he isn't good enough?' My mother bristled with indignation and I laughed.

'I think I am saying he's too good for her, Mum. She can be a bit odd at times – moody might be a better word to describe it. I just don't want him to be hurt.'

'I warned you not to expect too much from her.'

'I know, and I don't. I'm more sensible than you think, Mum. I'm having fun at the moment and there are lots of new customers coming to the shop because of Mary. It's good for business.'

'No, I don't underestimate you, Amy. You are like Joe – a deep thinker, except when you act on impulse, and you'll grow out of that.' She looked thoughtful. 'You are probably more able to take care of yourself than Terry is – so just keep an eye on him. He has another year at medical school before he can think about girls.'

'I'm sure he thinks about them, but as long as he doesn't get serious, it doesn't matter so much.'

My mother decided to change the subject. 'Do you listen to the wireless much in the evenings, Amy? The service has improved since they opened the new station in London, and I like some of the programmes they have on these days. There's one every afternoon I try not to miss called *Woman's Hour* – but that might not interest you.'

'I like to listen to the dance bands, but Lainie has a lot of good records and I've bought several jazz and blues recordings myself lately. We listen to them more than the wireless.'

We smiled at each other and I realized that we understood each other better these days. I also knew that she was as worried about my father as I was, though you would never guess it from the way she spoke to him. Her manner towards him was just as always, and I recognized the love beneath their sometimes sharp banter. A stranger might think they were having an argument, but it was just their way.

My father was laughing and joking throughout supper. He seemed to be as fit as he claimed, so perhaps his pain *was* merely indigestion and we were all worrying for nothing.

Lainie thought it was probably a storm in a teacup. 'Joe Robinson is as strong as a horse,' she said confidently. 'He will outlast us all.'

'I do hope you are right!'

'Bridget always fusses over us all.'

I nodded, knowing that was true. My mother had looked after her family all her life. She'd had to care for her difficult mother and her younger brother, and she'd been there for Joe Robinson when his sister was killed in a fire, before they were married.

I had never understood about the fire. I thought there was something more to it than an accident, something hidden that I had never been told.

'Have you thought any more about getting married?' I asked Lainie.

She shook her head, then hesitated. 'I've had a reply to my letter. John says he wants to meet me. I've spoken to him on the telephone and he's coming to tea tomorrow afternoon.'

'I shall be at Mary's. You will have him to yourself, Lainie.'

'Yes, for this first time, I think that's best.'

'It will be easier.' I got up and went over to

kiss her cheek. 'I'm so pleased for you, Lainie.'

'He sounds nice, not angry or bitter at all.'

'Why should he be? Harold said he was brought up in a nice home.'

'His adoptive parents are very ordinary people, not rich but not as poor as we were at the time. They gave him a better life than I could have done.'

'There you are then.'

Lainie was excited at the prospect of meeting her son. I knew she must also be nervous. They would be strangers, but that did not mean they could not be friends. I hoped for her sake that she would not be disappointed when they met at last.

'I'm glad you could come, Amy,' Mary said and kissed my cheek when we arrived. 'And it's lovely to see you, Terry. You must come and meet my friends. Amy knows everyone already.'

She slipped her arm through his, leaving me to mingle. It was only a moment or so before Paul came up to me.

'Who is the handsome stranger? Mary seems interested.'

'Terry is my brother. He's at college, training to be a doctor.'

'You have an uncle who is a specialist in treating burns I understand.'

'How did you know?' I looked at him in

surprise, sure that I had never mentioned Tom O'Rourke to him.

'My sister was friendly with Doctor O'Rourke during the war. I'm not sure who told me you were related, but someone did. You know that Eleanor was killed, of course?'

'Yes, Mary told me. You were very fond of your sister I believe.'

'I adored her. My father forced her to become a nurse. I blame him for her death.'

'Surely not? She was killed by the Germans.'

'Exactly. She should have been at home having fun. I hate my father for what he did to us. We seldom see each other. I won't touch his money. If he dies before me I'll give the lot to charity.'

'You sound bitter, Paul.'

'I am about him.' A smile of malice touched his mouth. 'He's terrified I shall marry Mary. I might just do it to spite him.'

'Why shouldn't you, if you want to?'

'That is another matter.' Paul laughed suddenly. 'What a grouch I must sound. This is supposed to be a party. Are you going to play tennis? We're hoping to make up a couple of mixed doubles matches.'

'I'm not dressed for it and I didn't bring a racket.'

'Mary didn't mention it, of course. That girl is so thoughtless!'

'It doesn't matter. I like to watch and I'm no Suzanne Lenglen.'

'None of us are!' Paul laughed. 'She just won Wimbledon again for the fifth time in a row. Besides, Mary isn't much good either. I'll have to ask Jane. One thing she can do is play tennis.'

Eight players were found to make up a little round robin, the winners of one match playing the winners of the other for the trophy. I was surprised to learn that there actually was a small silver photograph frame for the eventual winner. It was obvious that they intended to take the matches quite seriously.

Mary had chosen Terry, who apparently had his tennis things in the boot of his car. I hadn't even known he played, but it was something he had taken up at college. He was rather good and he partnered Mary to an easy win over Millie and Alan Bell.

Paul and Jane Adams played against a girl called Susan Hall and Jane's brother, Harry. The rest of us sat in chairs on the lawn and watched as Paul and Jane won their match.

They all came to sit down and have a cool drink before the final match of one single set.

'It's a knockout,' Millie explained as she sipped her iced lemon barley. 'Otherwise we would be here all night.'

'Amy's brother plays well,' Alan said. 'I

think we might have a new victor this time.'

'How often do they play this tournament?'

'We have three tennis afternoons during June and into July – and we've been playing for the trophy for three years. It's the culmination of our little tennis season, when Wimbledon is over. Did you get there this year, Amy?'

'Amy has to work.' Millie shook her head at him. 'She can't be idle all the time as we are.'

'I like working. My mother would rather I stayed home with her, but I enjoy what I do,' I said.

'Good for you,' Alan said approvingly.

'Jane showed me the embroidery on that dress she bought from your aunt's shop. I should love something like that. Would you do a design for me if I bought a dress from you?' Millie asked.

'I don't see why not,' I said. 'But I can't promise to make you a dress until Mary's are finished.'

'I'll come and see you next week.'

The final tennis match had begun. It was immediately clear that Mary wasn't a particularly strong player, but my brother was much better than I had expected. He and Paul were evenly matched, and they fiercely contested each other's serve. Both of them were too considerate to do the same on the ladies' serve, because that would have been considered bad form.

All four won their first service game, so it was two all. To everyone's surprise Jane then dropped hers because of a series of double faults. Even more surprising perhaps was that Mary held her nerve and won hers. So it was four games to two. The men then served again and it was five three. Tension was high as Jane served and managed to hang on to hers this time. Five games to four. Mary promptly dropped hers and it was level pegging. We all held our breath as Paul served again. It was a closely fought game and a collective sigh went round as he double-faulted at advantage against and dropped for the first time.

It was six games to five to Terry and Mary. It all depended on whether Terry could serve out for the match. The last game was hotly contested on both sides, all gallantry forgotten as the balls sung over the net and it went to several deuces, but in the end Terry managed to win and the trophy belonged to him and Mary.

Paul shook hands, seeming to accept defeat gracefully, but afterwards he disappeared into the house as tea was served to everyone else.

When he didn't reappear after a few minutes, I went inside. He was standing by the piano in the drawing room, running a finger over the keys, a moody expression in his eyes.

'What do you want, Amy?'

'Are you angry because you lost?'

'Yes – does that shock you?' He turned to face me. 'I like to win. Is there something wrong with that?'

'No, of course not. But you're not supposed to sulk when you lose.'

'Am I not? Thank you for telling me.'

'I didn't mean it like that.'

'No, of course you didn't. You see everything in black and white, don't you? I warned you I wasn't nice. Why did you bother to come looking for me?'

'I don't know. Obviously I shouldn't have bothered.' I turned to leave but he came after me, catching my arm.

The look in his eyes then was so tortured that I couldn't move away as he bent his head to kiss me. His kiss surprised me, because I had expected it to be hard and angry. Instead it was gentle and sweet, and it shook me.

I wasn't supposed to like Paul too much. He belonged to Mary, and I was going to marry Matthew.

'I am a rotten cad,' he said and smiled oddly. 'I shouldn't torment you. You are lovely, Amy. Inside and out. You're not like me – or Mary. It would have been better for you if you had never known us.'

'Why? I like being Mary's friend – and yours too, Paul.'

'You know we'll hurt you in the end, don't you? Mary is thoughtless and I'm cruel. It's our nature. We're both selfish and we deserve each other. You shouldn't have let me kiss you, Amy. I'm going to want to do it again. If you let me, I'll break your heart.'

'No, you won't. I like you, Paul. I'm fond of you as a friend, but I'm in love with Matthew.'

Even as I spoke I knew it was only partially true. The feelings I had for Paul were unlike those I had for Matthew, but they were too strong, too strange to be merely friendship.

Paul looked at me for a moment and I thought he was angry, but then he suddenly laughed. 'Bravo! Well done, Amy. I'm glad you have your Matthew – but you should still stay away from us. We are mad, bad, and dangerous to know.'

I ran my fingers over the keys, ignoring his remark.

'Do you ever play, Paul? I should love to hear you.'

'Would you? Perhaps I shall play for you one day, but not while the others are here. We had better go and have our tea or they will think I am sulking.'

'Or that we have run off together.'

'Then I had better protect your reputation, my girl.'

We were laughing as we went out into the evening sunshine. Jane glanced at us, a flicker of pain in her eyes, before she turned to her fiancé.

Paul had warned me to be careful of him. I wondered if he cared that he had inflicted so much pain on Jane. But he disliked her, and somehow I didn't think that Paul bothered much with people he disliked – which must mean that he liked me.

It gave me a warm feeling inside to know that Paul liked me more than most of the other girls he knew, and yet something in my head told me that I would be foolish to care one way or the other.

'I liked Mary and her friends,' Terry said as he drove me back to Lainie's that evening. 'But Paul Ross is a bit of a moody devil, isn't he?'

'Yes, I suppose he is. I can't help liking him though.'

'You're not being silly about him, are you?'

'No, of course not. I love Matthew.'

'That's all right then.' He grinned at me. 'I might as well tell you that the reason I came today was that Mum asked me to look your friends over for her. As long as you're not hiding anything I can tell her it's OK for you to keep visiting.'

'Cheeky devil! You just watch yourself with Mary.'

'Oh, I know she's a tease,' he said and grinned. 'I said I like her, Amy. I like a lot of girls. As far as I'm concerned, marriage – or even a serious relationship – is light years away. I've got exams and then intensive hospital training.'

'Well, I am sure Mum will be pleased to know that. I'm not the only one she worries about, our Terry!'

We laughed together, parting on the best of terms outside the shop. I'd asked if he wanted to come in and say hello to Lainie but he refused.

'I'd rather just get home. I know you get on well with her, Amy, and that's fine – but she's not my favourite person.'

'Why?' I stared at him in surprise.

'Dad told me something once. Lainie was very selfish when she was young. She behaved badly, got into trouble – and that led to trouble for Mum and Dad.'

'What kind of trouble?'

'It really isn't up to me to say. I only know that some people wouldn't have been as forgiving as Mum has been towards her sister.'

Terry wasn't going to tell me any more if he knew, and I didn't feel like telling him about Lainie and her son.

I wondered if John would still be there and what he had been like. But I found Lainie in the kitchen alone washing the tea things. She was humming to herself, so I guessed that the afternoon must have gone well for her.

'Everything was all right then?'

'Yes, I think so. John was a bit quiet at first, but after a while he started to talk about himself and his job. He wanted to know about my family and says he would like to meet you before any of the others.'

'I shall look forward to it. He doesn't hate you then?'

'He said he did when he was young. I think his parents were quite strict with him. He resented it and used to feel bitter about being adopted.'

'But now he doesn't?'

'He has grown up, Amy. He's older than you by several years, of course, and doing well working in a solicitor's office as a clerk. I think you will like him.'

'I'm sure I shall.'

'So how was your afternoon?'

'Oh, lots of fun. Terry and Mary played tennis together. They won the trophy. Mary kept it because they play for it each year.'

'And was there anyone else you knew at the party?'

'Yes. Millie and Alan and Jane – and Paul Ross, of course.'

'Well, I'm glad you enjoyed yourself.'

We parted and I went to my own room. I knew at once that someone had been in, touching things on the dressing-table, because the silver-topped pots my father had once given me as a birthday gift had been moved, the lid not replaced quite straight on one of them.

It must have been John. Lainie only came in if she wanted to polish the furniture, and mostly I did my room myself.

Why had John wanted to look at my things? It was puzzling but I soon dismissed him from my thoughts. He might be Lainie's son but he wasn't important to me.

I had other things to think about – like that kiss Paul had given me. Why had I let him kiss me again? Matthew would be terribly hurt if he knew, and there was nothing between Paul and me, never could be.

Paul was such a strange person. Why had he told me that he and Mary would hurt me in the end? They were my friends. Why should they hurt me?

Mrs Simpson came in for her final fitting midweek and declared herself satisfied with the almost-finished product. I told her she could collect it at the end of the week.

'The seaming is excellent,' she said. 'You told me the girl's name was Margaret, didn't you? Send her my compliments.'

Margaret was pleased when I passed on the message.

'I've only done what we always do,' she said, blushing a little.

'But you are very conscientious, and I always know I can rely on you. I was wondering if you would like to meet my family?' I asked. 'I'm going over on Sunday for tea and I thought we might go to a concert in the park if it's fine and then pay them a visit.'

'Oh, yes, that would be lovely,' she agreed at once. 'It's nice of you to invite me to your home, Amy.'

'It's not a particularly nice area, Margaret, but I think you will like Mum and Dad – my brother Terry, too.'

Margaret was a pretty girl and well brought up. The sort of girl I thought my brother should be taking out.

We talked for a while about various alterations that had come in that week, then about a musical show that Margaret and one of her friends had been to the previous evening.

'What I like best is the lovely costumes and the dancing,' Peggy piped up from her corner. 'I saw that Isadora Duncan once. She was wonderful.'

'She's started a school of dancing somewhere abroad,' Sally said. 'I read about it in the paper ... But I'd rather see a good variety show. Give me the good old Music Hall every time. I used to love Marie Lloyd. I cried when she died; they say she had a rotten time of it, one way or another, though she always made me laugh when she was on stage.'

It was nice gossiping with the girls in the workroom, but I had work of my own to do elsewhere. I was embroidering a band around the hem of Mary's latest evening dress and because it was such a big job I had decided to do some of it that morning. Lainie would call me if I was needed in the shop.

My embroidery things were kept in the second drawer of the chest in my room, and when I took the basket out to look for some special beads, I noticed the box I kept some money in was not quite shut.

Instinct made me open it and look at the notes. I realized almost at once that five pounds had gone. I knew exactly how much was there, because I had been saving to buy a new dress. I couldn't have made a mistake, nor had I taken money from the box recently.

Who could have taken it? Lainie wouldn't without telling me, even if she had wanted change for the shop, and none of the girls ever came up here. These were Lainie's private apartments and she would not allow anyone near...

It could only have been John on Sunday afternoon. I'd known immediately that he had been in my room, but I'd thought it was merely curiosity. I'd never thought to look and see if anything was missing.

I made a quick check through my bits of jewellery but as far as I could tell it was only the money that had gone. I felt angry and hurt that he should steal from me. I'd worked hard for that money and I needed a new dress for Mary's dance. She had asked me on Sunday.

'You will come down for that, Amy? You'll need to catch a train on the Friday afternoon and someone will fetch you from the station. I shall want you to stay until after Sunday lunch, then we'll put you back on the train.'

'That means two days off work.'

'Surely your aunt won't refuse you? It's not for a few weeks yet. You must be due for a holiday sometime?'

I tried to explain that you had to work for quite a while before you were entitled to take holidays, but I knew that Mary wasn't listening – and Lainie would let me have the time off if I asked. Mary had also asked my brother, who had told her he wasn't sure he would be able to make it.

When I asked Lainie about the time off she had looked at me in silence for a moment before agreeing.

'Don't do it too often, otherwise the other girls will think I'm favouring you because of our relationship.'

'It's a special occasion, Lainie. I'll work extra hours to make up for it.'

'You already do enough,' she said. 'I have to be a bit careful because of the others, but I really don't mind. I might ask John if he would like to stay for that weekend.'

Lainie was so happy that she had met her

son after all these years. I couldn't possibly tell her that I suspected him of being a thief...

Perhaps I had miscounted the money after all. In future I would put it somewhere safer.

Seven

My mother was delighted to meet Margaret that weekend.

'Amy has told us so much about you, Miss Price,' she said. 'She says she couldn't manage without you.'

'Please call me Margaret.' She blushed and glanced at me awkwardly. 'It's odd that you should say that, Mrs Robinson. I was going to tell Amy today ... I've had a letter offering me a new job. It's with a small fashion house making dresses for rich women, and they say they will pay me another two pounds a week. I wanted to know what Amy thought I should do.'

'When did that come?' I asked her. 'It seems very odd. Have you ever been sent a letter like that before?'

'No. I couldn't believe it when I read it this morning. There must be dozens of girls looking for work at a place like that. Why should anyone be interested in me?'

'You're very good at your job,' I reminded her. 'Don't forget what Mrs Simpson said the other day.'

'I try to please,' Margaret agreed. 'But I'm no better than loads of others. It's your designs and your ideas that make those dresses so lovely.'

'It would mean another two pounds a week for you.'

'Yes, I could do with the money.' Margaret frowned. 'But I should be letting you down, Amy.'

'I could find someone to do the sewing, but it isn't easy to find a girl who knows how to cut. How did you learn exactly?'

'My father was a bespoke tailor for years. He showed me, and then I worked for the same firm until he died.' Margaret smiled a little sadly. 'He was a good man but he died too young. My mother said he wore himself out working such long hours to make ends meet. She thinks I should take this new job, because the extra money is regular. I suppose I ought to at least find out a bit more.'

'Let me talk to Lainie. Perhaps we could pay you more.'

'Oh, I wouldn't want that, unless I did extra hours. If I stay it's because I want to.'

'You can't turn down two pounds a week,' my mother said. 'It's too much to lose, Margaret. If Lainie wants you to stay she will have to pay you.'

I agreed and yet I knew Lainie wouldn't be happy. Margaret was already paid a fair wage, but if she left I would just have to manage by myself. I could do it but it had made things easier with Margaret to help me.

The subject was dropped when Terry and my father came back for their tea. They had been out for a walk and had stopped to watch a local cricket match being played on the stretch of green by the river.

'It was just a few lads having fun,' Terry said, 'but it was good entertainment and Dad made the best catch of the day.'

'Life in the old dog yet, eh, son?' I caught a look between them.

Terry grinned and shook his head, and seeing them at ease together, my worries for my father were eased. My father looked as well as he was always telling us he felt.

'You're becoming a regular visitor, Amy,' he said. 'I shall have you wanting to move back in soon.'

'No fear of that,' my mother said. 'She's having too much fun, aren't you, love?'

I agreed that I was and told them that I had been invited to Mary's dance, which was at the beginning of September – just a few weeks away now.

'I need a new evening dress,' I said. 'I've been saving up but I'm not sure I shall have enough for the one I like. It's twenty pounds in the shop, rather expensive, but I haven't got time to make anything at the moment.'

'I'll lend you the money you need,' my mother said at once.'

'I could make you something,' Margaret offered. 'I've got a machine at home. I shan't leave for a month, anyway. I couldn't let Lainie down. I should have to give her time to get someone else to take my place. If we cut your dress out together I could do most of the seaming at home.'

'Surely Lainie doesn't charge you the full price for your clothes?' my mother said, and I could see she had been thinking it through.

'Of course she doesn't, Mum. But I'll need shoes and other things. If I'm going to stay for the weekend, I'll need at least one other new dress to take with me.'

'I'll help you if you need money,' my father said. 'Can't have you looking dowdy, Amy.'

'She never does,' Margaret said loyally. 'Even when Miss Adams and Miss Maitland come in, she looks every bit as nice as they do.'

'Who is Miss Maitland?' my mother asked. Her voice hadn't changed, but I thought she had gone very still, and I noticed something in her manner, the quick exchange of looks between her and my father.

'That's Mary's name. Haven't I ever mentioned it? I meant to tell you when I first found out, but it must have slipped my mind. I didn't think it important. She's just Mary to me.'

'I don't think you...' my mother began and stopped as my father frowned at her. 'You said you had met Mary's father, Amy. You thought he was quite nice, didn't you?'

'He isn't often around,' I said, wondering at the look in her eyes. She seemed nervous and almost frightened, definitely strained. 'Mary likes to keep her friends to herself. I seldom see Mr Maitland. I think he is away a lot.'

'It's a curious name,' my father said in a carefully measured tone that was supposed to make the enquiry seem casual, but didn't quite. 'I knew a Philip Maitland once – do you suppose he might be the same man?'

'I don't know, Dad. He did tell me his first name when we were introduced, but I call him Mr Maitland, or sir, and I'm not sure of his first name. He's a rich man and very busy, I know that much. Mary doesn't want to talk about him often and I don't ask questions. I think they live separate lives most of the time. It's not a nice thing to say, but I don't think she likes him.'

'Do you have any idea why she doesn't like her father, Amy?'

'I think he wasn't very kind to her mother, but as I said she doesn't talk about him often. Why do you want to know about him?

Is there something wrong?'

'Joe, I think we should...'

'No, Bridget, not just now, my dear.'

I saw the furtive exchange of looks again. They were both worried about something but they didn't want me to know. Yet it seemed it was because of Mary's father.

'The Mr Maitland you knew,' I said, meeting my father's gaze. 'You didn't like him, did you?'

'No, not much,' he said. 'He wasn't a nice person, Amy. If I thought it was the same man I might ask you not to go there again – but there must be other people with the same name, and I wouldn't want to spoil your pleasure for nothing. I expect everything is all right, but I shall make some enquiries.'

'Joe...' My mother looked at him anxiously. 'Shouldn't we tell her?'

'Not yet, love. It might not be him.' He glanced at Margaret, who was talking animatedly to Terry. 'Leave it with me for a few days.'

'I wish you would tell me if something is wrong.'

'Not today,' my father said and glanced at Margaret again. 'Best to be sure, Bridget. Don't worry, Amy. Your mother and I will have a little talk and sort things out. If there's anything to tell you, I'll do it next time you come over to see us.'

'I've been talking to Margaret,' Terry said into the silence that had suddenly fallen. 'She says that Ivor Novello is on stage next week. Shall we all go and see him? Margaret has already said she would like to go. You'll come, won't you, Amy?'

'Oh, yes, I'd love to,' I agreed.

My father said that he would think about it, and that we should certainly take my mother as she would enjoy herself, but she shook her head and said that she would rather not.

'You young ones go and enjoy yourselves. I prefer to listen to the wireless or the gramophone in the evenings these days.'

I was anxious about my mother. She looked really upset. Whatever Mr Maitland had done must have been very unpleasant. I wished they would tell me what was wrong. I wasn't a child any longer, but they seemed to think I must be protected. It was obvious that my father wanted to talk things over with Mum before saying anything to me.

Terry took us home later that evening in Dad's car. He dropped me off first and drove on with Margaret, though she had wanted to catch a tram.

'I'll take you home,' Terry said. 'It's no trouble. We might have a drink somewhere on the way.'

I waved goodbye to them and went upstairs to Lainie's flat. I could hear voices and as I went in I saw a young man sitting in a chair by the window. He stood up as I entered and looked expectant as Lainie introduced us.

'This is my son, Amy. John, this is Bridget's daughter.'

He smiled and offered his hand. 'I've heard so much about you, Amy.'

'I hope it was good.'

I shook his hand. His clasp was firm and his smile pleasant. If I hadn't suspected him of being a thief, I should have liked him very much. Yet perhaps I was being unfair.

'John popped over to see me on the spur of the moment,' Lainie said, looking happier than I remembered seeing her before. 'We've had a really good talk. He says that if I do get married he wouldn't mind coming to live near us in the country.'

'I think it would be a good idea for Lainie to make the move while she is still young enough to enjoy life. Why does she want to work all the time if she doesn't have to?'

'Oh ... No reason,' I said, surprised. 'Unless she wants to, of course. I thought you enjoyed having the shop, Lainie?'

'I do and I don't,' she admitted with a sigh. 'I've always had to work, Amy, but Harold is comfortably off and so am I when you think about it. He wouldn't mind if I sold up altogether.'

I felt disappointed. If Lainie sold the shop instead of letting me run it for her I would be out of a job, and I certainly couldn't live over the shop with Matthew then. I didn't remind her of her promise, but I wondered why she had changed her mind, and I thought John must have put the idea into her head.

'John says there are lots of way to invest the money from the sale,' Lainie went on. 'His firm do all that sort of thing for their clients and John knows all about it. He would help me if I wanted him to.'

'But only if you want,' he said quickly. 'It's your decision, your money.'

For how long? I wondered. Just as long as it took him to wheedle it out of her? It was a mean thought and I smothered it quickly.

'Yes, it's your decision, but I shouldn't make it too quickly if I were you, Lainie. You have always enjoyed the shop and you might miss it. I've got something to tell you later, but it will keep until the morning. I'm going to bed now. It was nice to meet you, John.'

'And to meet you, Amy. Perhaps we could go out one evening – get to know one another?'

'Perhaps, but not just yet. I'm rather busy at the moment. I have a lot of work to finish for clients. Goodnight.'

He looked disappointed. Had he thought I would be as easy to charm as his mother had been? Another mean thought! I was having them all the time about John Fisher.

I tried to smother my anger and my disappointment, and to think about Lainie's son in a fair-minded way. It was entirely possible that he was merely thinking about his mother. I ought to give him the benefit of the doubt, at least for the moment.

Besides, I had other things on my mind. I had been going to ask Lainie if she knew anything about Mr Maitland, but now I decided I wouldn't. Lainie had enough on her mind as it was, and she wasn't going to be pleased when I told her that Margaret might be leaving us.

'I couldn't possibly give her an extra two pounds a week,' Lainie exclaimed when I told her. 'It doesn't stop there, Amy. If the other girls found out they would all want more. Besides, I already pay her more than Peggy and Sally. It wouldn't be fair to them.'

'I knew you would think that,' I said, 'and I can't disagree, Lainie. You pay the girls good wages, and it wouldn't be fair – although Margaret does help me with the cutting for the special dresses.'

'I know, and I realize you will miss her if she goes,' Lainie said, looking doubtful. 'But I'm really not sure about carrying on this design thing, Amy. At the moment we are neither one thing nor the other. We can only make Mary's dresses and one or two other bits and pieces if you are willing to give all your time to the embroidery. It seems to me you can't carry on like that forever. Matthew won't want you to be working all the time when you are married.'

'No, I don't suppose he will,' I admitted, but the disappointment was sharp. 'I would like to carry on for a while though.'

'Yes, of course you should,' she said. 'I know I suggested that you might like to run this shop for me, Amy, and it would have been up to you what you did then – but if I do decide to sell ... Well, I can't see that we'd want to take on extra staff just for a few months.'

'No, I see that. So shall I tell Margaret to take the job if she wants?'

'I think it is best. We really only need two girls if we go back to doing just alterations anyway.'

I felt a little resentful and upset as I went down to the shop that morning. It was only natural that Lainie should think of herself, of course, but she hadn't been thinking that way until John put the idea into her head.

A part of me wanted to tell Lainie about the missing money, but I decided to keep it to myself for the moment. It would only sound like sour grapes.

Matthew came to see me that weekend. He

took me to a show and dinner on Saturday, and on Sunday we went over to see my parents, though we didn't stay to have lunch with them. Matthew wanted me to see a little house he had seen advertised for sale in a nice suburban area.

'I'm thinking of putting a deposit on it,' he told me. 'It has been for sale for some months now, and I think I might be able to get it cheaper – though it probably wants a bit doing to it, so you mustn't be disappointed.'

'How could I be disappointed?' I asked, feeling excited. 'Oh, Matthew! I thought it was going to be ages before we could buy a house – that's why I was so disappointed when Lainie said she might be selling the shop.'

'I might take a lease on the shop if she decided to let instead of selling,' he said, looking thoughtful. 'Not for a dress shop, though. I don't know enough about ladies' clothes – and Lainie's quite right. I would rather you didn't work once we are married, Amy.'

'You wouldn't mind me selling my designs to fashion houses if I could, though, would you?' I asked anxiously.

'No, of course not. I just want you to give most of your time to the home and me – and we may have children, though not too soon. I want you to myself for a while.'

When Matthew looked at me that way I melted inside, and my ambitions faded into the background. I clung to him when he kissed me and felt the desire surge between us.

This was right for me; this was how it should be. It was foolish to mind too much about other things when I had all this.

The house was about the same size as the one Matthew's parents owned, but in a rather rough state. My heart sank when I first saw it – there was so much to do! Matthew saw it through different eyes.

'I know it looks pretty bad now,' he said. 'But most of it is easy enough to put right. It wants completely stripping out, new plaster on the walls and ceilings and a new bathroom and kitchen. It will look very smart then, I promise you – and it is a nice area, Amy. Just what you wanted.'

'Yes, I like the area,' I agreed. The suburb was not much bigger than a village, with a shop, post office and a doctor all within reach. There was also a playing field for the children and a pond with ducks swimming on it. It was within easy reach of the town by train. Ideal for Matthew to get to work. 'The neighbours aren't too close, and they look friendly – that woman waved as she saw us come in. Yes, it will be nice when it's done, but isn't that going to cost a lot of money?'

'I had a word with your father,' Matthew

said. 'He knows some people who will do it for us at a reasonable rate. It might be ready for Christmas.'

'Does that mean we could get married?'

'Yes, I think so,' he said and smiled as I hugged him. 'I thought that might please you.'

'It does. Of course it does. You know that's what I've always wanted.'

'You haven't changed your mind then?' He looked at me oddly. 'I wondered if all this talk of dress designing and mixing with Mary and her friends had made you think again.'

'No! No, of course it hasn't.'

I blushed and hugged him, but I couldn't quite meet his eyes. I was still in love with Matthew, of course I was ... But I liked being Mary's friend, and I liked the new world she had opened up for me. And even Matthew's surprise about the house hadn't quite eased the disappointment I'd felt over Lainie's change of heart.

I suppose the praise from Jane Adams and a few others had gone to my head, making me think I was something special. Of course I wasn't really, just a very ordinary girl with a small talent for designing clothes to suit people.

I tried to put my disappointment behind me, and think about how lucky I was to have Matthew. He loved me very much, and I knew he was buying the house sooner than he had really wanted to because he wanted to make me happy.

'I'm not sure if I can, but I might come up again the week after next,' he told me just before we parted. 'If I get the house I might meet Joe there and hear what he has to say about renovating it. Your father knows a lot of stuff like that, Amy.'

'Yes, I think he's done up a few properties in his time,' I said. 'I'm going to stay with Mary in the country that weekend, Matthew. It's her special dance and I shall need to be on hand for any last minute fittings she might need...'

Matthew frowned as he saw the faint flush in my cheeks.

'You weren't going to tell me that, were you?'

'I didn't want to make you cross,' I admitted.

'Then you admit I might have reason to be?' The look in Matthew's eyes made me feel guilty. 'I'm not going to ask if there's someone else, Amy. I just want you to think very carefully about what you want. If it's not me, then I hope you will be honest and tell me before things go too far.'

'Matthew! Of course there isn't anyone else, not like that. I just enjoy being friendly with Mary, that's all.'

'Then tell me what you're doing. Please

don't hide it from me, Amy – or I shall think the worst.'

'Don't look at me as if I've committed a crime.' The hurt in his face was making me squirm inside and I kept thinking about the way I'd let Paul kiss me. 'I do love you, Matthew.'

He reached out to touch my cheek. 'I love you, Amy – but I don't want to hold you if what I can offer isn't enough. Think about it and tell me next time I come. I shall not come for a week or two, but I'm still going to offer for the house, because I think it's a good investment.'

I didn't answer and Matthew walked away, leaving me to go home alone.

'Oh, I do like to be beside the seaside,' Sally sang over her work that Monday morning. 'Beside the seaside, beside the sea...'

She was not particularly tuneful, but she was happy. Margaret smiled at me as I handed her the back panel of Mary's dress, which I had embroidered with beads.

'That's beautiful, Amy,' she said. 'I can sew both panels together now and it will be ready for her to try on when she comes in.'

'I think I shall take a break before I start on the next one.'

Margaret hesitated. 'We've got a social evening on at the church hall tonight. All the money we collect is going to charity. It's for ex-servicemen who were gassed in the war. The tickets are two shillings. I don't suppose you would like to come?'

'Yes, I would,' I said, smiling at her. 'I was wondering what I might do with myself – and it's for a wonderful cause.'

So many ex-servicemen had become part of the 'forgotten army': men who had returned after so much suffering and self-sacrifice to a grateful nation but had soon discovered there were no jobs and none of the benefits that had been promised them. Just after the war it had been common to see them on the streets hawking cheap goods from trays they carried about their necks. It was seen less often now but they still stood on street corners, jobless and hopeless, their faces reflecting the kind of despair that only poverty brings.

'Oh good,' Margaret said. 'It's always nice to see a new face at these things, and as you say it's for a worthwhile cause.'

'I'll come an' all,' Sally chipped in. 'I can spare two bob for 'em. My cousin Billy were gassed. He near enough coughed his bloody lungs up afore he choked to death. What about you, Peggy? Are you comin' wiv us?'

Peggy looked at her for a moment and then back at her sewing.

'I can't manage it. There's no one to look after the baby at night. 'Sides, it takes me all me time to keep body and soul together. Leave charity to them what can afford it, that's what I say.'

She shot an accusing look at me.

I saw the exchange of glances between Sally and Margaret and wondered. It seemed to me that they didn't much like the newcomer to the workroom.

I enjoyed my evening. After leaving Margaret and the others that morning, I telephoned my mother at home and left a message for my brother, asking if he would like to accompany me to the social evening.

'Tell him to pick me up at seven if he wants to come, Mum.'

Terry was there on the dot. I knew from his expression that he was keen to see Margaret again, and I was glad I had asked him.

The entrance fee paid for a cup of tea, but sandwiches and sausage rolls were extra. There were lots of other things we could spend our money on, including draw tickets and toys made by disabled servicemen.

Between us, Terry and I spent three pounds, which pleased Margaret and her mother no end.

'Mum is thrilled,' Margaret told us towards the end. 'We've never done quite so well. I think you've brought us luck, Amy. We've raised quite a bit for the charity. I'm so grateful.' She spoke to me but I noticed that her large brown eyes were on my brother most of the time.

I sensed a blossoming romance between them, and I wished that everything could be as pleasant. Why had I quarrelled with Matthew when I didn't really want to?

I asked Terry how my father was when he took me home afterwards.

'He seems all right, but I don't like to see him looking so tired all the time ... But don't worry too much, Amy. He'll be fine if he slows down a bit, takes things easy for a while.'

That was easier said than done. I'd never known my father to take things easy.

Terry dropped me outside the flat. I went upstairs to find Lainie sitting over her accounts. She looked up and smiled.

'Did you enjoy yourself?'

'Yes, thank you. There was a bit of dancing and some party games for the children. It was very much a family evening.'

'Yes, these things usually are.' She frowned. 'I think we shall have to charge more for the next dress Mary orders. It's all very well for Mrs Holland to insist on a discount but you're working all hours for nothing.'

'I haven't minded,' I said. 'Mary has been nice to me.'

'Well, as long as you don't mind, but I'm sure she could afford to pay the full price. Just don't let her use you too much, Amy.'

'No, I shan't,' I said and went to kiss her cheek.

I was thoughtful as I went to my room. Was Mary using me? Or was she really my friend?

I was introduced to Harold Brompton for the first time that weekend. He had come up to visit Lainie, and he took us both out for a special dinner at the Savoy Hotel. I had never been there before, and I was thrilled to see how grand it looked.

'I wanted to take you both somewhere special,' he told us. 'I've come into a little money, you see. It's not a huge fortune, but a nice house and some land. I'm hoping to persuade Lainie to come down and take a look soon. It's bigger than my own house – and just crying out for a mistress.'

'Well, we'll see,' she said. But I could tell she was thinking very seriously about it. 'Not this weekend, Harold, but perhaps in a few weeks.'

'You could come too if you wanted, Amy.' He smiled at me. 'I've told Lainie that all her family will be welcome once we're married.'

'I haven't said yes yet,' she reminded him, but she was smiling and I guessed that she was very near to making up her mind.

Harold was a decent man and I thought he would look after my aunt, but I knew that when she did marry him I might well be out of a job.

* * *

My mother came into the shop on the Thursday afternoon of the following week just before lunchtime. She had a look through the rails and picked out a dress she liked, which Lainie took away to have wrapped for her.

'It's time I had a new dress,' she said when we were alone. 'Joe is always telling me I should spend more on myself.'

'That isn't why you came though, is it?'

'I thought we might go out to lunch, if you have time?'

'Yes, of course. We can pop out and have a sandwich just next door. I mustn't be too long, because I have a client coming in for a fitting in an hour, but we'll go now. You can collect your dress when we come back.'

There was a nice little café next door to Lainie's where the girls sometimes went for tea and sandwiches. They made simple things like salads and omelettes, too. I had an egg and cress sandwich and my mother had an omelette with salad.

She didn't eat very much, just picked at it with her fork.

'Isn't it very nice?'

'Yes, of course it's fine.' She laid down her fork and gave me a straight look. 'Would you be very disappointed if I asked you not to go to Mary's this weekend?'

'Oh, Mum,' I said, stunned. 'You know I

would. I've been looking forward to it so much. Why don't you want me to go? Is it something to do with Mary's father?'

'Yes...' She sighed. 'Joe said I wasn't to spoil your fun. He says I worry too much and that you're too sensible to get involved with him. You wouldn't get involved with an older man, would you, Amy? Only Mr Maitland isn't a very nice man and I would be very unhappy if you did.'

'If that's all you're worried about...' I laughed. 'I promise you I shan't, Mum. I know that older men sometimes like young girls, but I wouldn't give him the chance. He suggested something about me finding a backer for a fashion house based on my designs, but I told him I wasn't interested because I was going to get married.' I smiled at her. 'If Matthew and I get married at Christmas I shan't see much of Mary then anyway.'

'Good.' She laughed at herself. 'I know I worry too much, Amy – and your father doesn't want me to tell you why, not at the moment – but just be careful of Mr Maitland, please.'

'I promise I won't let him get me in any dark corners. He probably won't be there anyway.'

'Terry has decided he's coming with you for the weekend,' she said. 'He will be there if you need him, love. Your father told him he could have the time off. He'll drive you down tomorrow and bring you back when you're ready.'

They had arranged it between them. Mum had tried to persuade me not to go, but they had a back-up plan to cover all emergencies. I wasn't sure whether to laugh at them for fussing over me like old hens or to be annoyed that they thought I needed looking after.

'I wish you would tell me what Mary's father did to you, Mum.'

'It wasn't to me,' she said. 'There were other people who were hurt. I would tell you all of it, but Joe says we shouldn't – and I suppose he is right. But remember that Mr Maitland isn't nice and he isn't kind, Amy. I think you are safe enough if you keep your distance, but don't trust him.'

'Mary has told him to leave me alone, Mum. I'm her friend, and I think he respects that. It's almost as if she draws a line and he can't cross over it for some reason.'

'Yes. He told me once that he respects decent women,' my mother said. 'But if he ever thought you had crossed that line...' A little shiver went through her. 'I would still rather you didn't go, Amy – but if you're set on it I shan't forbid you.' She smiled as she pushed her plate away. 'Have you got everything you want? We've got time to go shopping if you need some new shoes.'

'I bought them yesterday. If you've got time to come up to my room, I'll show them to you. And Margaret has almost finished my dress. She is going to bring it to work with her in the morning. We'll decide on any last-minute changes before I leave. It will make things easier if Terry is taking me down. I'll phone Mary this evening and tell her.'

'I believe your brother has already done that,' she said. 'Come on, we'll pay for this and go. I should like to see your new shoes.'

Eight

I was thoughtful as I selected my things to take to Mary's that evening. What was so terrible about Mr Maitland that my father had forbidden my mother to tell me about it?

Did Mary know things about her father? Was that why she seemed not to like him, why she had told me I couldn't be her friend and his?

I knew that I was going to have to think very seriously about continuing my friendship with Mary. I liked her and I had enjoyed being a part of her world, but if it was upsetting my parents then I might not be able to see her any longer.

It was another disappointment, but perhaps it was inevitable. After all, we were from completely different worlds.

Margaret brought my dress in with her the next morning. It needed one small adjustment at the back but otherwise it was perfect. Very sophisticated – like something out of a Paris fashion magazine.

'It's beautiful,' I said and kissed her. 'I love it. You are so clever, Margaret – and I think you are worth the extra money those people have offered you.'

She blushed and looked at me oddly. 'I'm going to see someone this afternoon,' she said. 'It's my free afternoon...'

'I'm sure you are right to do so,' I said. I hadn't told her that Lainie might be selling the shop, because it wasn't certain yet and it might mean that we should lose several of the girls. Besides, I thought it wasn't likely to happen just yet. 'If you like the people you will be working with, the money would be much better for you, Margaret.'

'Yes, I could use the extra money,' she agreed. 'But I enjoy working with you – we've become friends, haven't we?'

'Of course we have, and we still can be,' I replied. 'I shan't hate you if you go. We can still meet up sometimes.'

'It wouldn't be the same, though.'

'You must do what is right for you, but be sure it's what you want, Margaret. It still seems a little odd to me. It would be awful if they didn't keep you for long.'

'That's what I told Mum, but she says I can find plenty of jobs with my skills.'

'That's very true.' I looked at my dress. 'If I was still designing dresses I would always have work for you.'

'Might you do that when you get married – design and make clothes for friends?'

'It would be one way of continuing,' I said and sighed. 'We shall have to see what happens.'

I went upstairs to pack my gown with my other things ready to take with me when Terry called later. Lainie was standing by her desk in the sitting room, looking bothered about something.

'Is anything wrong?'

'I've mislaid some money,' Lainie said. 'I was sure I had left ten pounds in this top drawer. I wanted it for change in the shop.'

'Yes, I saw it a week or so ago,' I said and frowned. 'Have you ever had money go astray before, Lainie?'

'No...' She looked up, eyes narrowed. 'Why, have you lost some?'

'I think I may have done. I'm not certain, but I think five pounds went out of my chest of drawers a couple of weeks ago.'

'Why didn't you tell me?'

I stared at her in silence, then said, 'I wasn't sure.'

'You should have told me.' Lainie's mouth drew into a thin line. 'You think it was John, don't you?'

'I don't know. I thought it was missing, but I might have miscounted. I couldn't be certain, and I didn't want to upset you for nothing.'

'That was money you were saving for your dress. I'll give it back to you when I get some cash from the bank.'

'No. I don't want you to, Lainie. I told you I'm not sure.'

'Yes, you are. You think it was John but you don't want to upset me by saying so. You think John has taken my money as well, don't you? Is that why you don't like him?'

'I didn't say I didn't like him.'

'No, but he sensed it. He told me he thought you didn't trust him. It isn't like you to be so unfair, Amy.'

'I haven't accused him.'

'Not in so many words.'

'Well, if you have money missing as well ... Who else could it be? The girls know they aren't allowed up here. I've never seen any of them going up or down the stairs. I don't think they would dare – and customers never go through the back.'

'The girls could go when we're both busy. If you were in the shop and I was working in the office, one of them could slip up here without being seen.'

'I think that's a bit unfair, Lainie. There was never any money missing before...'

'Before John came?' She looked angry. 'I think that makes your feelings pretty clear. My son has to be the thief, of course. I suppose your mother told you that I took something of hers once, so you think John is the same.'

'No, of course she didn't. I had no idea.'

Lainie's eyes glistened and then fell as I looked at her.

'That was unfair of me, I suppose – but John is all I have, Amy. You don't understand.'

'Of course I do,' I said. 'And I'm sorry if I've been unfair. I couldn't be sure, but if your money is missing too...'

'Perhaps I took it for change,' Lainie said. 'Yes, I might well have done. I'm always doing it. I expect we both made a mistake.'

'Yes, we probably did,' I agreed, because I knew it was what she wanted to hear. 'I'm going to get ready now, Lainie.'

She nodded, but I knew she wasn't listening. She might try to convince me that she had taken the money and forgotten, but Lainie was too careful about these things. She couldn't lie to herself.

It was the first time we had come close to quarrelling and I felt upset. Everything was changing and I hardly knew what to think any more.

But I wasn't going to let anything upset me today. I was going to Mary's party, and I was going to enjoy myself. I would think about the future when I came home.

It was obvious that it was going to be a big party from the moment we arrived. Several of Mary's closest friends were already there, although many more would travel down the following day. Despite the twenty-odd bedrooms the house boasted, the girls were sharing two or three to a room. Some of the men were staying at hotels or other houses in the area.

'I told Mary I would share with you,' Millie said. 'I hope that's all right, Amy?'

'Yes, of course. It will be almost like being back at art college again.'

'Can you draw people?' Millie asked, and when I nodded, she said, 'Would you do a sketch of me?'

'Yes, why not? I can do two or three while I'm here and you can choose which one you like best.'

Millie took me up to show me the room we would be sharing. It was not one of the larger guest rooms and might actually be a bit cramped for two when we were getting ready for the evening. Millie told me it was often like this when there was a big Society affair on.

'Sometimes they even put spare beds in,' she said. 'It's quite fun really, as long as everyone gets on.'

We went down to have tea, which had been laid in the conservatory because there had been a shower of rain earlier in the afternoon. It had cleared up again, and people were wandering in and out to help themselves to the lavish tea laid out on tables, or standing in little groups on the terraces.

I walked out on to the terrace to see if Terry had come down yet, but I couldn't see him and I was about to go in and have some tea when a voice spoke behind me, making me jump.

'Let's hope it stays fine for tomorrow. It will be miserable in that marquee if it's wet. I can't stand damp marquees.'

'It looks as if it will keep the elements out,' I said, looking round at Paul. 'You're thinking you might get a game of tennis in the morning if it's fine, I suppose?'

'Oh no, that's over for the moment,' he said and grinned. 'We're back to the cricket now and then there's a regatta coming up at Henley soon. Then of course there's the racing, hunting and shooting ... and a trip to the French Riviera if one can afford to stay in a decent hotel.'

'It's impossible to keep up with you!' It seemed to me that he was describing a totally idle and wasted life. 'Don't you ever do any work?'

'Work? Now that *is* a shocking suggestion.' His eyes gleamed with self-mockery. 'It's all part of the social whirl. Shall I tell you what I really enjoy, Amy?'

'Is it fit to be heard?' I teased.

Paul chuckled. 'Oh yes. I meant sport, you wicked girl. In particular motor racing. That is my true love. I'm taking a run down to Brooklands next weekend, and there's a ride going begging.' He arched his brows at me suggestively.

Was he inviting me to go with him? I wasn't quite certain, but I couldn't think he meant it – unless he intended to invite my brother, too.

'You can tell me later,' he said softly. 'Now isn't the time to discuss such matters. Excuse me, I must mingle.'

I stood watching for a moment as Paul moved off, turning to go into the conservatory, but as I did so I almost bumped into Mary's father. It gave me quite a shock to find him standing so close, especially after the warning my mother had given me.

'Oh ... Mr Maitland,' I said, feeling flustered. 'I didn't realize you were there.'

'I startled you, forgive me.' His eyes were narrowed, intent on my face. 'I couldn't help overhearing what Paul was saying to you just now, Miss Robinson, and I feel it my duty to warn you to be careful of that young man. He is an idle fellow and not the kind of companion I think your parents would approve.'

My cheeks burned as I heard the disapproving note in his voice.

'I believe Paul was merely teasing, sir. He could not think I would go to Brooklands with him.'

'I understood you were engaged, and yet I believe I've seen you out with two young men.'

'One of them was my brother, sir. As a matter of fact he is here this weekend...' I saw Terry come out of the house with Mary and waved at him. 'He is with your daughter. Perhaps you would care to be introduced?'

'Your brother?' He glanced at Terry, smiling slightly. 'How interesting. Yes, please do introduce me, Miss Robinson.' He offered his arm, which I felt obliged to take. 'How very nice it is to have another member of your family as a guest in my house. I feel quite honoured.'

I sensed that he was amused, and a question hovered on my lips that I did not dare to ask. If something had happened between Mary's father and mine in the past it was best forgotten, at least for this weekend.

Terry shook hands with Mary's father. He seemed to take the introduction in his stride, and there was no change to his expression, so perhaps my mother hadn't told him her secret either.

Mr Maitland's visit to the gathering was brief. He greeted everyone and then went into the house, disappearing until dinner that evening. As I was seated a long way down the table, between Alan Bell and a gentleman I had met for the first time that afternoon, Mary's father did not bother me. He disappeared soon after dinner with some of the older gentlemen, none of whom were seen again that evening.

'He has taken his friends off to play billiards,' Mary told me. 'I wish he hadn't come at all, but he said he couldn't miss my dance, and Aunt Emily says it would look bad if he did, so I suppose I shall have to put up with it.'

Mrs Holland had been pleasant but reserved in her manner to me the whole evening. I knew she did not approve of Mary having taken me up in her circle of intimate friends, but I was discovering that Mary took only as much notice of her 'aunt' as was forced on her. Millie had warned me that Mrs Holland wasn't Mary's real aunt at all.

'It's a courtesy title,' she told me in confidence as we were freshening our gowns after the long and lavish dinner. 'She was asked to sponsor Mary into Society, because there is no one else who could do it now that Mrs Maitland is dead. Paul's mother might have taken her up, or Eleanor Ross – but of course they are both dead. Mary's father isn't exactly the thing in polite circles, you know. My father wouldn't invite him to dinner at his home, though he might mingle with him at his club or some large function. But Mary is different, because her mother was a lady, so she is accepted as long as Mrs Holland accompanies her and not her father.'

'What is wrong with Mr Maitland?'

'I don't know,' Millie admitted. 'My father hinted that I should have as little to do with him as possible, though he didn't say I should cut him altogether. I think there was some kind of scandal a few years back, and he was asked to leave one of his clubs – but he's still accepted at others and whatever happened was brushed under the carpet. He probably bought his way back in to the fringes of Society somehow, but he wouldn't be asked to the best houses. Even Mrs Holland hasn't been able to get Mary into the very best circles.'

'I didn't know any of this.'

'No, I don't suppose you would,' she said. 'And it is a bit mean of me to tell you – except that I like you, Amy, and I think you should be careful.'

'Of Mr Maitland?'

'Not just him...' Millie frowned. 'Jane wanted to tell you, but thought you would think she was being spiteful ... Mary has a habit of picking up girls like you and then dropping them suddenly. She has done it once or twice.'

'Girls like me?'

'That sounds awful. I don't mean it to, Amy. I really like you – but you must know what I mean.'

'Yes, of course I do,' I said and smiled at her. 'I'm aware that I don't belong in your world, Millie.'

'Oh, you belong in mine,' she said. 'My family isn't all that well off you know, though Daddy is one of the old school. Ex-army – but a perfect poppet. He would love you. In fact he told me to ask you over for tea one day. He thinks you have a lot of talent, Amy. He says you should be designing your own clothes rather than working in a shop.'

'That is very kind of him,' I said, but I didn't say that I would like to be invited for tea. I didn't think Millie was trying to be spiteful, but I did wonder why she had taken it into her head to warn me about Mary and her father.

Jane was just one of the girls who were asked to play the piano that evening, and Paul disappeared as soon as they began their party pieces. After a few minutes, I got up and wandered out to the conservatory. I found him at the door, staring out into the night, smoking his cigarette. There was something about him then that reached out to me, some echo of loneliness, of despair that touched my heart.

'I hoped you might come,' he said without looking round. 'Will you walk in the gardens with me, Amy?'

'Will you promise to behave?'

'Yes, if you will come.' He flicked his cigarette into the bushes and turned to hold out his hand to me. 'You can trust me if I give my word, you know.'

'Word of a gentleman?'

'Yes, of course.' His eyes gleamed with laughter. 'You do amuse me, Amy. You don't really know what that means, do you? It's actually quite sacred in my family.'

'I've been told that true gentlemen can always be relied upon to keep their word,' I said as I went to take his outstretched hand. 'No kisses tonight, Paul. It's strictly friends.'

'For this evening, I promise.'

I tucked my arm through his and we left the house, walking across the lawns to the summer house at the far end, which was almost hidden amongst a clump of weeping ash trees.

'It is a beautiful night, isn't it? Fresher somehow for the rain we had earlier. Do you ever walk at night, Amy? I find it relaxing to walk alone in the darkness; it frees the mind and refreshes the spirit.'

'Are you lonely, Paul?' I asked. 'I see sadness in your eyes sometimes and I've wondered. You must miss Eleanor terribly still.'

'She was like a part of me,' Paul said. 'It's as if I'm missing a rib or something vital inside. I try not to brood on it, but on nights like this I tend to miss her more. We used to walk together.'

'Is that why you asked me – as a friend?'

'Yes, because I can talk to you, almost as I did to Eleanor. We shared the same jokes and the same passions about most things. There is no one else I can talk to in the same way, except you sometimes – but I don't see you often enough.'

'You may not see so much of me soon. Matthew is buying a house and that means we shall probably marry by Christmas.'

'Are you still going to marry him?'

Paul stopped walking and looked at me in the moonlight.

'Why shouldn't I? I love him and he loves me.'

'But that kind of life isn't enough for you, Amy. You are bright and clever and you have so much to offer. You shouldn't marry and bury yourself in suburbia with half a dozen children before you're thirty. It's a waste of your talent.'

'I can design a few clothes for friends, and I may sell some ideas to a fashion house.'

'Is that enough for you?'

'Yes...' I knew that I sounded doubtful. It

had been enough for me once, but I had since discovered a different world, new ideas. 'I don't know. It's what I've always wanted. I do love Matthew, Paul.'

'But you also love me a little, don't you?' Paul lifted an eyebrow and I looked away from that mocking gaze. 'Why won't you admit it, Amy? You know I adore you.'

'I thought you were going to behave.'

'I haven't touched you, and I won't – not this evening. But that doesn't stop me trying to prevent you making a mistake.'

'You don't know it is a mistake.'

'I feel it,' he said. 'God knows I'm not right for you, Amy – I'm not right for any decent woman – but I do love you. If things were different, if *I* were different, I would ask you to marry me. You are the woman I should marry – decent and wholesome and—'

'Don't, Paul,' I said. 'Please don't say another word. You know I like you – perhaps it's more than that – but it wouldn't work. We are from different worlds, and you need to belong to this set. You wouldn't like the way I live, the way my family lives.'

'Your family definitely wouldn't like me,' he said. 'Terry is very suspicious of me. I dare say he will forbid you to be alone with me when he gets a chance. I'm definitely out of bounds for a girl like you.'

'I choose my own friends, Paul.'

'You won't stop liking me, Amy? No matter

what anyone tells you about me or my family?'

'I don't think I could stop liking you.'

Paul smiled. We resumed our walk, returning across the lawn to the conservatory. Before we parted, Paul took my hand, saluting it with a chaste kiss.

'I believe I kept my word.'

'Well, almost,' I said and smiled.

'Think about what I've said, Amy. It's not for my sake. I know there can never be anything serious between us – I'm quite frankly not good enough for you, my dear. I just want you to be happy.'

'Thank you, Paul, but I am happy. Goodnight now. I think I shall say goodnight to the others and go to bed.'

'Goodnight – and thank you for the walk. I enjoyed it, but then I always enjoy your company.'

I turned and walked out of the conservatory. As I went into the drawing room to join the others and say goodnight, I caught a glimpse of Mr Maitland talking to a lady at the foot of the stairs. I knew he had seen me and I was conscious of his eyes following me, but when I came out to go upstairs he had gone.

I spent the morning drawing quick sketches of the guests for Mary and those who had chosen to rise before noon, which was most of the younger ones.

'It's too good a day to spend in bed,' Millie told me. 'Besides, I want to show Alan the sketch you did of me. It's really good.'

Alan thought it was marvellous and immediately wanted one of him and Millie together so I had to fetch my pad and draw them both. Mary wanted her picture done after that, and so did some of the other girls.

Several of them told me they admired the dresses I had made for Mary and asked whether I would design something for them. They were disappointed when I told them I wasn't sure if I would be able to continue much longer.

'I hope you're still going to do some of my trousseau?' Jane asked.

'Oh, yes, I think I can manage that – it's just that I can't take on too many new clients until I know for sure whether my best girl is leaving us. She was going for an interview yesterday, so I may hear on Monday when I return to work.'

'It doesn't matter about them,' Mary told me just before I went up to freshen up for lunch. 'As long as you keep making dresses for me I shall keep asking you to my house.'

Was that a threat? Or was I allowing Millie's warning to cloud my judgement?

'I shall keep making things for you as long as I can,' I promised.

Several of the men and a couple of the

younger ladies decided to make up a cricket team on the lawn after lunch. Mary didn't join them. Cricket bored her and she preferred just to sit in one of the basket chairs and relax.

'It's all just too tiring,' she complained. 'Besides, I want to be fresh for my dance this evening.' She gave me a look that was a little sly. 'I'm going to persuade Paul to ask me to marry him this evening. I've made up my mind and I don't care what my father or anyone else thinks. I want Paul and I'm going to have him.'

'I thought you told me he said it wasn't a good idea for cousins to marry – something about your family being too closely intermingled already?'

'Oh, that's just rubbish,' she said. 'Besides, I've made up my mind and I usually get what I want.' Her eyes seemed to convey a message, as if she were warning me of something, and I wondered if she knew I had been for a walk with Paul the previous evening. 'I told you Paul was mine, Amy. He flirts with other girls all the time, but I have him on a line and when I pull the line he will come back to me. I want him, and I'm going to have him.'

Remembering some of the things Paul had said to me the previous evening I thought that he might have something to say about Mary's plans. He told me that he did not intend to marry anyone, but that if he *had* been able to take a wife he would have chosen me.

Of course, I didn't tell Mary that; it would have been useless and unfair of me. I didn't want to marry Paul. There was definitely a bond between us, an invisible string that seemed to draw us together sometimes, but it was an impossible dream. He wasn't for me and never could be.

Paul was out second ball, having scored no runs. Obviously he wasn't as good at cricket as at tennis, I thought, until I heard someone say that it was unlike him to be out so easily. He disappeared into the house and when he came back out he had changed into an open-necked shirt, a dark blazer and slacks. He came and sat next to me, watching for a while before saying anything.

'I'm going for a drive,' he said. 'Would you like to come with me, Amy?'

'Do you think we should? Won't you be needed when your side is fielding?'

'I've told the captain I don't feel up to it. I need to get away from all these people – are you coming or not?'

'Yes, if you want me to. Shall I tell Mary?'

'No. Just come if you are coming.'

I got up and followed him. Terry was batting as I left and I didn't think he noticed, but Mary did. I saw her frown and sensed she was angry that I was leaving with him.

It was reckless to go with Paul, I suppose. I knew I was risking a breach with Mary, and a part of me was sorry for that – but I also knew there was unfinished business between Paul and me.

His car was a sports model with an open top, dark green in colour and very fast on the road. He opened the door for me to get in, saying nothing as he began to drive.

We went very fast, especially after we left the estate and ventured out on to the open road. I wondered if Paul was trying to scare me, and a couple of times I had to hold my squeal of fright inside as he cornered recklessly, but after half an hour or so, he drew to a halt on an open stretch of common land and turned to grin at me.

'That's better. I should have exploded if I had stayed there another minute.'

'Has something happened to upset you?'

'No – should it have?' He stared at me for a moment then leaned towards me, kissing me softly on the lips. 'My promise was only for last night, Amy. I've been thinking all night about what we were saying.'

'We didn't say anything sensible.'

'I told you that I loved you, and that I thought you loved me a little.'

'But you were teasing, weren't you?'

'I was then – but I'm not now.' His eyes seemed to burn into me. 'If I asked you to marry me – just run off somewhere now and get married – would you?'

'You don't mean that.'

'Yes, I do. I'm quite serious. I love you, Amy. I'm not good enough for you, and I haven't the right to ask ... but I am asking anyway.'

What was he asking – that I should throw everything into the melting pot to go off with him on some mad adventure? For one wild, foolish moment I almost said yes, but then sanity returned.

'I couldn't, Paul. I couldn't do that to my family – to Matthew.'

'I was afraid you would say that.' He smiled oddly. 'That's it then, isn't it? I shan't ask again. It was now or never, while I still had the courage.'

'Oh, Paul...' I said. 'You know I do love you as a friend.'

'As a friend?' He nodded and I saw a flash of pain in his eyes. 'Yes, of course. We are friends, Amy. I love you, too, as a friend. You will think kindly of me, won't you – whatever happens?'

A shiver went down my spine and I was suddenly cold. I was frightened for Paul, though I wasn't sure why I should be. He looked like a man for whom the net was closing in, a man whose only hope of escape had been denied him.

'I'm sorry.'

'Why should you be? You were very

sensible to turn me down, Amy. I warned you that I wasn't good for you, didn't I? And I'm very glad that you heeded my warning.'

Paul started the car and drove us home at a sedate pace. He didn't speak as he opened the car door for me to get out.

'Good luck, Paul,' I said, feeling somehow that he needed it.

'Thank you, Amy. I wish you happiness.'

'Thank you.'

I was thoughtful as I walked into the house. Paul was in a very strange mood. What had prompted him to suddenly ask me to run off and marry him? He must have been desperate, because he must surely have known that I would never do something like that.

Lost in my thoughts, I had not noticed Mr Maitland until he spoke to me. I jumped as I heard his voice, feeling uneasy though I wasn't sure why – except that he seemed almost to be spying on me these days.

'Good afternoon, Miss Robinson. I trust you enjoyed your outing with my wife's nephew?'

'Oh yes, thank you, sir,' I replied, because there wasn't really anything else I could say.

I tried to go past him but he caught my arm, detaining me. I noticed an odd gleam in his eyes that disturbed me, making me remember my mother's warning.

'I was hoping we might have a private talk,

Miss Robinson.'

'I really think I should join the others, Mr Maitland.'

'I have a suggestion that you might find of advantage to you.'

'A suggestion?' I wanted to escape but it was difficult without being rude.

'I have been told that your hopes of continuing as a dress designer may be coming to an abrupt end...'

Who had told him that? I did not even know for certain myself.

'I may not be able to do as much in that direction as I'd hoped in future, but I shall be able to complete Mary's commission.'

'In this instance I was thinking of you rather than my daughter, Amy.'

It was the first time he had used my Christian name and I thought I detected a subtle change in his manner towards me; it seemed not quite as respectful, and more intimate than before.

'Excuse me, sir. Mary will be wondering where I am.'

'I doubt it. I asked her earlier and she made it clear to me that she was no longer interested in you. You have seriously displeased Mary, and I'm afraid that was a mistake. You are either my daughter's friend or you are not.'

'I must go.'

'Not before—'

'Amy! Where on earth have you been?'

My brother's impatient words had an instant effect on Mr Maitland. He stood aside for me, a flicker of annoyance on his face.

'Another time, Miss Robinson.'

I walked quickly to join my brother, who frowned at me.

'Have you been with *him* all the time?'

'No, of course not. Paul asked me to go for a ride with him. I know we've been more than an hour, but he was in a bit of a mood and he needed to calm down.'

'You should stay away from Paul Ross. I don't trust him.'

'Paul would never hurt me. You don't understand him. As a matter of fact...' I had been about to tell my brother that Paul had asked me to marry him but I changed my mind. 'Oh, forget it. I'm going up to rest before I get changed for the evening.'

'Most of the other girls went up half an hour ago. Mary was looking for you and she wasn't pleased when she couldn't find you.'

'Mary gets altogether too much of her own way as it is!'

I left my brother staring after me as I ran upstairs. I was feeling upset by Mr Maitland's behaviour and half regretting the answer I'd given Paul. His suggestion that we should run away had stunned and shocked me and I had replied defensively, but I knew that he meant more to me than he should.

If he had asked me to get engaged in the conventional way, would I have agreed? At this moment I wasn't sure, and that was very disturbing. I felt guilty, as though I had betrayed Matthew, and I almost wished that I had never met Mary or Paul, that my life was still as simple and uncomplicated as it had been before I began to design dresses for Mary.

Millie looked at me oddly as I entered our room. She was dressed in only her underwear and was obviously nearly ready for the evening. I realized that it was even later than I had thought.

'Mary asked me if I knew where you had gone. I think she is very angry with you, Amy.'

'Because Paul asked me to go for a ride with him in his car?'

Millie hesitated, then said, 'Paul has been paying you too much attention. We've all noticed it but didn't like to say. Mary has always thought she owns him. It's as though she has some kind of hold over him. I think he will marry her in the end.'

'Paul doesn't think that's a good idea, because their family has inter-married too often in the past.'

'Mary won't care about that. I know she seems shy and unsure of herself when you first meet her, but underneath she's tougher than either of us. When she wants something she usually gets it.'

'I'm not stopping her. Besides, it isn't really my affair. I'm not going to marry Paul.'

'I never thought you were. He couldn't afford to marry you, Amy. You don't have any money.'

I almost told her that he had asked me to run away with him, but something stopped me. Paul wouldn't want everyone to know that I had refused him.

Millie turned away when I didn't answer, fastening her necklace, and I went into the bathroom to wash before changing into my evening dress. I thought Millie might have gone down without me, but she was still fiddling with her hair in front of the mirror. When I returned, she asked if I would fasten a hook at the back of her dress, which I did. She watched as I went to the wardrobe and took my own gown out, slipped it on and then took her place in front of the mirror to put some lipstick on and comb my hair again.

'That is a very smart dress,' she said. 'Did you make it yourself?'

'I designed it and helped cut the material, and I did the embroidery on the bodice.'

'It suits you so well. Very ... sophisticated.'

I glanced at myself in the mirror. I had chosen a stiff crimson satin and a very simple design for my gown that fitted closely to the shape of my body and was cleverly draped to emphasize the waist. It had a dipping neckline at the front and the back, thin shoulder straps and a beaded flower motif across the bodice. When I'd tried it on with Margaret I had thought it perfect, but looking at it again now I realized it was a little too daring, too sophisticated for a young girl's dance.

'It makes me look older.'

'I think you look lovely,' Millie said loyally.

I was doubtful, but it was too late to change my mind now. I had nothing else suitable. Even as I went downstairs with Millie I knew I had made a mistake. The dress would have looked right in a London nightclub, but it was out of place at a country dance, especially for a girl of my age. If my mother had seen it she would have said at once that it was too old for me.

I saw the expression on the faces of some of Mary's guests and I guessed what they were thinking. Most of the other young girls were wearing pastels or white, and I stood out like a sore thumb.

I could have died when I saw the lustful gleam in the eyes of one or two of the older men and I wished I had worn my old blue dress again.

'Where did you get that dress?' Terry asked when he saw me. 'It's pretty, Amy, but a bit over the top for an occasion like this, don't you think?'

'Yes. I can see now that it was a mistake.'

'Why didn't you wear something else?'

'I made this especially for this evening. I haven't got anything else suitable.'

'Oh well, you will have to make the best of it then.'

Nine

Mary was in the drawing room, receiving her friends as they came down, but when she saw me she turned her back on me and spoke to someone else. I took hold of Terry's arm as we filed past her, sticking my head in the air defiantly. I wasn't going to let her or anyone else see that I was hurt.

Most people were making their way across the carpet that had been laid on the lawn to the marquee to protect our shoes, and Terry and I followed the others. There was music playing as we entered the huge tent. People were already dancing and Terry asked me if I would like to dance with him. I accepted gratefully. If it hadn't been for my brother, who was looking very debonair in his evening suit, I thought I would have turned tail and gone to hide in my room rather than face Mary's guests.

I was dancing with Terry when I saw Mary come in with Paul. She had her arm linked with his and looked both pretty and excited, the beautiful diamond necklace she was wearing flashing in the light of the chandeliers. She looked exactly what she was: the spoiled and indulged daughter of a very wealthy man.

Paul glanced across the room at me. For a moment his eyes seemed to linger, intent and hungry, and then Mary tugged at his arm and he looked down at her. The next minute they were dancing.

I danced two dances with my brother. When the music ended, Terry took me over to where Mary, Jane and Millie were standing with Paul and Jane's brother. Mary gave me a hard, malicious look but said nothing. Terry asked Millie to dance and Jane's brother led Mary on to the floor. Paul glanced at me but then asked Jane if she would like to dance.

For a few minutes I was left standing alone, but then Alan Bell came up to me.

'You look rather splendid this evening, Amy. Quite a dark horse, aren't you?'

'What do you mean?'

'All the chaps are admiring you from a distance,' he said. 'You look like a Hollywood actress, Amy. Very glamorous and ...

Well, very nice indeed. I hardly knew you at first.'

'It's just the dress. I haven't changed.'

'Exactly my thoughts ... But some of the other chaps may have other ideas. I wouldn't go walking in the gardens this evening if I were you. Might get the wrong idea, what?'

Alan's warning was meant kindly but it made me blush. I might have gone up to change my dress after our dance, but pride made me stubborn. If they wanted to think ill of me, it was up to them. I was the same girl, even if I had chosen to wear a dress that was a little too sophisticated for me.

I had already decided that I would think long and hard before I came to another of Mary's parties – if I was even invited. From the looks Mary had been giving me, I probably wouldn't be. She had warned me she intended to have Paul for herself, and she was angry because I had gone for that drive with him. But it was more than that, of course. She must know that there was a special feeling between Paul and me – and she was jealous.

I danced with a succession of gentlemen after Alan, some of whom I had never met before that evening. Some were friendly and scrupulously polite, others held me too close and gave me suggestive leers that made me shudder inside.

And all because of a dress! I just hadn't

realized what a difference it would make. I wished I'd bought the dress I'd been thinking of having from my aunt's stock, which was a pale blue silk and very like the dresses that most of the girls were wearing. What had possessed me to design something so outrageous for myself? And why had I chosen crimson? I knew it looked fabulous on but it just wasn't right for this evening. Or for a girl of my age.

The evening wore on but neither Mary nor Paul came to speak to me, which made me feel like an outcast. I knew Mary was angry, but why had Paul abandoned me? I was hurt by his apparent disapproval, just when I could have done with some support. He must have known that I was feeling uncomfortable. It would have eased my embarrassment if he had spent just a few minutes talking to me. After his usual assiduous attention it looked so odd that he hadn't even said hello.

Mary's father paid a brief visit to the marquee about halfway through the evening. I had hoped he would ignore me, but instead he came over almost as soon as he saw me.

'You look beautiful this evening, Amy. That wonderful dress must have been made for you – your own design, of course.'

'It is too old for me. I made a mistake.'

'Not at all,' he said, an intimate note in his voice. 'If I had any say in the matter you would always wear gowns that show off your unique beauty. I was always aware that you were different from the others – those foolish little girls my daughter collects. There is something special about you, my dear.'

'Oh, no, I am quite ordinary...'

I wanted to escape and looked desperately for my brother, who was dancing with a very pretty girl I did not know. He was supposed to be here to protect me!

'Allow me to differ. You are special – could be very special indeed with a little help from a friend. You have more than one talent, Amy. I could help you to develop them all.'

'Please ... You must excuse me.'

I left him abruptly, not caring that I was being rude. I could no longer doubt the nature of his interest in me, and was determined to give him no opportunity to force his unwanted attentions on me.

Leaving the marquee I went into the house, hurrying up to the room I shared with Millie. After a moment's hesitation I took off my new dress and replaced it with a plain black skirt and a white blouse with long full sleeves that I had worn for dinner the previous evening.

I had no intention of going back to the marquee and decided that I would get something to eat from the buffet tables in the dining room and then go to bed. It was still quite early but the evening was over as far as

I was concerned.

As I approached the door of the dining room I heard laughter coming from inside. Jane, her brother, Millie and Alan Bell were obviously in a merry mood, talking loudly – about me.

'I always thought she was a little tart,' Harry Adams drawled.

'That's a bit unfair, old chap,' Alan protested. 'I've always liked the girl. Mind you, that dress was a mistake for an affair of this kind.'

'I thought she had good taste,' Mary said with a spiteful note in her voice. 'I've decided to drop her. I'll buy my trousseau from Worth's.'

Her trousseau! Had she managed to persuade Paul to marry her?

I turned away from the dining room, making my way to the conservatory via the hall. Paul was standing looking out into the night. I hesitated but he knew I was there and turned to face me.

'So they got to you after all,' he said, noticing that I had changed my dress.

'I made a mistake with that dress.'

'It would have looked better in town, but I liked it. You shouldn't let them get to you, Amy. Underneath they are rotten – like the stinking filth you find in the sewers. You're worth ten of any of them, including me.'

'Why didn't you give me some courage

earlier?'

'Mary forbade it. If I had taken your side...' He shrugged his shoulders. 'Will you congratulate me, Amy? I am going to be married.'

'To Mary?' I stared as he nodded, a wry, slightly bitter expression on his face. 'Why? Are you in love with her?'

Paul gave a harsh laugh. 'Love doesn't come into this. Mary owns me, my dear. I need money rather badly and I won't go to my father. She knows that. Besides, Mary knows things about me, things that I would rather the rest of the world didn't...'

'What kind of things?'

'Things I would never tell you, sweet Amy. The kind of thing that haunts my dreams and would give you nightmares. I was drunk when I confessed it all to Mary like a fool. She has never let me forget it since.'

Now I understood why Mary had been so sure of him.

'But that's blackmail, Paul.'

'Yes. Nasty, isn't it? I did tell you we were not very nice people.'

'What would you have done if I had said I would run away with you this afternoon?'

Paul laughed softly. 'But of course I knew you wouldn't. I was desperate, and I might just have gone through with it if you had agreed, my dear. However, I was quite safe. Neither of us is brave enough to make that break for freedom, are we? We both cling to what is safe and known.'

'So you will marry her knowing...'

'That we must never have a child. Of course you've worked it out, haven't you? There is madness in my family, Amy. My sister and I escaped the curse, but my mother was suffering from dementia when she died – though it was hushed up of course. Eleanor never knew the truth, thank God. My father told me when I came back from the war. He thought I was a coward and he made no bones about the reasons for my lack of fibre. All my mother's fault, of course. Apparently, the madness goes back several generations, but had missed a few, so it wasn't generally known when they married. Father found out afterwards, as Mary's father did – but Mary's mother had a different weakness, a fondness for alcohol possibly induced by her husband's cruelty.'

Paul's face worked with emotion. He looked drained, a man in torment as he finished speaking. I felt the sadness and pity swell inside me so that I wished I could go to him and comfort him, but there was something in his manner that warned me to keep my distance.

'You're not mad, Paul.'

'Not yet, no – but I may end up that way. As I told you, it goes back quite a way. So you can see what a lucky escape you've had, my sweet girl. I would have ruined your life if you had let me.'

'I don't believe that. I don't believe you would hurt anyone deliberately.'

'Precious, innocent Amy. How I love you. Go away now, my dear one, and don't come back. Mary doesn't want you any more, and she can be vicious if she feels inclined. Take my word for it.'

'You shouldn't marry her, Paul. You will both be unhappy.'

'I don't think Mary cares about having children.'

'I didn't mean because of that. You don't love her.'

'As I've told you before, love doesn't come into this.' He turned his back on me, staring out at the night once more. 'Goodbye, Amy. We shall not meet again.'

'Goodbye, Paul.'

I hesitated for a moment, still drawn to him, still caught by this feeling between us, then I turned and went out. It was impossible, had always been so. I had my foot on the bottom stair, intending to go up to my room, when I heard my brother's voice call out to me.

'I was worried about you, Amy,' he said when I turned and waited for him to come to me. 'You've changed then?'

'Yes, I should have worn this in the first place.'

'Come back to the dance with me?'

'No, I don't think so. I have a headache. I'm going to bed.'

'Are you sure?' He looked anxious. 'You were looking forward to this party so much.'

'I know, but Mum was right. I shouldn't have come. I don't belong with these people.'

'Thank goodness you've come to your senses at last.' Terry grinned at me. 'Shall we go home?'

'In the morning,' I said. 'I'm not going to run away like a thief in the night, but I shan't stay for lunch. Mary wouldn't want me to. I think she may cancel her last gown. She has decided to drop me.'

'A good thing, too,' Terry said, walking up the stairs with me. 'I'll see you to your room, love, and then I'll turn in. These things aren't really my kind of affair.'

'You liked dancing with that pretty girl I saw you with earlier,' I teased.

'I like pretty girls. But Margaret is more my sort. I've asked her to go out with me next week. I'm going to take her to a show.'

'Good. I like Margaret.'

We had reached the door of my room. Terry kissed my cheek.

'Cheer up, Amy. It isn't the end of the world.'

'Of course not. Both Lainie and Mum warned me it would happen. I should have listened to them at the start, but I was having fun. It was fun for a while, Terry.'

'Just as well this happened when I was with you. Maitland is an odd fellow, Amy. If I were you I should lock your door. Don't open it unless it's Millie. She seems the best of this bunch.'

'Yes, I think she probably is. Goodnight, Terry. I'm going to pack. We can leave by eight in the morning if you like.'

'The sooner the better as far as I'm concerned.'

I laughed, kissed his cheek and went in, locking the door behind me. I would take Terry's advice and open it only for Millie.

I left a note for Mary on the hall table the next morning. We had decided not to bother with breakfast but find a café on the way home to have a bite to eat. No one was about when Terry and I took our things down to the car, except for one or two rather exhausted-looking servants.

A very sleepy Millie bade me farewell.

'I'll come into the shop to talk to you another day, when I'm not so tired. I hope we can still be friends.'

'Yes, of course, if you want to.'

'Oh, yes, I don't care what Mary says, and nor does Alan.'

'Goodbye for now then.'

Terry looked at me as he started the car.

'No regrets, Amy?'

'No, of course not.' I had no regrets about leaving, and only a slight ache in my heart when I thought of Paul.

I thought I would always carry the faint scars of my brief friendship with Paul and Mary. Paul had warned me at the start and I should have heeded his warning. But it could all have been so much worse...

Mary had turned against me because she had sensed the attraction between Paul and me, but I wasn't sure what that attraction actually was. Paul had spoken of love, but it wasn't the kind of love I felt for Matthew. It was something wilder, strange, inexplicable, a fatal attraction that I had always known was wrong. I knew we could never have married. Paul would never allow himself to have children and that would have broken my heart – his too if he truly loved me. He was right when he said that he should never marry.

How big a burden it was to carry the knowledge of his mother's dementia, to know that the thread of madness was in his blood, waiting like an evil seed to be passed on to his children.

But perhaps it didn't matter to Mary. She wanted Paul, had used blackmail to get her own way. Perhaps she didn't care that he would never give her a child.

'You're very quiet, Amy,' Terry said when I

had been silent for a long time. 'What's on your mind?'

I couldn't tell him the truth; it would have been disloyal to Paul. 'Nothing really. I was wondering what I shall do if Lainie sells the shop, that's all.'

'Is she thinking of selling?'

'She might if she gets married. I don't know for sure yet.'

'You could always find another job. I am sure Dad would help out. He has loads of contacts, probably knows a few people in the rag trade if you asked him. There are openings with small fashion houses for designers like you, Amy.'

'I've sent loads of designs out but no one has answered.'

'Maybe you've been trying the wrong places,' Terry said. 'The bigger houses probably wouldn't be interested, but there are scores of small manufacturers in the East End. Dad is bound to know a few. He could maybe ask around a bit, find out if anyone is looking for a great young designer with new ideas.'

'Oh, Terry,' I said, and laughed as he had intended I should. 'You make me feel so much better.'

'As I've told you before, it isn't the end of the world, Amy. Mary and her friends aren't the only ones who would appreciate your designs. If I were you I'd have another go at sending them out, but to different places.'

'Yes, perhaps I shall,' I said. 'I hadn't bothered because I was too busy doing the embroidery for Mary's gowns, but now I shall have more time to myself again.'

My spirits had lifted and I knew Terry was right. I had enjoyed my time as Mary's friend, but it was over and I would just have to think about other things now. Not least what I was going to say to Matthew when he visited the following week.

Lainie asked me if I'd enjoyed myself that weekend. I told her it had been a nice party but that I didn't expect to be visiting Mary much in future.

'Well, you've had some fun,' she said apparently not particularly interested. 'If Mary cancels that gown we'll put it on the rails, Amy. I'm sure we can sell it to someone else.'

'Yes, I should think we probably can. I'll tell Margaret to carry on then?'

'Yes...' She looked at me thoughtfully. 'Amy, I've made up my mind to marry Harold, but not until next year. I need some time to decide what to do about the shop. I've got several choices. Matthew has offered to lease it from me for a men's outfitters and I might let him have it. Or I might sell.'

'You're the only one who can decide that, Lainie. You've ruled out keeping the shop and employing someone to run it then?'

'I think I would rather lease or sell.' There was a hint of apology in her eyes as she looked at me. 'I know I did say that you could run it for me, Amy, but I've decided it's best to be in or out. John was right about that. I don't need to work and I don't see why I should.'

'I see. Well, thank you for telling me. At least I know where I stand.'

'Oh, don't look so stricken,' she said a little impatiently. 'You'll be married by Christmas anyway, that was one of the things that decided me. Matthew won't want you to be running a shop once you're his wife. Some men expect their wives to stay home, and he's definitely one of them.'

'Supposing I decide I don't want to get married for a while?'

'Have you quarrelled with Matthew? Oh, Amy, I hope it wasn't over that stupid dance. Matthew loves you and I thought you loved him.'

'I do but I'm not sure I want to get married just yet.'

'I don't understand. You were the one pushing for marriage. It was all you wanted.'

'Yes, I know. But now I'm not sure. I might prefer to wait for a while.'

'You will be a fool if you lose Matthew,' Lainie told me. 'I thought you had more sense, Amy. If your head has been turned by all this nonsense with Mary you need to straighten yourself out quickly, my girl.'

'It isn't anything to do with Mary.'

'Another man then?' Lainie frowned. 'I was a fool once, Amy. There was a man I cared about who loved me very much. But I let someone else turn my head with false promises and it led to heartbreak. Don't let it happen to you. This dress designing is all very well, but a good man, marriage and children are far more worthwhile. I know what I'd do if I had my time again.'

'Did John come to stay this weekend?' I asked because I wanted to change the subject.

'No. He telephoned to say that he had to work and couldn't make it, so you needn't check to see if anything is missing.'

'I wasn't going to.' I stared at her unhappily. 'Are we going to quarrel over this again?'

'No, of course not. I'm sorry if I was touchy – but it would hurt me a lot if I thought—' Lainie broke off as the telephone rang and she got up to answer it. 'Bridget? Yes, of course she is here. Oh, I see. I'm so sorry. I'll hand you over to her now.'

I was waiting for the phone even before Lainie turned round.

'Mum, what's the matter?'

'Now don't panic, Amy. Your father has had a slight heart attack. He is all right. The doctor came and examined him and he said he was better off resting at home rather than going to hospital, but I wanted you to know.'

'I'm coming home now.'

'No, don't do that this evening. Joe is asleep and you would only worry him if you turned up late at night. Come over tomorrow if you want.'

'I shall come home to stay for a while, Mum. I'm sure Lainie can manage without me for a few days.' I looked at my aunt and she nodded emphatically. 'I can help you at home while Dad is ill. Just for a few days.'

'You know there's nothing I would like better than to have you at home, love – but what about the dresses you are making for that girl?'

'She will have to wait,' I said. 'But I think that is probably over, Mum. You were right about the Maitlands; they are not very nice people. I don't think I want to design anything for Mary any more.'

'He didn't do anything to harm you?' My mother sounded alarmed and I laughed.

'I had Terry there to protect me, remember? No, nothing happened for you to worry about, Mum. I'm fine. Just worried about Dad – and you.'

'Well, you don't need to worry about me, darlin',' she said. 'And the doctor says your father will be fine if he takes things easy for a while. That's going to be the hard thing, keeping him from going off to do one of his deals. If you are here he may be more content to sit around and rest for a few days.'

'I'll be there in the morning. Take care of yourself, Mum.'

'Bless you, me darlin',' she said, suddenly sounding very Irish, which told me that she was desperately upset and trying to hide it. 'There's not the least need for you to be worryin' your head over me.'

'I love you, Mum. I love both of you.'

'And we love you, Amy. I'll see you tomorrow then.'

Lainie was looking at me oddly as I turned to her. Her face was very pale and I could see that she was concerned.

'Mum says he's going to be all right. He just needs to rest for a while.'

'That's good,' she said. 'Did I hear you say that Mary's name was Maitland just now?'

'Yes. I've known for a while now, but I didn't think it was important...' Lainie sat down abruptly, her hand shaking on the arm of her chair. 'What's wrong? You look as if you've seen a ghost.'

'Is her father's name Philip – Philip Maitland?'

'Yes, I think so.' I frowned at her. 'Did you know him too? I've been told my father did – and he didn't like him much.'

'I hate him,' Lainie said. She raised her head and looked at me, her eyes dark with remembered grief. 'If I had known ... If I had guessed that she was his daughter, I would never have let you go there. You must promise me that you won't go there ever again, Amy. He is evil – a wicked man.' She gave a little cry and covered her face with her hands. 'To think that you have been staying in his house...'

'Terry was there. Besides, I was quite safe. He respects Mary's friends...'

'You must never go there again,' she repeated. 'Please promise me you won't, Amy. I should never forgive myself if...'

'If he tried it on with me? He has already made suggestions,' I said and frowned. 'At the dance last evening. He said that he could help me develop my talents as a dress designer and other things...'

Lainie shuddered. 'Don't listen to him. Whatever he promises you, don't listen, Amy.'

'I shan't,' I said. 'Stop worrying, Lainie. I have already made up my mind not to go there again. I don't trust Mr Maitland; he seemed nice at first but I've realized that he probably isn't. I don't want anything to do with him, but he doesn't frighten me. If I wanted to continue my friendship with Mary I would simply ignore him, but I don't think there's much point to it now.'

'Philip Maitland isn't the kind of man you can just ignore,' Lainie said. 'But if you stop going there he may forget about you.'

'Of course he will,' I reassured her. 'And if he does try to make me an offer, I shall simply tell him I'm not interested. Besides, I'm not going to be here for a while, am I?'

'No, and perhaps that is just as well,' she said.

'I'm sorry to let you down, but I think Mum needs me more at the moment.'

'Yes, I am sure she does,' Lainie said and smiled. 'I shall miss you, Amy, but you needn't take all your things. You can come back when your father is better – if you want to?'

'Yes, of course I do. I have enjoyed working for you – and I'm sorry we quarrelled over John.'

'Yes, so am I,' she agreed. 'I haven't forgotten that you had money missing too, Amy. I'm going to get to the bottom of this, but it will keep until John comes to see me next time.'

'I'm sure it was all a mistake,' I said, and I genuinely hoped it was, because it would hurt her so much to know that her son had stolen her money.

'The money was there,' she said. 'Someone took it, Amy. I'm just not certain who that someone was...'

Mum held me in her arms for several minutes when we met the next day. Both of us had tears trickling down our cheeks. My mother took out her handkerchief and wiped mine away, just as she had when I was a little girl.

'I'm so glad you're here, Amy,' she said. 'Your father seems not too bad this morning, just a bit tired. I've told him you're coming and he asked me to send you up straight away.'

'I'll go up then,' I said. 'And then I'll do the ironing for you.'

'There's no need for that, love. Just having you here is tonic enough for me.'

'I would like to do it as we talk,' I said. 'Just the two of us, in the kitchen.'

'All right. I'll make a start on the dinner then.'

I left her smiling and went up to my father. He held out his hand to me and I walked over to the bed to kiss him on the cheek.

'What are you doing home?' he challenged. 'Shouldn't you be at work?'

'I'm taking a few days off to help Mum.'

'Yes, that's a good idea,' he said approvingly. 'Just as long as you haven't come to make a fuss over me.'

'As if I would!'

'As if,' he repeated and grinned. 'I dare say I've been overdoing things a bit. The doctor says this is a warning to slow down, so maybe it's time. I shall probably rest for a while and then start to sell off some of my interests. See if I can persuade your mother to retire to a country cottage with roses growing round the door.'

'Some hope of that,' I said, and laughed because I knew he was only teasing. 'Besides, it would drive you mad after a week.'

'Never was one for gardening much,' he agreed. 'But I shall certainly take things easier. I've been thinking of asking Matthew if he will come in with me and help out. I know he wanted his own shop, but I've got three of them and I need someone to run them for me.'

'You've got three shops? Men's outfitters? Where? It's the first I've heard of them, Dad.' I stared at him in amazement and he grinned.

'Up West, as a matter of fact, a little chain of them. That's surprised you, hasn't it? I keep things close to my chest, Amy. Always have, always found it best. A still tongue makes a wise head in my estimation – but now things have to change. Your brothers are not interested in running my little empire for me. They both have better things in mind, but I'm hoping Matthew might. He's an enterprising lad, you know. He isn't always going to be a dogsbody for someone else to order around.'

'I never thought he was,' I said. 'Does he know any of this?'

'I dropped a few hints when we had a little

chat the other week. He said he would consider working for me. I haven't told him the whole of it yet, but I made it clear that I wasn't going to do him any favours. He'll start off as a manager but there's a partnership in it for him if he deserves it.'

'Supposing I didn't want to get married for a while?'

'Quarrelled with him?'

'No, just thinking I might want to wait for a while.'

'That's up to you, love. There's no rush, and it makes no difference as far as me taking Matthew into the business is concerned. He is intelligent, honest and hard-working – just the man I've been looking for for a while now. I shall give him his chance, even if you decide you don't want to marry him.'

'I haven't changed my mind. I'm just not sure that I'm ready to get married yet.'

'Changed your tune, haven't you?' My father's eyes narrowed. 'Something wrong?'

'No ... But Mum was right about Mary Maitland. I shan't be visiting her house again, Dad.'

'Well, I can't say I'm sorry about that. I was sure you would make up your own mind without us interfering. He didn't do anything to you, did he?'

'Don't worry, Dad. He said he could show me how to be special if I let him help me, but

I made it clear I wasn't interested.'

'I'd kill him first! If that man ever touched you...'

'Now, don't get upset,' I said and smiled. 'It's over as far as I'm concerned. I think Mary will probably cancel the last dress she ordered, but Lainie says it will sell in the shop anyway.'

'I know someone who might help you,' my father said. 'I didn't want to interfere, but if you need an introduction...'

'Terry said you were the one to ask.' I smiled at him. 'For the moment all I want is for you to get better.'

'I'll be on my feet in no time,' he promised. 'Go down and give your mother a hand now, love. I feel a bit tired. You can come up and see me again later.'

'Is there anything you want?'

'No, nothing for the moment.'

I smiled at him and went back down to the kitchen. My mother was making a stew for dinner, and the smell of it made my mouth water.

'No one cooks like you, Mum,' I said as I went to pick up the iron from the fire. 'This is a bit hot. I had better let it cool down before I start on those sheets.'

'I'll make a cup of tea,' she said. 'It is nice having you here, Amy. Tell me all about your weekend.'

'Oh, it was all very grand. There was a

huge marquee with boards on the grass for dancing, and a carpet across the lawn so that we didn't get our shoes wet. An expensive caterer supplied the food, but it didn't taste half as nice as that stew will. I'm hungry already.'

'Good.' She smiled at me. 'What were the clothes like then?'

'Oh, mostly pale pastels, very pretty. My dress was crimson and it was all wrong for the occasion. It was more suitable for a nightclub in London.'

'Oh, dear,' she said and laughed. 'It's a pity you didn't show it to me first, Amy.'

'It wasn't finished or I would have done.'

'Well, never mind. I'm sure you looked lovely.'

'It did suit me, but it was too old for me and wrong for Mary's party. I'll save it for the right occasion – one day when I'm older and wiser.'

'I think you are quite a wise young lady now,' she said and smiled at me. 'Your father was quite right to say we shouldn't interfere. You've made up your own mind without any help from us.'

'I'm glad you warned me though, Mum. Mr Maitland did try it on a bit and if I'd been a silly young girl with no one to care about her, I might have fallen for it.' I was thoughtful for a moment as I looked at her. 'He did something to Lainie, didn't he –

something bad? She wouldn't tell me anything, but she was very upset when she discovered who Mary's father was. She went as white as a sheet.'

'Yes, he did something bad to her,' Mum agreed. 'I can't tell you, Amy. Your father said it wasn't our secret to tell. If Lainie wants you to know she will tell you.'

'He isn't John's father, is he?'

'No, I don't think so,' she said and frowned. 'It was much worse than that, but Lainie must tell you herself.'

'What did he do to Dad – can you tell me that?'

She hesitated for a moment. 'You know that Joe's sister Mary was killed in a fire, don't you? It was the eve of her wedding to my brother Jamie, and she had insisted on sleeping alone in the rooms above her flower shop. Someone set fire to the shop that night, Amy, and she was killed.'

'Oh, Mum!' I looked at her in horror. 'I thought it was an accident. You mean someone did that on purpose? That's wicked!'

'Yes, it is. The man who did it – Hal Burgess – was killed some days later – a kind of execution ordered by the man he worked for, because he had made a mess of the job. Joe was supposed to be sleeping there – it was your father's shop. I think he was the one they hoped to murder, but they killed Mary Robinson instead.'

'Wanted to kill Dad...' A chill ran down my spine. 'Are you saying it was Mr Maitland? Is he the one who gave the order?'

'We believe so,' she said, and I saw the grief in her face. The memory of Mary Robinson's cruel death still cut deep after all these years. 'We could never have proved it of course. The man who set the fire was dead, and the man they called "Mr Big" was safe as usual. Joe had been trying to unmask him, show him for the evil creature he was, but after that he let it go. He was afraid I would be next if he didn't draw back...'

'Has Mr Maitland ever tried to harm you?'

'He threatened me once, but that was before the fire that killed your father's sister, Mary. I think that shocked him, because it was Hal Burgess that set it and it wasn't supposed to happen like that. It was Joe who Maitland wanted dead, not Mary. Philip Maitland is an odd man, a bad man, but he has his own strange code. He respects women he thinks are decent. He used to buy flowers from our shop and I think he respected Mary. I believe he was genuinely sorry for what had happened – and Hal's execution, which I'm certain he arranged, was his way of saying the feud between us was over. But I've always been afraid he might decide to have another go at us one day.'

She looked thoughtful, her finger moving

about the table, drawing patterns.

'Is there something more I should know, Mum?'

'You remember Billy Ryan, don't you? Do you remember he was killed in a fight with the police?'

It was a name I vaguely recalled from the past, though the face was not clear in my mind. 'I think so. He was Maggie Ryan's son and married to Kathy – our Kathy. Tom's wife. But what does Billy have to do with this?'

'I think Maitland had Billy Ryan killed,' she said, her eyes meeting mine across the table. 'I'm almost sure he had been working for Maitland – and Billy stepped out of line. That police raid was set up and I think Billy was meant to die that night.'

I remembered all the talk about Billy Ryan so vividly. It had caused a terrible scandal in the lanes, and upset Maggie Ryan for months. She had even fallen out with my mother for a while, although I had thought that was something to do with Kathy. Billy and some others had broken into a factory on the docks, but the police had been waiting for them.

'That makes Mary's father a very dangerous man,' I said 'Is that why Kathy and Tom went to live in America after they got married?'

'Yes.' My mother looked anxious. 'I was

worried that Maitland might come after Kathy, because she knew Billy had been working for him. Tom had always liked working out there in America, so he took her off, and they're very happy from what I hear of things.'

'Yes, I know you said they like it out there.'

'Tom wants us to go out for a holiday...'

'Dad was joking about retiring to a country cottage with roses round the door.'

'I think I would rather go to America,' my mother said, pulling a face. 'But Maggie Ryan is seriously thinking of going back to Ireland – her husband has wanted to retire there for years – and if she does, I might think about moving somewhere different. Perhaps a nice little house in the suburbs, somewhere not too far from you and Matthew, Amy.'

'I'm sure a house like that would be much easier for you than this old place, Mum – even though Dad has made it a little palace for you inside. There's always dirt off the street whenever you open the door.'

'I was happy here,' she said. 'But things are different now. If I can persuade your father to retire...'

I told her about his plans for Matthew and she nodded.

'Yes, we've talked about it several times. I think this has been coming on for a while, Amy. Your father knew he wasn't right, but he wouldn't admit it.'

'He seems not too bad.'

'I think we've been lucky,' she said. 'Joe was always lucky. And I intend to make sure that he doesn't work too hard in future.'

'Kettle calling the pot black?' I suggested, using one of my father's favourite phrases to tease her. 'Perhaps you should think about getting some help, Mum.'

'Well, I might,' she said, surprising me. 'Just someone to do all the things I find more difficult these days. And I might sell my market stalls. I've had an offer from a nice young man I think deserves the chance to get on. He reminds me of Joe when he was young. Yes, I might let him take over the stalls before this winter.'

I had begun the ironing now that the iron had cooled down a little. She poured herself another cup of tea. I saw that she was smiling and wondered what she was thinking.

'A penny for them?'

'I was just thinking I could get used to this,' she said. 'I remember how I used to grumble when my mother made me do the ironing after I got home from work at night. I was so tired, Amy. Especially when she was ill and had me running up and down the stairs all day.'

'Well, I'm here to help so you won't have to do that for Dad.'

'He wouldn't call me a dozen times for

nothing,' she said. 'Ma wanted her whisky and I wouldn't give it to her all the time. We couldn't afford it in those days, and it was killing her. We had some right old battles over that, I can tell you.'

'It must have been very hard for you then, Mum. Have you heard from Uncle Jamie recently?'

'He writes once in a blue moon,' she said. 'But I hear about him from Kathy now, and she says he's the most popular man for miles. It made him, going out there, but he's never got over Mary's death. He told me when he was here last time that he would never marry.'

'It was such a tragedy,' I said. 'Such a wicked thing to do. It makes me angry to think that Mr Maitland got away with it. Why should he be able to carry on, living his life as he wants without being punished for what he did?'

'I've asked myself that a thousand times,' Bridget said. 'I don't know the answer, Amy. It isn't just the money – not all rich people are bad. Your father is a warm man as they say, but he has never hurt a soul in his life.'

'I know that,' I said. 'But Mr Maitland is an evil man. I think that is why Mary is too ashamed to tell people her second name. She never does, you know. I wondered about it at the start, but it didn't seem important.'

Mum looked at me curiously. 'Does she

know what kind of a man he is?'

'I'm not sure. I think she knows something. Perhaps that is why she seems to have a hold over him...'

Mary had seemed to control her father in some strange way. She had certainly warned him to leave me alone that day at her house. I remembered the way she had used blackmail against Paul and I knew that she wouldn't hesitate to use it against her father if need be.

'What are you thinking about, Amy?'

'Oh, nothing. It isn't important any more.'

'Then we'll forget it,' she said. 'Let's talk about something else. I understand that Matthew is coming up again this weekend?'

Matthew was a little subdued when he came to visit that weekend. He spent a couple of hours talking to my father in his room, and we had lunch when he came down. Afterwards I helped my mother with the dishes and then we went out for a walk.

Matthew was quiet to begin with, and then he turned his head to look at me and smiled as I walked in silence at his side through the lanes. We headed towards the river, sitting on a wooden bench on the grass verge to watch the boats as they passed. As it was Sunday the river traffic was fairly slow, with just the occasional barge passing in the distance and the hoot of a horn from a pleasure boat. Yet the water was grimy with oil floating on the surface, and clogged with rubbish from the big ships that used the docks, reminding me of the true nature of the river here.

'Joe told you he'd asked me to work for him, I suppose?' Matthew said at last. It was the first remark he'd made since leaving the house, except to answer a neighbour who had called out that it was a fine afternoon.

'Yes, he talked about his future intentions. He needs someone he can trust, Matt. I know he likes you a lot. What did you think of his offer?'

'I've thought it over and I've decided it makes sense. It would take me years to work my way up to the position your father is offering me. And I'm not particularly happy where I am – the firm is now talking of my staying there for another six months, which I don't want to do, if I can help it.'

'So you're going to accept then?'

'Yes. Yes, I have already. Joe made it clear that his offer had nothing to do with us. He still wants me even if...' He broke off, looking at me oddly. 'I was a bit harsh with you last time I was home, Amy. It upset me because you so obviously didn't want to tell me about your plans for the weekend.'

'That was wrong of me,' I admitted. 'I should have been open with you, Matt. I'm sorry I didn't tell you that I was going to Mary's house – but I thought you wouldn't like it and I didn't want to quarrel.'

'You should have told me.'

'Yes, I should have. It was silly and wrong, and it won't happen again.'

'Are you going to keep visiting her?'

'No, I don't think so. I don't think either of us wants that. I still like Mary, but there are reasons why I probably won't be seeing so much of her in future.'

'Would you like to tell me about them?'

'Her father has started to take an unhealthy interest in me,' I said. 'And she was jealous because her cousin liked me too much.'

'Liked?' Matthew looked at me intently. 'Is that all it was, Amy?'

I knew I had to tell him the truth, and I took a deep breath.

'Paul told me he was in love with me. He suggested we should run off and get married, but I don't think he really meant it – it was just a mad idea.'

I couldn't bear to look at Matthew, because I knew I would see hurt in his eyes.

'And what did you tell him?'

'I said I couldn't do that to my family or to you.'

'That was good of you,' he said, a note of bitterness in his voice. 'But I dare say I would have got over it. I think I'm man enough to accept it if you've changed your mind about us.'

'I never meant to hurt you, Matt. I simply got caught up in something I couldn't control.'

'And this Paul Ross? What do you feel for him?'

I turned to face him. 'I don't love him the way I love you.'

'But you do feel something for him?'

The hurt was in his eyes once more, making me feel like some sort of criminal, forcing me to look away because I couldn't bear the accusation I saw there.

'I feel something for him but I can't explain it. We would never have married, but there was a strong feeling between us.'

'Did he kiss you?' I heard jealousy and anger in his voice now. 'Tell me the truth, Amy.'

'Yes.'

'More than once?'

'Yes.'

'Anything else? Did he have you ... sexually?'

'Of course not!' I was shocked. 'How could you ask? You can't think I would do that.'

'Why not? Other girls have in similar situations. He could give you all the things I only dream of giving you.'

'Paul doesn't have money,' I said quietly. 'That's why he's marrying Mary, because she has quite a bit of her own. Her maternal grandfather left it in a trust for her until she marries, and of course her father is a wealthy man.'

'He sounds a really nice chap,' Matthew sneered. 'And you're in love with him!'

'I'm not in love with him. Besides, you don't understand. Paul is trapped. Mary has him on a string – he has no choice but to marry her. I think he was desperate, that's why he asked me to run away with him. He was trying to escape, but he didn't quite have the strength to make the break.'

Matthew looked disbelieving, and I could see that he despised Paul – and me for caring about him. But I couldn't tell Matthew the reasons for Paul's decision to marry a girl he didn't love, nor could I explain my own feelings. I didn't really understand them myself. I just knew that a part of me had felt it belonged with him.

'There is always a choice, Amy.'

'You don't understand about Paul.'

'And I don't want to. I've no time for people like that. They disgust me. They are rich, idle and worthless. If he needed money he should have pulled himself together and found a job. You said he was talented – why couldn't he play the piano for a living?'

'I've never heard him. He was scarred by the war or some private hurt and he no longer plays in public.'

'He sounds like a wastrel to me.'

'That's unfair. You know nothing about

him or why he is the way he is.'

'As far as I'm concerned there's nothing to know.'

'You're pig-headed and too sure of yourself. You think you're always right and that other people don't have a right to live their own lives in their own way.'

A pleasure boat was passing. It hooted its horn and the people on board waved. Neither of us waved back, we were both feeing too miserable.

'And you are a spoiled, silly girl who doesn't know what she wants.'

I glanced at Matthew. He was glaring at me.

'There's nothing more to say then, is there? I think we'll postpone the wedding, Matt. We are obviously not suited.'

'My thoughts exactly.' His eyes flashed with temper. 'You need to grow up before you're fit to marry anybody.'

'I'm not sure I want to get married anyway. There's more to life than washing shirts and changing nappies.'

'Just as well we found out before it was too late then.'

I jumped up and walked quickly away, leaving him sitting on the bench alone. The tears were very close and I felt wretched, but there was no point in continuing the argument. Matthew was so sure he was right, and perhaps in a way he was. Perhaps I was just a silly girl who didn't know what she wanted from life.

I only knew that I was hurting inside, but I wasn't sure why.

Ten

After more than a week of complete rest my father seemed much better and I decided to return to work. Lainie had visited with flowers and fruit, spending most of her time chatting to my mother over a cup of tea in the kitchen.

'Everyone has been asking after you,' she told me before she left. 'Are you coming back to us soon, Amy?'

'You should go,' my mother said. 'Joe says he's coming downstairs tomorrow, so I shan't be up and down all the time.'

'I'll go then,' I agreed. 'If you want me you can always telephone me at Lainie's.'

'I'm sure Joe is much better. There's no need for you to worry about us, Amy, love.'

'No, of course not.'

My mother had friends who would help her if necessary and my father was looking less tired. Lainie obviously wanted me back, and I'd missed working with the other girls and the customers.

'A letter came for you the other day,' Lainie said as she was leaving. 'I meant to bring it for you but I forgot. I hope it wasn't important.'

'I'm not expecting anything in particular.'

'Oh well, I'll put it in your room and you'll find it there when you come.'

The only person who wrote to me as a rule was Matthew but my aunt would recognize his hand, so it must be from someone else. Besides, I didn't think he would write for a while after our quarrel. So far I hadn't told anyone the wedding was off but I would have to soon – unless we both thought differently after we'd had time to calm down.

I was reflective as I went to bed that night. A part of me wanted time to live my own life and sort out my feelings, and another part of me missed Matthew so much that it hurt.

It took me ages to get to sleep that night. My mind kept running over and over the things that haunted me, keeping me restless, and when I did finally sleep it was only to toss restlessly on my pillow.

I woke from the dream with a start, hot and sweating, staring fearfully into the darkness. It was the first time I'd had the dream in months. I had thought it gone completely, but this one was worse than all the others, because I now knew the man with the staring eyes.

And he was dead.

Terry took me to Lainie's in the car the next morning. He studied my face thoughtfully for a moment or two as he took my case from the back and handed it to me.

'You're looking a bit peaky this morning, Amy. Something wrong?'

'I didn't sleep well, that's all – a bad dream.'

'Do you still have those? I remember you screaming as a child. Got a lot on your mind?'

'No, not really.'

'Have you heard from Mary at all?'

'No, but I didn't expect to while I was at home. She doesn't know where I live. Besides, I expect she's still angry with me.'

I had wondered if my letter might be from Mary but I didn't mention that to Terry. I wasn't sure how I would feel if she *had* written to me. Our friendship was over. I doubted it would be sensible to try to renew it.

'You won't go running after her again if she does?'

'I've never run after her,' I told him. 'I don't intend to start now – but I shan't be rude if she wants to be friendly.'

I gave my brother a quick hug, told him

not to worry and waved him off, then used the back stairs to go up to Lainie's flat. As I went into the sitting room I saw a girl standing by the desk. She had the top drawer open and was looking for something, and I knew she hadn't heard me come in.

'What are you doing, Peggy?'

She whirled around, fear and guilt in her face.

'Miss O'Rourke sent me to fetch something for her.'

'No, I don't think I believe that,' I said. 'You were looking for money, weren't you? You took money from the desk once before – and from my bedroom.'

'I didn't! I didn't steal anything. I was only going to borrow...'

'I think we had better go and ask Lainie why she sent you up here, don't you?'

'No! Please...' Peggy burst into a flood of noisy tears. 'I'll lose my job, and I needed the money so badly. My baby has been ill. I took the money to pay the doctor. It's all right for you, Amy. You've never known what it's like to be desperate.'

'I'm sorry...'

'Don't believe her.' Lainie's voice was harsh as she came out of her bedroom. 'I suspected Peggy as soon as I knew money was missing, but I hoped I was wrong, that we'd merely mislaid it.'

'It's a trap,' Peggy said, her face deadly

white. 'You said you were going out. I heard you telling Margaret...'

'Yes, it was a trap for a thief and you fell into it,' Lainie said. 'I'm not a hard woman but I won't keep a thief on my premises. I'll give you your wages and you can leave now, immediately.'

'Please...' Peggy sobbed. 'How am I going to find another job? No one decent will employ me without a reference. I shall 'ave to go back to that sweatshop I worked in afore, and that'll be the death o' me.'

'You should've thought of that before you stole from me. You're lucky I don't hand you over to the police.'

'Amy! Help me!' She looked at me fearfully. 'I can't go back to that dreadful place...'

I felt pity for her plight as she sobbed but I knew there was nothing I could do to help her. Lainie had given her a chance and she had abused her trust.

'Go down and collect your things,' Lainie said. 'In a few minutes I shall come and give you your wages.'

Peggy looked at her in silence for a moment, then turned away, leaving without another word.

'I'm glad you saw that, Amy,' my aunt said. 'I hope you're convinced now that it wasn't John who took your money.'

'Yes, of course. I apologize to you and to

John. I jumped to conclusions and I should not have done. I'm sorry.'

Lainie nodded her satisfaction. 'We'll forget about it now. I didn't say anything to him, so he doesn't know he was under suspicion. I would appreciate it if you didn't tell him.'

'Of course I shan't. I feel awful.'

'There's no need for that. I wondered if it might have been him myself for a while, but then I remembered Margaret saying they were short in their tea money in the workroom just after Peggy first arrived.'

'Well, I'm glad you've sorted it out. What will happen to her now?'

'She'll find work or she'll have to go into the workhouse.' Lainie shrugged her shoulders. 'Don't waste your pity. Peggy isn't our worry. There are hundreds of girls who would give anything for the chance I gave her.'

'Yes, I know. She let you down. You couldn't do anything else but let her go – but I can't help feeling sorry for her. Especially if her baby was ill.'

'She made that up to get your sympathy.' Lainie frowned. 'I've got something else to tell you. Mary Maitland came in this morning asking about her dress. I told her we wouldn't be making it for her and asked her not to come here again.'

'Oh, Lainie! You were a bit harsh. Besides,

the dress is almost finished.'

'I've already sold it to Miss Adams. It needs some alteration but Margaret is working on it. Miss Adams bought two dresses from the rails, on which she would like some embroidery – and she wants you to make something special for her if you will.'

'Of course I will – for as long as I can.'

Lainie was silent for a moment, then said, 'Margaret has decided not to leave us. She was suspicious of the working conditions at that other place. She thought she might be expected to put in extra hours for nothing whenever they needed her, and she can earn as much here if she does extra work for you.'

'Until you sell the shop.'

'*If* I do,' Lainie said. 'I was hurt and angry when I made my decision to sell, Amy. Harold says I shouldn't be too hasty. London isn't so far by train these days, and until you have children ... That's if you want to carry on?'

'You know I do! Oh, Lainie!' I hugged her. 'You don't know how much this means to me. Especially now...'

'What do you mean?'

'I'm not going to marry Matthew, not for a while anyway. It's not that I've stopped caring for him, I'm just not ready yet.'

'Well, that suits me. It's selfish to say so, I know, but you're young, Amy. You've plenty of time to marry later on.' She looked at me thoughtfully. 'This doesn't mean you're going to start up with Mary again, does it?'

'Not as a friend, no. But if we're going to develop the design side I wouldn't turn her down as a customer.'

'You'll have plenty of those. I've had six ladies in asking about you while you were away. They were older women, not young girls. One of them told me she saw the dress you wore to Mary's dance and loved it. She wants you to make something similar for her.'

'Good gracious! Are you sure?' I was so surprised that I stared at her with my mouth open like a fish out of water. 'I thought everyone was saying I looked like a tart that evening.'

'Well, apparently some of them thought you looked divine – her words, not mine.' Lainie smiled. 'People are talking about you, Amy. You undoubtedly have talent and Mary isn't the only one who knows a good thing when she sees it. We shall charge more for your work in future. If there is a demand for something it's worth its price.'

Lainie looked quite excited and I thought the upsurge in business was probably one of the main reasons she had changed her mind again.

'It sounds as if we are going to be busy. We shall have to take on another seamstress again.'

'Next time I'll make sure she's honest.'

'Yes, please do.'

Lainie said she had things to do in her office and I carried my suitcase into my bedroom. The letter Lainie had told me about was lying on the dressing table. I picked it up and opened it, frowning as I read it through twice.

Apparently, one of the fashion houses I had sent a design to had decided they wanted to use it in their next collection and were offering me twenty pounds. It was a considerable sum of money – far more than I had ever earned before – but that wasn't all. I had been invited to take along a portfolio of my work. If it was satisfactory I might be offered full-time employment.

I felt a surge of excitement, but then I read the letter again and began to wonder. I did not recall submitting a design to a firm called Rosemary Fashions. It seemed a little odd and I decided to take my letter downstairs and show it to Margaret.

Sally and Margaret were having an earnest conversation when I went into the workroom, but they stopped when they saw me.

'Has Peggy gone?'

'She was crying,' Margaret said, looking upset. 'She wouldn't tell us why she'd been dismissed. I thought it might be because I had decided to stay on.'

'No, of course not. If anything we shall

need at least one more girl, perhaps two. We're going to expand the design and made-to-order business if we can.'

'Oh, good,' Margaret said, looking happier. 'I'm glad I decided to stay then. I felt guilty when Peggy was so upset.'

'Why was she sent off?' Sally asked.

'She was caught trying to take money from Lainie's desk upstairs. It wasn't the first time she'd done it, so Lainie had to let her go.'

'She'd borrowed from both of us,' Sally said. 'Told us her mother was dying once, and her rent was overdue another time. I reckon she was a liar as well as a thief.' She sniffed her disapproval. 'If you want another girl I've got a cousin looking for a good place. She don't like it where she is 'cause 'er boss is a bit nifty wiv 'is 'ands if yer know what I mean?'

'Yes, I do,' I agreed. 'Where does she work now?'

'It's a classy manufacturer's down the Portobello Road. Knows all the tricks of the trade, does Alice. She'll be able ter 'elp wiv the cuttin' as well as the sewin', I reckon.'

'Ask Alice to come and see us. If Lainie likes her she sounds just what we need.'

I turned to Margaret, taking the letter from the pocket of my skirt to show her. 'I wasn't sure ... Is this the firm that wrote to you?'

She glanced at the letter in surprise, then nodded. 'Yes, just the same. Miss O'Rourke told you I've turned them down? I didn't like the look of things there – something not quite right about it. I thought it was odd right from the start, offering me all that money.'

'What do you mean exactly when you say you didn't like the look of things?'

'I'm not sure. I just felt uncomfortable.' Margaret frowned. 'I think I've seen the woman who runs the place before. She didn't interview me, but I saw her in her office talking to a man. I was told he had recently bought the business.'

'Where had you see the woman, Margaret? Was it here?' She looked doubtful. 'Could it have been Mrs Simpson – the customer we made that afternoon dress for?'

'It might have been. Yes, now you say that, I think it was.' Margaret nodded vigorously. 'I knew I'd seen her. It was when I brought something through to the shop for you one morning. She was just leaving the shop but I wasn't sure who she was. You mentioned her having been in to ask about that dress.'

'Then she must have sent both our letters. She did ask a lot of questions at the time. I did wonder if she might have had something to do with your letter, but now I think...'

Suddenly the answer came to me in a flash. I hadn't sent a design to that fashion house; I hadn't even heard of it until now. Mrs Simpson must have taken something from my portfolio when I showed it to her. But why should she do that? Unless she was acting on behalf of the man who had recently bought her firm...

I knew only one man who might go to such lengths to get me to work for him. It must be Mary's father. Of course – I had seen Mrs Simpson with him the night Terry took me out to dinner!

It all slotted into place. They had tried to entice my best worker away and then made that generous offer to me – but why? I shivered as I wondered about the motives behind Mr Maitland's devious activities. Why was he so interested in me?

Without being vain, I knew I was attractive and I did have some talent, but there had to be more to it than that. There were hundreds of pretty girls out there, so why choose me in particular? Was it for another reason, perhaps? A form of revenge against my father? It hardly seemed possible, but I could not think that he had fallen in love with me.

He was far more likely to want to use me for reasons of his own. A shiver went down my spine as I realized Mr Maitland was even more dangerous than I had first believed.

'You won't work for them, will you?' Margaret asked, breaking into my thoughts.

'No, certainly not. I shall sell them the design if they want it and say that I am not looking for a job.'

'Good for you,' Margaret said. 'But you might have been if Miss O'Rourke had sold the shop.' She blushed. 'Terry mentioned it...'

'And you still decided to stay with us?'

'I could find another job if I had to, but I wanted to stay, Amy. We're friends – you, Terry and me.' Her cheeks were bright red. 'I've invited him for tea this weekend.'

'Good,' I said and smiled. 'You, Sally and I should all go out together one evening. We ought to celebrate.'

'Only if it's the Music Hall,' Sally said. 'I don't want to go to one of them fancy concerts.'

'We'll go wherever you want; it's my treat,' I replied. 'And now I really must do some work.'

I woke from the dream trembling and sweating that night. It was the first time I'd ever had it at Lainie's and it frightened me, perhaps because the man's face was so clear to me now. His eyes were wide and staring and there was blood all over him.

It was a horrible nightmare, the more so because I knew it was Mary's father who lay there staring up at me with his dead eyes. And I knew that I was frightened of him, frightened that he might not take my refusal to work for him as an answer.

My mother and Lainie had both warned

me that he was an evil man, and for some reason I did not understand he wanted me. I knew that I must stay well away from him. I must give him no opportunity to harm my family or me.

I had been back to work for a week when Millie Fairchild came into the shop. I was serving a customer so she took her time looking through the rails and waited until I had finished.

'I came in when you were away,' she said, seeming anxious.

'Yes, I know. My father wasn't well and I had to take time off to help my mother look after him.'

'Is he better?'

'Yes, much better, thank you,'

'I'm glad,' Millie said, then hesitated. 'I want a new evening dress ... But there's something I have to tell you, Amy.'

She was clearly on edge and somehow I guessed it was to do with Mary. 'It's obviously private. You had better come into my aunt's office. She is out this afternoon so we shan't be disturbed.'

Millie followed me inside and closed the door. Her face was strained as she looked at me, and I could see she was struggling to stay calm.

'I thought you might have heard, but you haven't...' She took a deep breath as I shook my head. 'It ... It's Paul. He had a terrible accident in his car last night. They took him to hospital, but my father says there isn't much hope.'

'Paul ... Paul Ross?' I was in shock, unable to take in what she was saying for a moment. I must have misheard her. She couldn't have said what I thought, but I could see by her face that she had. I sat down suddenly as my legs went weak, my head spinning. 'Paul had an accident? Was it on the road or at Brooklands? He told me he liked to race his car there.'

'On the road. I don't know much but they say his brakes must have failed. He skidded off the road and hit a tree head on. I'm sorry to have to tell you this, Amy. I know you liked him...'

'Yes. Yes, I did.' I felt sick and dizzy. It was terrible, terrible news. I couldn't take it in, didn't want to believe it was true. 'I can hardly believe it. You say he won't recover – there's no hope?'

It couldn't be true! Paul dying? It was too much to take in, too terrible to accept.

'My father says he's unconscious. They think there's brain damage. If he lived...' Millie broke off, a sob in her voice. 'I can't bear to think about it. Paul was strange sometimes but I did like him.'

'Poor Mary,' I said. 'She must be suffering so much.'

'How like you to think of her. She was very unpleasant about you after you left, Amy.'

'She loved Paul. She was afraid I might take him away from her.'

'Hardly an excuse for her behaviour.' Millie frowned. 'But I do feel sorry for her. She always wanted Paul. Her father was furious when she announced their engagement. They had a terrible row about it that Sunday. He said he would stop the marriage, and she ... Well, I couldn't possibly repeat what she said, Amy, but it wasn't nice. I've decided that I shan't visit Mary again. I'll speak to her if I see her out, but I shan't go to her home. My father is pleased, and Alan agrees that I should drop her. I think Jane feels the same. Alan and I are getting engaged next month.' She smiled at me. 'It won't be a grand affair like Mary's, of course, but I should like you to come.'

'Oh, of course, if you want...' I stared at her. I hadn't been concentrating. All I could think about was Paul lying in hospital, dying. 'Do you know where they've taken him?'

'Paul? Yes, it's a small private hospital. I'll write the address down for you.' She took out a leather notebook, wrote the address carefully and tore the page out. 'Of course. You will want to see him.'

I struggled to contain my impatience. How could she talk about her party at a time like this?

'I must. Would you excuse me? One of the girls will take your measurements – ask for Margaret, and she will make an appointment for a consultation. I shall be happy to design your dress, Millie, but I have to go to Paul.'

'Please don't let me delay you. I'm so sorry...'

I was no longer listening. Hurrying upstairs to collect my bag and coat, my mind was denying the terrible news. Millie was wrong. Paul would live, of course he would. My eyes were smarting with tears as I remembered the last time we had spoken. He had been so desperately unhappy – and now he was dying.

Paul was dying and I wanted – I needed – to say goodbye.

'Are you a relative?' the nurse asked when I told her why I had come. 'Mr Ross is very ill. Doctor says only relatives.'

'I was a very close friend. Please, I must see him! It means so much to me.'

'I am very sorry, Miss Robinson. I cannot let you see Mr Ross without permission from his family.'

I gave a sob of despair and turned away. It made things worse to know that Paul was so near, so close to death, and I could not say my farewell to him.

As I walked towards the door once more someone called my name. I turned and saw

Mary. She looked awful. Her dress was creased, hair tangled, face red from weeping – but it was the wild look of despair in her eyes that held me rooted to the spot. As I stood there uncertainly she came running towards me and I could see that she was in terrible distress. Without thinking, I opened my arms and she ran into them.

'Oh, Amy,' she sobbed. 'He's dead ... A few minutes ago. He never even knew I was there and I loved him so. I loved him so!'

'I know, I know,' I said and stroked her hair as I felt her pain, her despair. The arrogance, the selfishness and the spite had all gone. She was the vulnerable, lonely girl I had taken to my heart when we first met. And I knew what I had to do. 'He cared for you, Mary. He would have known you were there. I am sure he would have known.'

'I want to go home.' Mary was shaking violently, clearly in shock. 'I can't go alone. The house is empty; the housekeeper left us last week, and the maids went with her. Come with me, Amy. Please don't let me be alone now. I can't bear it. Paul was all I had. I know I was rotten to you, but I was afraid he might choose you, and I loved him so much. I don't know what to do. I'll die if I'm alone. I can't bear it. I can't!'

'Yes, of course I'll come.'

I didn't hesitate. Mary couldn't be left alone in this state and there was no point in staying at the hospital. Paul was dead. They wouldn't allow me to see him while he was still alive, and now it was too late.

The pain of loss that swept over me then was almost unbearable. If I had been alone I might have broken down as Mary had, but somehow I had to get through it; I had to take her home. The thought that she mustn't be left alone in an empty house was paramount in my mind.

I wondered briefly why Mary's housekeeper had left them, but it wasn't important. Nothing mattered but our shared grief.

Tears were slipping down my cheeks as I led Mary outside. The sun was shining. How could the sun still shine when Paul was dead? It seemed all wrong somehow. I was hurting so dreadfully inside but I knew I had to be strong. I had to take Mary home and look after her until she was feeling better.

I saw a taxi and hailed it, then paused for one moment.

'Is your father at home, Mary?'

'No. He's away on business. He won't be back for ages. I don't care if he never comes back. I hate him. He's cruel and ruthless. It should have been him that died. I wish it had been. Oh, God, I wish he was dead and Paul was alive!'

She was near to collapse as I helped her into the taxi. If Mr Maitland had been at home I couldn't have taken Mary to her house, but neither could I have deserted her in this state. It seemed that I had no choice but to go with her.

She sobbed all the way there, in such a state that I had to deal with paying the taxi and getting her into the house. She told me that the back door was unlocked. She had rushed out in such a hurry when she heard about Paul's accident that she hadn't bothered to lock it.

I could hear the dogs howling as I took her round to the back of the house, and realized that they probably hadn't been fed. If the housekeeper was away and there was no one here to look after them they must be in a terrible state.

'Who has been feeding the dogs?'

Mary blinked and looked at me stupidly. 'Paul fed them yesterday, I suppose. I didn't think. I daren't go near them. Let them starve. I don't care what happens to them. They are *his* ... I hope they die. I hope *he* dies!'

'It's not their fault, poor things,' I said, remembering the way Paul had controlled the dog when I'd first come to the house that day. He at least had cared about their welfare. 'I'll see if I can find them some food in a while, after I've got you to bed.'

'Don't go in to them,' she warned. 'They would tear you to pieces.'

'I'll see what I can do. Isn't there someone

you can telephone to help you, Mary? Someone who would come and see to things for you?'

As we passed through the house I could see that it looked neglected. No one had cleaned up for a while, and I could see Mary's things lying about where she had dropped them.

'You can't go on like this for much longer. You need someone to look after you.'

'Don't leave me, Amy.' She clutched at my arm. 'Stay with me, please. I need you. You're my only real friend. The others only came because I gave them a good time. They never really liked me. You liked me, didn't you?'

'Yes, you know I did, Mary. You were the one who turned against me.'

'I'm sorry, so sorry,' she said. 'I'll make it up to you. I'll give you anything you want – the diamonds my father gave me for my dance if you like.'

'Don't be silly! I don't want your diamonds. I'll stay with you for a while. You need to sleep. When you're calmer we'll talk about this sensibly. You can't stay here in this house alone, especially while you're so upset. Could you stay with your aunt?'

'She isn't my aunt. She only sponsored me because *he* paid her. She wouldn't come near me if he didn't pay her – and I told her I didn't need her any more. Why should I put up with her nagging? She was always telling me not to do things, and she didn't approve of my marrying Paul.'

'But there must be someone – your mother's relatives?'

'There aren't many and they hate my father. Everyone hates him, Amy. He isn't a gentleman. He bought my mother with his filthy money, but he couldn't buy respectability – not once they knew what he was really like.'

'What do you mean?'

She gave a shrill laugh. 'Why do you think I never use my father's name? I'm ashamed of him, that's why – ashamed of what he does, of his rotten money.'

'What does he do, Amy?'

'All the nasty things you can think of,' she said bitterly. 'He is a crook and a thief, a pimp and a gangster – and probably a murderer, for all I know.'

'You don't mean that? You can't!' I stared at her in horror. 'Your father can't be all those things, Amy.'

'Oh, yes he can,' she said, her eyes gleaming with hatred. 'I heard him telling my mother once when they quarrelled. She had accused him of something, and he stood there laughing, telling her exactly where the money that paid for her clothes had come from.'

'But you may have misheard...' I was

fighting the horror, not wanting to accept that such evil could really exist, yet in my heart I knew it did. 'When people quarrel they often say terrible things.'

'I know what he does,' Mary said and her voice was hard, full of hatred. 'I listen when he doesn't know I'm around. I hear what he talks about to those men – the ones who do his filthy work for him. Oh, his hands are clean, Amy. He doesn't actually do these things himself. He just gives the orders and other people do it for him – but that doesn't make him any the less guilty.'

'Oh, Mary...' I stared at her, not knowing what to say.

'I found proof of something,' she went on, a small cynical smile on her mouth now. 'I hid it where he could never find it, and I told him – I told him I knew what he was and that I could prove it. I made a bargain with him. He was my father but we were to live separate lives. He wasn't to interfere with me, and I wouldn't interfere with him – but if he ever touched any of my friends or did anything to harm them or me I would go to the police and give them my evidence, tell them what I knew. And I know a lot, Amy – names, dates, and places. If I told the police they would throw him in prison and never let him out.'

It was blackmail, exactly as she had used against Paul. For a moment I was revolted and wondered why I was there in her house with her, but then I began to see what it must have been like for her, growing up with a father who was steeped in crime and a mother who drank to forget what her husband did.

She had used blackmail to protect herself against her father, and in a way I applauded her courage.

'Didn't you ever think he might...'

'Get rid of me?' Mary laughed bitterly. 'If he did, my evidence would find its way to the police. Besides, he says he loves me, accuses me of being cruel to him. I don't believe him, of course. He doesn't know what love is...' Tears filled her eyes once more. 'The only people I ever had to love me were Eleanor and Paul and now they are both dead.'

'Come and lie down for a while,' I said. 'You should try to rest, Mary. You are exhausted.'

She allowed me to persuade her up to her bedroom, which was far more untidy than the rest of the house and it convinced me that Mary couldn't stay here alone. I had to find somewhere for her to stay – but where? I knew Lainie had told her she wouldn't be welcome at the shop again, and she would hardly welcome her to her flat – which wasn't big enough for all of us anyway.

Mary clutched at my hand as I drew the

quilt over her.

'You aren't going to leave me? Please, Amy. I'm afraid of being alone. The nightmares will come back if I'm alone.'

'I have nightmares too,' I said and sat beside her for a moment. 'Will you drink something if I make it?'

'I don't want anything.'

'Some warm milk if there is any – or tea. You should have a cup of hot sweet tea, Mary. Will you let me call a doctor for you? He might give you something to help you sleep.'

'I don't need a doctor. I just need someone to be with me.'

'I'm not going to desert you. You can't stay here alone. I'm going to telephone my aunt and ask if I can take you there.'

'She hates my father,' Mary said. 'I can't go there.'

'Let me think about it for a while. I'm going down to make you a cup of tea. I wouldn't mind one myself.'

'Oh, all right,' she said. 'I wasn't thinking about you. You cared about Paul too, didn't you?'

'Not in the way you did. He was a friend, a special friend, nothing more, Mary.'

'You won't leave me here?'

'No, I shan't do that.'

I went downstairs, finding my way to the kitchen after some trial and error. At least in the kitchen there was a semblance of order, and I thought that perhaps Paul had taken care of things while he...

A wave of grief swept over me as I felt the shock and pain of loss all over again. I had loved Paul, more than I had realized at the time. It was not the nice, safe, conventional feeling I had for Matthew, but I knew that it existed. The ache in my heart was almost more than I could bear.

Tears filled my eyes and spilled over, and for a few minutes I sat at the kitchen table and sobbed, but then I pulled myself together. This was doing no good. Besides, I didn't want to stay in this house a moment longer than necessary.

As I made the tea and carried a tray upstairs I realized that the dogs had stopped howling. Had someone fed them? Perhaps a man came in to do so each day without Mary knowing. She had never taken much notice of them. They had certainly gone quiet, which was a relief. Like Mary, I was frightened of the dogs.

I went into Mary's room and, seeing that she had fallen asleep, I smiled. I put a cup of tea on the chest by her bed in case she woke up and went out, taking my own tea downstairs to the small sitting room we had used on the two occasions I had come to the house.

I drank my tea and then sat thinking for a

long time. What was I going to do about Mary? She couldn't stay here. The house was too big and I knew how she must feel about being here alone. But would Lainie accept her? I looked at the clock. It was nearly five o'clock. Lainie would be wondering where I was. I ought to telephone her.

I got up and went to the telephone, picking it up and asking the operator for my aunt's number.

'I am sorry, miss, that number is engaged. Please try again later.'

I replaced the receiver and started towards the door. I would wake Mary and risk taking her to my aunt's. If Lainie refused to let her stay even for one night, I would take her somewhere else...

I was still pondering the problem when the door of the sitting room opened and I saw a man standing on the threshold. My blood ran cold and I was paralysed with fear. Mary's father! But she had said he wouldn't be home for ages.

His eyes narrowed as he saw me, and then he smiled – a cold, unpleasant smile that made me shiver.

'What a nice surprise, Miss Robinson – or shall I call you Amy? Yes, I think that is very much better, don't you?'

'I prefer that you call me Miss Robinson, sir.'

'I wondered who was in here. I thought it

must be Mary or Paul – but of course it wouldn't be him, would it? He's dead – but you know that, don't you? That's why you are here. You came to look after my poor deserted daughter, didn't you?'

'I met Mary at the hospital. She was naturally upset, so...'

'You brought her here. It is what you would do, of course. You are very like your mother, Miss Robinson. I liked Bridget O'Rourke, you know – until she started to interfere in my business. After that I had to teach her a lesson.'

Without thinking, I blurted out the truth. 'I ... I've been told that you had my Aunt Mary murdered.'

'Tut-tut, Amy. That is a terrible accusation. I was very upset about what happened to Mary Robinson. I called my own daughter Mary in memory of her, did you know that? Do you have proof that I was involved in that regrettable incident? Your father never did manage to find any, you know. I could sue you for malicious slander, my dear – but I shan't, of course. You are much too pretty. I have far nicer things in mind for you.'

He took a few steps towards me. I drew back with a shudder.

'Please do not come near me. I am not interested in any of your plans.'

'I have been told you refused my generous offer to work for me. That was a mistake,

Amy. I would have been so good to you – I could make you famous and rich, you know. I have influence in many spheres, and if I used it to help you...'

'I do not need or want your help, thank you.' I raised my head and looked him in the eyes. 'Why should you want to help me? Or is it that you were hoping to ruin me? Was it some kind of petty revenge against my parents?'

He laughed softly, his eyes gleaming with amusement.

'How adorable you are when you are angry, Amy. Shall I be honest with you, my dear? Yes, I think I shall. There was some element of that at the start. It amused me that you had walked into my home like a fly into a spider's web. I told you my full name but it was obvious that you knew nothing. You were so innocent. I could have harmed you then had I wanted, but you were my daughter's friend and it amused me to have you in my home. I knew that one day your parents would discover the truth and I felt that it would be interesting to see what happened.'

'They asked me not to attend Mary's dance, but I wanted to come. If I had known as much as I know about you now...' A shudder ran through me. 'Please excuse me, I have to speak to Mary and then I must leave.'

'Oh, but I don't think I'm ready to let you go yet, Amy. I am enjoying our little chat too much.' His eyes narrowed, hard and cold. 'Just what is it you think you know? What has Joe Robinson been telling you – or perhaps it wasn't Joe. No, I think he is too sensible, too cautious. Mary, then...' He looked at me intently, then nodded. 'My foolish daughter. I fear I have been too easy with her. It's time she was brought into line – you too, Amy. I cannot have the pair of you running round telling silly tales, now can I?'

'Mary could have you put behind bars,' I said. 'You are an evil man, Mr Maitland. I think it's time you were punished. You have got away with things for too long.'

'And what do you intend to do about it?' His voice was quietly menacing. 'Foolish girl! I admired you, Amy. I would have been good to you. It is so stupid to defy me. Mary thought she could defy me. She thought she could marry her cousin against my wishes, but I think she knows now that it is not wise to carry defiance too far.'

'What do you mean?' The coldness was spreading down my spine. 'I was told Paul's brakes had failed ... It was you! You did something to his car!'

'I was in France until a few hours ago, Amy,' he chided, a hateful smile on his lips. 'How could I possibly have done such a thing?'

'Someone did it for you,' I said. 'It's the way you always do things, isn't it? You paid someone to set fire to my father's shop thinking he was inside and then you had the man who did it killed, because you were afraid he might talk. And you paid someone to interfere with Paul's car because you wanted him dead. You are an evil, wicked man and I'm going to the police. I won't let you get away with this.'

I tried to go past him, determined that I would unmask him at last. Mary had proof of his crimes; if she knew that her father had ordered Paul murdered she would help me to put him behind bars where he belonged.

'You silly bitch,' he hissed as he caught my arm, swinging me round so that I had my back to him and his arm was about my waist. I could feel the heat of his breath, the steel of his grip. He was so strong! 'Do you think I shall let you bring me down? A chit of a girl like you? I've chewed up powerful men and spat them out, and you're less than a fly on the wall to me. I'll teach you to defy me. I'll have you crawling, begging me to spare you before I've finished – and it starts now.'

He gave my arm a twist that made me scream with pain and then he sent me flying forward so that I stumbled and almost fell. I whirled round to face him, clawing at his face with my nails as I fought to defend myself. He cried out as I drew blood and then he hit me across the face, sending me staggering backwards. I fell against a table and then to the floor on my knees. He bent down and pulled me roughly to my feet, then forced me to the settee. My legs gave way as he pushed me down on it.

I looked up at him as he stood over me breathing hard and I saw the lustful expression in his eyes. I knew instantly what he planned to do and I tried to jump up but he knocked me back, his hand chopping against my throat in a movement that winded me. I lay where I'd fallen, unable to move. I could see him unfastening the buttons of his trousers and I screamed long and loudly for help.

'There's no one to help, you silly bitch,' he muttered and then he was on me, clawing at my dress as he dragged it up over my face. There was to be no tender seduction, no kisses or lovemaking. This was meant to be a lesson, to teach me that I couldn't stand up to a man like him, to shame and humiliate me. I felt his hand between my legs, touching me, forcing my thighs apart and then the weight of his body, the heat of his swollen penis thrusting at me and I screamed again.

'Stop it! Stop it! I hate you!'

But I was helpless beneath him. He was far too strong for me and I knew that he was going to rape me in the most brutal way possible. There was nothing I could do.

'Oh, God, help me,' I prayed. 'Please help me.'

But even as I prayed I knew that it was hopeless. There was no one to help me. I was alone.

Eleven

'Get off her, you filthy pig, or I'll kill you!'

Mary! I had forgotten Mary upstairs in her room. Her words cut through my fear like a knife through butter, giving me the courage to fight back. I pushed against him, bringing my knee up sharply and he groaned, then rolled off me and sank to his knees on the floor next to the settee. I pulled my dress down and sat up, gasping as I saw Mary. She was standing a few feet away from us, pointing a small handgun at her father. He had seen it too, and was staring at her in fear.

'Get away from him, Amy,' she told me, her voice icy cold, her manner calm and controlled. She was no longer the hysterical girl who had been on the verge of collapse when I brought her home from the hospital. 'I'm going to kill him. He deserves to die for what he's done. He killed Paul and he tried to rape you. He isn't fit to live.'

I moved away from the settee quickly. Mary's father seemed to have recovered from his shock. He was fastening his trouser buttons, getting to his feet, a hateful smile on his mouth.

'Don't be foolish, Mary,' he said. 'You're upset. You don't know what you're talking about. Amy and I were just having a bit of fun – and Paul's accident was just that.'

'Don't lie to me,' she said, her face twisted with hatred. 'I heard everything you said to Amy. I was coming downstairs to find her and tell her I was ready to leave – and I heard you tell her what you had done to Paul.'

'Mary, listen to me...' He looked at her uneasily. 'You thought you heard something but you're wrong. Perhaps I was a little rough with Amy, but she deserved it. She tried to take Paul away from you – you told me you hated her. You told me you didn't want her as a friend any more.'

'That was a mistake,' Mary said. 'Amy is my only friend. She cares about me. You are the one I hate. I should have done this long ago, when you drove my mother to an early grave...' She lifted her arm, pointed her pistol at his chest and fired as I screamed for her to stop.

'Oh, Mary!' I stared at her in dismay as I watched her father crumple into a heap and fall backwards on to the floor. His eyes were wide open and staring – just as I'd seen him in my dream. 'What have you done?'

'What someone should have done years ago,' she said. 'He's dead, isn't he?'

'Yes, yes, I'm sure he is.' I could hardly bear to look at him, but I forced myself to do so. His eyes were staring at me accusingly, his expression one of horror mixed with disbelief. Mary was just standing there, apparently calm and uncaring. 'What have you done? You needn't have killed him!'

'He was hurting you the way he hurt my mother.' Her voice was flat, emotionless. I was revolted by her apparent indifference to what she had done.

'But don't you realize – it's murder. You murdered him!'

Suddenly the realization of what she had done hit her. I saw her expression change, saw the calm stripped away to be replaced by fear. Her hand trembled and the gun slipped from her fingers. She looked at me helplessly, all the arrogance and bravado gone.

'What shall I do, Amy? They'll hang me!'

It was true, they would hang her. She hadn't killed in self-defence but in cold blood – except that she was half out of her mind with grief. She hadn't really known what she was doing even though she had appeared to be in control. If they didn't hang her they would lock her away in a mental institution for the rest of her life.

My mind was working frantically. If Mary hadn't threatened him with the gun her father would have finished what he'd set out to do. What he *had* done to me was bad enough. I had suffered the humiliation but not the pain of rape. A part of me was sick to my stomach and wanted to give way to hysterics, to cry and scream and abandon all responsibility, but another, saner part of my mind had taken over, carrying me on as if I were somehow outside looking in. None of this was real. It was just part of a bad dream and soon I would wake up. But it wasn't a dream and I had to look after Mary, because it was obvious that she wasn't capable of doing anything for herself.

'No, they won't hang you,' I said. I was the calm one now. Mary was staring at me helplessly, her whole body shaking with fright. 'Not if I can help it.

I knelt down beside Philip Maitland and took the white handkerchief from his top pocket, then, holding it with the cloth, I picked up the gun and began to wrap it carefully.

'What are you doing?'

'I'm going to take this away and get rid of it.'

'It's his gun. I took it from his bedroom.'

'Throw a few cushions about, and knock a lamp to the floor. We have to make it look as if there has been a fight.'

Mary nodded, moving like an automaton to do as I said. She was almost like a wooden puppet on a string, obeying me with no will of her own. I knew that I was the only one who could get us out of this. Left to herself, Mary would just stand there until someone came and found her.

'You said you'd packed a bag?' She nodded, seeming lifeless, as if she didn't care. 'Good. We'll take it with us. You've got to get away from here. You haven't been back to this house since we left the hospital together. Don't forget that, Mary.'

'But someone may see us...'

'We'll just have to hope that they don't.'

'Why are you doing this for me? You'll be an accomplice.'

'I already am. Besides, what do you think it would do for my reputation if this got into the newspapers? Everyone would think I had brought it on myself. I should be branded a whore. They might even think we planned the whole thing together.'

'But where shall we go?'

'To my parents' house,' I said. 'My mother has never turned away anyone in trouble yet.'

'But they will hate me. I heard what he did to your family...'

'They hate your father, not you, Mary.'

I prayed I was right as I took hold of her arm and steered her from the room, but I couldn't think what else to do. I was barely holding myself together, fighting the panic that threatened to sweep over me.

We carried the small bag Mary had packed between us. She had wanted to telephone for a taxi but I wouldn't let her.

'You weren't here, remember? No one will notice us on the tube. Just try to act naturally.'

I had made her put on a dark coat and wear a scarf over her head. It was getting dark and there was rain in the air. Everyone seemed in a hurry to get home that night. There were people about but they scarcely glanced at us. Why should they?

Mary was too shocked to speak and I was nearly as bad. The gun was burning a hole in my pocket. I was tempted to throw it into some bushes as we made our way to the tube station, but I told myself not to panic. I wasn't sure why I had brought the gun away. Something at the back of my mind had warned me that it might be used against Mary if I had left it there.

I was trying not to think about what had happened in that room, to forget the horrible, humiliating experience of attempted rape. The fear and the shame were locked away somewhere at the back of my mind. They would come back to haunt me when I was alone, but Mary's future was more important. We had to make up a story that would satisfy the police if they asked questions.

It was just like a part of the nightmare that had haunted me for so long. My heart raced every time someone glanced our way and I was terrified that we would be denounced as murderers, but of course no one knew that we had left a dead man lying on the floor in Mary's house. I felt sick and frightened, my mind still reeling from all the shocks it had received that day.

What kind of a girl could kill her own father in cold blood?

Paul had told me she could be ruthless, and yet I could still find it in my heart to pity her and I thought I understood what had made her this way. She was an emotional, highly strung girl and for years this hatred of her father had been building inside her. Paul's death – and her father's part in it – had pushed her over the edge. I wasn't sure she was quite sane. She needed to see a doctor but I knew she would never agree.

I became more and more nervous as I approached my parents' home. What if they were angry because I'd brought Mary there? Supposing they refused to have her in the house?

My father was sitting in a wooden rocking chair by the fire when we went into the kitchen, and my mother was pouring tea into two cups. There was no sign of my brother.

'Amy! What's wrong?' my mother cried. 'Who is this young lady?'

'Where is Terry?'

'He has taken Margaret to the cinema.'

'Good – the less he knows for the moment the better.'

'Who is she?' my father asked. 'You had better tell us, Amy.'

'Mary Maitland. We met at the hospital. Her fiancé, Paul Ross, has been killed in a car accident. I couldn't leave her alone so I took her home...' I was removing my coat as I spoke. My mother gave a cry of alarm as she saw that my blouse was torn.

'What happened to you?'

'Mr Maitland tried to rape me while Mary was lying down in her room. But I'm all right...'

'Oh, Amy!' My mother had gone white with shock.

'I'll kill the bastard!'

I looked my father in the eyes. 'Mary has already done that, Dad. She heard me screaming. She took his gun from his bedroom and shot him. She was in time to save me from the worst of it.'

'Why have you brought her here?' my mother said.

'Bridget!' My father was on his feet. 'Sit here by the fire, lass. You look exhausted.' He helped Mary to his chair. She obeyed but didn't speak. She hadn't spoken once since we left her house.

'Joe...'

'Think about it, Bridget. Amy is involved. The police might think it was a plot between them, especially if Amy wasn't actually raped. At the very least she could have her picture flashed all over the papers and a lot of nasty things written about her.'

'Oh, no!' My mother stared at me in distress. 'Why did you go there? You said you wouldn't go to her house again.'

'Mary was in a terrible state after Paul died, Mum. She loved him. I couldn't let her go home alone to an empty house. Their housekeeper left them a week ago and the place was in a mess. Besides, she said her father was away. I didn't expect...' I shuddered. 'It was horrible, like something out of a nightmare. He was laughing at me – at you and Dad. He thought he was so clever. He wanted to use me against you. He was going to humiliate me and ... and ... he did. I feel so awful...'

Tears stung my eyes but I held them back.

'Leave Amy be, love,' my father said. 'She's not in much better state than this poor lass.'

Mary was staring straight ahead of her. I didn't think she was aware of what was going on. The shock of Paul's death, followed by what she had done seemed to have robbed her of her senses.

'Are you all right, Mary?' I knelt by her side and took her hand in mine but she stared straight through me. 'She hasn't spoken since we left her house, but I hadn't realized she was this bad until now.'

'It's shock,' my father said. 'She may come out of it but I can't say for sure. We ought to get a doctor to her.'

'Not yet,' my mother said, and I could see that she had recovered from her own shock. 'Leave her for a few days. Let's see what happens. We don't want her babbling away in some mental hospital.'

'Take her upstairs and put her to bed, Bridget. I want to talk to Amy.'

My mother smiled at Mary and held her hand. Mary clung to her. She was like a small trusting child as she allowed my mother to take her from the room.

'You're sure you're all right, Amy? That bastard didn't hurt you?'

'Not in the way you mean, Dad. Mary came in time – but I feel so dirty. I'm sorry if I've made trouble for you. I knew Lainie wouldn't have Mary there and I didn't know what to do.'

'You did the right thing, love. I'm your father and it's my place to look after you when you're in a spot of bother.'

'It's more than a spot of bother!'

'We'll get through it, love.'

'I brought the gun with me. I'm not sure why.'

'It's as well you did, Amy. They have what they call forensic tests these days and they might be able to use fingerprints to prove who fired the gun. That was quick thinking, Amy. Give it to me. I'll see to it for you.'

I handed over the gun and he slipped it into his jacket pocket. 'Not a word to your mother about this. She worries too much as it is.'

'We threw some cushions about, knocked a lamp over. I thought it looked as if there had been a fight.'

'Maitland was a crook. The police have suspected it for years. If we do this right they may think it was his past misdeeds catching up with him. God knows he deserved what he got, Amy. If Mary hadn't killed him I would have for what he tried to do to you.'

'Oh, Dad, don't talk like that. I didn't want anyone to kill him. Mum is right. I was a fool to go there but I couldn't think what to do when Mary was so upset. She said there was nowhere she could go and no one who cared about her.'

'You should have brought her here then,' my father said. 'But it's easy enough for me to say that now. You wouldn't have expected her to be welcome here, but you can't blame the lass for what her father did.'

'I don't know what she'll do, even if this all

blows over and she's in the clear. She has no one, Dad – no real friends, no relatives who would own her.'

'We'll think about that when we come to it. For the moment we have to get your story straight, Amy. I think you should tell the police that you came straight here after you left the hospital. We've been on our own all afternoon, no one will know any different. Besides, folk don't split on each other round here. The police can ask all they like, they won't hear a word about us from folk in the lanes. If we say you've been here all afternoon, then that's where you were.'

'Doesn't that make you and Mum accomplices to the crime or something?'

'Something like that,' he said and chuckled. 'You know my motto, Amy. In for a penny, in for a pound!'

'Oh, Dad...' A sob rose in my throat. He was such a good, dear man and he didn't deserve to have this trouble pushed on him. 'I shouldn't have come here.'

'Nonsense! There's still enough go left in me to sort this out, love. It will take me out of myself, stop me feeling like an invalid. I've got plenty of friends to help me out, including a cabby who will swear to the time he brought you here if need be. That gun never existed. It will be in tiny pieces before the police start to search for it. Don't you worry, Amy. All you have to do is phone your aunt, tell her you brought Mary here after you left the hospital, and that you'll go back to work when you feel up to it.'

'I should probably go in tomorrow, Dad. It might look odd if I didn't.'

'If you feel you can face it,' he agreed.

'I shan't feel any better if I don't.'

'Work is always a help. You mustn't feel ashamed, Amy. None of this was your fault. You did what you thought was right and got caught up in something that ought not to have concerned you.'

'He was so horrible...' I shuddered as the memory of Mr Maitland's hateful words and what he had tried to do to me came sweeping back. My father stood up, opening his arms to me. He held me as I sobbed against his shoulder, the tears I had held back breaking from me in a flood. 'He made me feel so dirty...'

'Shush, love. It's over.' My father stroked my hair with his big, gentle hands. 'He was a wicked man and you're not the first he's hurt. I know you feel shamed, but there's no need. He was to blame, not you.'

I moved away from the shelter of his embrace, wiping my face with the handkerchief he had given me. I knew that what he was saying was right, but the horror and humili ation was beginning to sink in. I had held my feelings in check for Mary's sake, but now that the immediate crisis was over they had come back to haunt me.

'I have to telephone Lainie,' I said and went out into the hall.

My aunt was horrified at the news.

'I'm sorry about Paul Ross, of course I am,' she said. 'It is a terrible tragedy and I know you liked him, Amy. But as for the rest...'

'I know you never trusted Mary, and I can understand why – but I liked her and she needed me. I could hardly leave her alone in that state, could I?'

'Surely she has someone to help her?'

'No, I don't think so.'

'What about her father?'

'They ... They don't have much to do with each other. I think he's too busy, away on business or something...' My voice trailed away as I lied. 'And she doesn't have many real friends, Lainie.'

'Well, I still think you're a fool, but it's up to you. When are you coming in again?'

'Tomorrow I should think. I'm just staying here for the night.'

'Well, that's a relief. We've been inundated with enquiries.'

'I'll see you tomorrow then.'

'Yes. Oh, I nearly forgot – there's a parcel here for you. It was delivered just after you went rushing off apparently.'

'I wasn't expecting anything. Unless it's some material or beads for my embroidery.'

'It feels quite heavy,' Lainie said. 'Mary isn't your responsibility, you know. You should send her home as soon as possible. That family is trouble, Amy. You don't know what you're dealing with.'

The tears had dried by the time I finished my phone call. Lainie's matter-of-fact tones had banished my feelings of self-pity and shame. They would come back to haunt me in the night, but for the moment they had gone.

'Mary is sleeping,' my mother said as she came down the stairs just as I replaced the receiver. 'She was exhausted, poor girl. Your father was right, Amy. I've carried my fear and hatred of Philip Maitland for a long time, but Mary isn't to blame for what he did – and in a way we owe her something. I'll be honest with you, I shall rest easier in my bed now that man is dead.' She crossed herself and looked guilty. 'Jesus! What a sinner I am, to be pleased by a man's death – but I can't be sorry for it, Amy. He deserved what he got and more.'

'That's what Dad said.' I went to put my arms about her and we hugged. 'I'm sorry for causing you so much trouble.'

'Sure, you know you're never a trouble to us, me darlin'. This will give your father something to think about, help him back on his feet again I shouldn't wonder.'

She was always at her most Irish when she

was distressed, and I knew she was worrying – for my father, for me and for Mary, too, because she always had looked after us all.

'It was a terrible thing to happen,' Margaret said when I saw her the next morning. 'No wonder Miss Maitland was so upset, her fiancé dying like that.'

'Her father was away and she was alone in the house, so I had to take her home with me. I couldn't leave her to cope alone like that, could I?'

'No, of course you couldn't,' Margaret said with a warm smile. 'I think it was kind of you, Amy, and just what I'd expect you to do.'

'She may be a bit of a cat sometimes,' Sally remarked, breaking off a cotton thread with her sharp white teeth. 'A lot of them rich girls are – but she's human same as the rest of us. You done the right thing, Amy, and don't you let no one tell you no different.'

Each time I told the lie it got easier. I thought that I would believe it myself in time.

Lainie hadn't been so easy on me.

'You look tired to death,' she said. 'Perhaps you should have stayed in bed instead of coming to work.'

'I would rather be here. I just didn't sleep very well, that's all.'

I had lain awake reliving the moments

when I had been crushed beneath the weight of Philip Maitland's body, feeling helpless as he thrust at me with his throbbing member and believing that there was nothing more I could do. What would have happened if Mary hadn't come? Perhaps I should have fought harder. Perhaps it was my fault that he tried to rape me ... Men didn't do that to decent girls, did they? Perhaps it was because of the dress I had worn to Mary's dance. He had thought I was easy...

My thoughts had tormented me half the night, and when I did eventually fall asleep I had soon woken again from the nightmare – a nightmare that had grown out of all proportion and now haunted me during the day as well.

A part of me wanted to shrink away into a dark corner and hide. I felt dirty, used and unworthy somehow. Yet I knew that I mustn't give way to my feelings of shame. I had to fight them or I would never be able to face life again. My mind wasn't properly on my work, even though I tried hard to concentrate when people were telling me what they wanted, and I jumped every time the doorbell went, expecting it to be the police.

What would they do when they discovered Mr Maitland's body? They were bound to want to find Mary, but she wasn't in a fit state to talk to them yet. I had gone in to see her before I left for work, but though she was awake and seemed to know me, she hadn't spoken a word.

'My parents say you can stay here until you feel better,' I'd told her. 'And then we'll help you decide what you want to do, Mary. You don't need to worry. Everything is being taken care of.'

She had looked at me blankly. I didn't know whether she'd heard or understood me, but when my mother brought her a cup of tea and some breakfast she had eaten a few mouthfuls of the bread and honey and drunk all her tea.

I bought a newspaper on the way to work, scanning it for any mention of Mr Maitland's death, but there wasn't even one line. So perhaps the body hadn't been found yet. It was possible that no one would go near the house. Their housekeeper had left them a week earlier – but I'd forgotten the dogs. The dogs had to be fed. I remembered that they had stopped howling just before I took a tray of tea up to Mary's room. Someone must have fed them – perhaps it was Mr Maitland himself.

We had left the tea tray there! Panic swept over me as I wondered if the police would think that was strange, but then I realized they wouldn't know when the tray had been left there. It could have been before Mary left the house to go to the hospital.

But what about those dogs? Supposing no

one fed them? Their howling was sure to bring someone to investigate – and it might be that Mr Maitland employed a man to go in and feed them.

My thoughts went round and round in confusion. I felt like a criminal, uneasy and on edge. Lainie looked at me oddly a few times that day, though she didn't say much until we closed the shop.

'Something is wrong with you, Amy. You've been like a cat on hot bricks all day.'

'I'm just anxious about Mary,' I said, not meeting her eyes. 'She has taken this badly. She was just lying there this morning, not speaking a word.'

'She'll get over it,' Lainie said. 'Have you opened your parcel yet?'

'I'd forgotten about it.'

'It's on the dressing table in your room.'

'Thanks. I'll go and have a look.'

It was an excuse to get away from her suspicious eyes. She knew that I was hiding something, but I didn't want to tell her the truth. She thought I was a fool for taking Mary home as it was.

The parcel was oblong in shape and quite heavy. I didn't recognize the handwriting, though I saw that it had been delivered by special messenger. It was unusual for the people I dealt with for my sewing materials to use a special messenger.

As the strings fell away I saw that the

parcel contained a wooden case. Taking it out, I was surprised at the beauty of the wood, which was highly polished and inlaid with what looked like silver. I opened the lid and discovered that it was an artist's box with various paints, chalks and pencils. Then I saw a small envelope in the wrappings. It must have been underneath the box.

Opening it, I read the brief message:

For a beautiful girl with the soul of an artist. Remember me when you use this.
I love you, Paul.

'Oh, Paul,' I whispered and I felt as if I had been punched in the stomach. 'Oh, Paul...'

All the anxiety over Mary, the horror of the rape and then the murder and the frantic journey to my parents' house had somehow blunted the grief I'd felt over Paul's death. Now it came back and I lay on the bed sobbing out my grief and my pain.

After a few minutes the door of my room opened and Lainie came in. She stood by the bed looking down at me for a moment, and then she sat down and held her arms out to me, holding me close as I went into them.

'Shush, love,' she said as she stroked my hair. 'You'll be better for a good cry. You've been holding it inside all day, haven't you?'

'Yes.' I wished that I could tell her everything, that Paul's death was only a part of my grief, but it was best that she didn't know just yet. Perhaps one day when this was all over. 'Yes, I shall be better for a good cry.'

In a way Paul's gift did help me. The storm of tears released some of my tension and the next day I was more able to concentrate on my work.

Terry came to see me at lunchtime the following day. He took me next door to the pub and bought me a sandwich and a ginger beer, and then gave me a straight look.

'Dad hasn't told me all of it,' he said. 'But I reckon I can fill in the bits that I don't know. I thought you ought to see this...' He handed me a newspaper, and at the bottom of the page there were two lines to say that a Mr Philip Maitland had been found shot dead at his home and that the police were looking for witnesses. 'Dad is going to wait another day or so then he'll go to the police and tell them Mary is staying with us.'

'Is Mary any different?'

'She got up this morning, but she hasn't said much. I don't know what happened, Amy, and maybe it's best I don't – but I'll help in any way I can.'

'Thank you,' I whispered. 'Please don't say anything to Margaret.'

'As if I would – but I think you ought to speak to Matthew.'

'Has he started to work for Dad yet?'

'Yes. He started yesterday, and he was asking after you, Amy. I think he wants to see you.'

'No! I don't want to see him – not yet.'

'You've fallen out with him, haven't you?' Terry frowned at me. 'He's very cut up over it, Amy. Don't you think you ought to see him and talk to him? I thought you wanted to marry the man?'

'I did ... I still might one day. I don't know. I'm not ready to see him yet, Terry. I can't...'

How could I face Matthew after what had happened? I felt so ashamed, unclean.

'Well, that's up to you, I suppose. Don't forget what I said. I'll help out in any way I can.'

'Yes, I know. Thank you.'

It was a relief to know that the police had found the body, but I wondered how long it would be before they came looking for me.

My father phoned me the next day and told me that he had been to see the police. He had told the sergeant he'd spoken to – a man he knew quite well – that Mary was staying with us because she'd been unwell after the tragic death of her fiancé.

'They asked when she came to us and I told them it was early afternoon, then I said that I had told Mary about her father's death and that she was in shock. They said they would need to question her at some future date, but to be honest, love, they didn't seem very interested in Mary. They did ask about your friendship with her, and they might want a statement, but they don't seem in any hurry.'

I wished in my heart that they would come and get it over with, and my guilt in the cover-up pricked at my conscience. But it was another three days before a rather young and subdued constable came to ask very politely if he could have a word with me.

'I'm sorry to trouble you, miss,' he said when I took him into Lainie's office. 'But it's a nasty business and we have to ask questions.'

'Yes, of course,' I said, feeling terrible. 'I'm not sure what happened. I read in the paper that—'

'Mr Maitland was shot in his home,' he finished for me. 'Yes, there wasn't much in the paper for a very good reason. We wanted it kept quiet – but I dare say it will all come out soon enough.'

'Do you know who...?'

'It's a gangland killing, miss,' he said, glancing over his shoulder. 'I shouldn't be telling you this – but I don't expect you know any gangsters.' He laughed and I smiled. 'A war over territory, we think. There was another similar killing a few weeks back.'

I swallowed hard. 'How could Mr Maitland be involved in something like that?'

'I can't tell you that bit, miss. I don't

suppose you would know about him or what he did. He kept it pretty quiet and I dare say his poor daughter hasn't the first idea – it's going to be a terrible shock to her when it all hits the papers. That was one of the reasons we held it back, so that she could be told first.'

'Mary isn't well. She's been in shock since her fiancé died.'

'That makes it even worse, poor lass.'

'She has no family to speak of, and few friends.'

'Then it's lucky your family took her in, miss – and a good thing you took her home with you when you did. If she'd been at her own home she might have been killed too.'

'Oh, no!' The colour drained from my face as I remembered what had happened. I saw Mary's face as she shot her father and felt the guilt strike me once more.

'Well, now don't upset yourself. It didn't happen and you can congratulate yourself for that, miss.' He closed his notebook and stood up. 'I shan't take up any more of your time. I'm sorry to have troubled you, and I hope you won't have nightmares over what I've told you.'

'No, I shan't.' I smiled at him. 'You've been so kind.'

He had asked me hardly any questions, giving out more information than he'd gained.

'Well, it wasn't likely that you'd know anything, was it, miss?'

'No. I'm sorry I couldn't be of more help to you.'

'Never expected you could, miss. Goodbye then.'

I shivered as he left, feeling that it was all a bit unreal. Had we got away with it so easily? But of course there was still Mary – how would she react when the police interviewed her?

I took the tube and went to see my parents that evening after work. Mary was sitting in the kitchen drinking a cup of tea. She looked up as I went in and smiled at me.

'Hello, Amy,' she said. 'It was good of you to come and see me.'

I glanced at my mother, who shook her head and indicated that I should go through to the parlour.

'I'll be back in a moment, Mary love. I'm just going to do something for Amy.'

'She isn't quite right in the head,' my mother said as she joined me. 'She seems to understand what I tell her, and she's as good as gold, no trouble at all – but she doesn't know what's going on and she doesn't remember anything. The police inspector who questioned her said that in his opinion she ought to be in a mental home. He thinks she's had a nervous breakdown brought on by the death of her fiancé, and he advised us to seek medical help. I've had our doctor to her a couple of times, but he says there's nothing he can do. He thinks she might come out of it in time, but he says there's a place she can go for tests and treatment. Your father said I should ask you before we decide.'

'Do you mind having her here, Mum?'

'I told you, she's no trouble – but don't expect her to talk to you much. She will ask for what she wants now, and she says thank you when I do anything for her, but that's about it.'

'She isn't just pretending not to remember?'

'No, I don't think so and neither does your father.'

'Where is Dad?'

'He went out with Matthew somewhere. He seems back to his old self now, but he's promised he won't do so much, and he won't have to now that Matthew has taken so much of the load from his shoulders. That young man of yours is a marvel, Amy.'

'He ... He isn't my young man any more, Mum. I should have told you – we've postponed the wedding.'

'I did think he seemed a bit glum when I mentioned you. Why did you fall out with him?' My mother frowned. 'It wasn't over what happened the other day? You're not being silly, are you?'

'It happened before that,' I said and then felt my cheeks go hot. 'But it has made me feel dirty, Mum. How could I marry anyone after that?'

'Now that's nonsense, Amy Robinson. Nothing so very terrible happened – nothing that *my* daughter can't cope with, I hope.'

'Oh, Mum...' I laughed as she had intended. 'It does make me feel ashamed when I think about it, but it isn't just that. I'm not sure if I want to get married yet. I like working for Lainie, and I'm so busy with my designs and my embroidery.'

'Talk to Matthew then,' she said. 'Explain how you feel and ask him to be patient for a while if that's what you really want. Don't lose him, Amy. There are good men and bad – and that one is a treasure. You should be catching hold of him with both hands.'

'Perhaps ... if he was willing to wait.'

'Well, I've told you what I think and I shan't lecture you. It's your decision now, my love.'

'I'll think about it,' I said. 'But for the moment we have to decide what to do about Mary. The police think her father's murder was a gangland affair. I should imagine they will be investigating his business very thoroughly now. I don't know how she stands concerning his money.'

'Your father says most of it will be tied up

in legitimate stuff they can't touch, which means she won't be short of money. There will be sufficient to pay for her stay at this place I've told you about. It's privately run and the patients are tended by nursing nuns, so I've been told. I understand it is in the country and very peaceful. It isn't an institution, Amy – just a pleasant home for people who have been damaged by life.'

'Give her a little longer with you,' I said. 'And then we'll decide.'

'Yes, that's what I thought you would say, love.' My mother smiled at me. 'Now come and talk to her again. She might respond to you more than she does to us.'

'Perhaps,' I said. But in my heart I knew that the only person she would truly respond to was dead. Paul was all Mary had ever wanted and without him she had simply lost the will to live.

I sat by her side in the kitchen and talked to her for more than an hour. I told her about all the dresses I was designing, and that Jane Adams had been into the shop and asked after her.

'Millie is getting engaged soon,' I said. 'If you're well enough, Mary, I'm sure she would invite you to her party.'

Mary stared at me without a flicker of interest. I saw that nothing I could say would rouse her, and in the end I bent to kiss her cheek and left her there.

Unless there was a change in her soon we would have no choice but to send her to the nuns.

'Do you think it's too casual for me?' Lainie asked, turning so that she could see the back of the new winter costume she was trying on. We were alone in the shop and she was getting ready to go down to visit Harold the next day. She had finally agreed to stay with him for a few days and help him decide whether to sell or keep his inherited property. 'I normally wear a more tailored style.'

'I think it looks lovely on you,' I told her. 'But don't let me persuade you if you're not sure. There was a waisted suit in your size, it came in this morning.'

'It's grey, isn't it?' She frowned as I nodded. 'I don't really want grey. I like this blue – as long as I don't look like mutton dressed up as lamb.'

'Everyone will be wearing this style before long,' I told her. 'I am sure Harold will think you lovely. Besides, he won't care what you wear as long as you are with him.'

'It isn't too young?' She laughed as I pulled a face. 'I feel almost like a girl again ... Excited and happy.'

'Well, why shouldn't you? I think it's time you had some happiness – and you really do look lovely, Lainie.'

'No wonder we've been so busy since you

came, Amy. If you are this persuasive with all the customers I'm not surprised they buy more than they intended.'

'But you aren't a customer and I really do think it suits you.'

'Yes, it does,' she said. 'I shall take your advice and wear it this weekend.' She smiled and looked oddly nervous, unlike herself. 'Wish me luck?'

'Of course I do – but you don't need it. Harold loves you. He's only waiting for you to name the day.'

'If I do decide to marry him, will you design a wedding dress for me? I want something suitable for a woman of my age, nothing like the young girls wear, just elegant and easy to wear.'

'You know I shall – and I shall want to be your maid of honour.'

Lainie looked at me, the smile fading from her eyes.

'Are you going to be all right here on your own?'

'Yes, of course I am.'

My mother had wanted me to stay with them while Lainie was away, but I had insisted that I would be perfectly safe at the flat.

'You are all right now, aren't you, Amy?'

I turned away from the anxious look in Lainie's eyes as I answered that I was fine. It wasn't strictly true. I had stopped worrying about imminent exposure and arrest by the police, but I was still haunted by what had happened that afternoon. Perhaps if I had done something differently, Mary's father wouldn't have tried to rape me – and then she wouldn't have killed him. And perhaps she wouldn't be the way she was now.

I woke with a start from the nightmare, lying shivering and afraid for some minutes before I could pull myself together enough to get up and make a cup of cocoa.

It had been horrible, but it was just a dream, something I must learn to live with or conquer. I couldn't go back to sleep after that, so I went to the desk in the living room and got out my folder of designs.

A new idea was forming in my mind. I drew a blank sheet of paper towards me and began to sketch in the outline of a new dress – not the kind of thing I had designed for Mary, but a very sophisticated, expensive dress that one of my new clients might like.

As it began to take shape on the paper, the horror of the nightmare receded into the background. Work was my salvation. It was what I needed, the only thing that could drive away my fear and my shame.

I was reading the newspaper when Lainie came in that Sunday evening. I laid it down, looking at her expectantly.

'Anything interesting in the paper?' she asked.

'Oh the usual – inflation in Germany and some trouble with that man Hitler again. I think they've arrested him.'

'Oh, I don't like the look of him,' Lainie said. 'Harold is sure he will cause a lot of trouble before he's finished. He thinks there will be another war if we're not careful.'

'Oh, I do hope he is wrong!' I cried. 'Surely we couldn't go to war with Germany ever again?'

'Harold says we should keep them under. If they get on their feet again, they will be back for more.'

'So what else did Harold say?' I asked. 'What is his house like? And have you made up your mind about whether you are going to marry him or not?'

'I think I decided on that months ago,' she said. 'It was just a question of time.'

'So...?'

'I've told him I'll marry him after Christmas.'

'Oh, Lainie, that's wonderful news!' I jumped up and hugged her. 'I am so very pleased for you.'

'Yes, I'm pleased now,' Lainie said. 'It took me a while, but now I'm looking forward to the whole thing.'

'Wait until I tell Mum. She will be over the moon – unless you want to tell her yourself?'

'I'll let you do that, Amy.' She smiled at me. 'I've told Harold he should sell the house he inherited. It's very big and far too grand for me. He thought I might like it, but I prefer his own. It has four bedrooms – plenty of room for guests. You will come and visit us sometimes, Amy?'

'Just try stopping me.'

'Do you think Bridget might come now and then?'

'You know how difficult it is to get my mother away from her own house, but I think she might be persuaded now and then.'

The telephone rang then and I went to answer it.

'Oh, hello, Millie,' I said, a little surprised. 'No. No, I haven't seen Jane – why?'

'She was asking if Mary was any better. I told her I would ask you.'

'I saw her this morning, and she's about the same.'

'Oh dear. Well, give her my love when you see her next time – and I'll be in on Wednesday for my fitting.'

'Yes. I think your dress will be ready by then.'

I replaced the receiver and went out to the kitchen where Lainie was boiling the kettle.

'Is that girl still with your mother?' she asked and frowned. 'Don't you think it's time you did something about her?'

'Yes, I suppose it is,' I agreed. 'My mother said she would see how she was this week, and then she would have the doctor to her again.'

'In my opinion she should have sent her away at the start. That sort always takes advantage. Give her an inch and she will take a mile.'

'I don't think Mary even knows where she is most of the time, Lainie. Besides, she doesn't have anyone but us.'

Several weeks passed and Mary improved a little, but she was still listless – unable to concentrate or have a proper conversation. I sat with her one Sunday afternoon and told her about the place my mother had been recommended.

'It's very nice there, Mary,' I said. 'You will have a garden to walk in and people to look after you. If you agree to go there the doctors will make you well again.'

For a moment she looked directly at me. 'Will you come and visit me there, Amy?'

'Yes, of course. I shall always be your friend now, Mary.'

She smiled at me. 'It sounds nice,' she said. 'Will you and Paul take me there?'

'Terry and I will take you,' I said. It wasn't the first time she had spoken of Paul as being alive, and I believed that she was blocking out his death because she couldn't bear to remember. Perhaps that was why she was also blocking everything else. 'And I promise I shall visit you sometimes.'

'I should go then,' she said and for a moment I saw perfect understanding in her eyes. 'I can't stay here forever.'

'No, you can't. It wouldn't be fair to anyone, Mary.'

'When shall you take me?'

'One day next week, as soon as it can be arranged.'

'Good.' She smiled and then stared blankly into space. I knew that she had gone back into her own little world, a place where there was no pain and no regret. I was sad and yet I felt that perhaps it was better this way. At least she was not forced to face the pain.

I was unable to forget either my own grief over Paul's death or the humiliation of Mr Maitland's attempt to rape me. They came to haunt me at night when I lay sleepless, although the old nightmare seemed to have faded. It had been replaced by others.

The only time I could forget was when I was with other people, working and talking. I went out often with Margaret, who seemed to understand that I was hurting inside but made no attempt to pry into my private grief.

As yet I hadn't found the courage to see Matthew, though he had telephoned me once or twice asking if we could meet up.

* * *

It happened the afternoon Terry and I returned from taking Mary to her new home. We had gone early in the morning, and stopped for lunch on the way back.

'She seems to have settled in quite nicely,' Terry said. 'I had a chat to one of the doctors. He says that she could come out of it at any time.'

'Or stay like that for the rest of her life. I talked to him too, Terry. He told me that victims of trauma can often be like Mary, and he wasn't too hopeful in her case, because there is a history of mental instability in her family.'

'Did you know that her father's lawyers have been in touch with Dad? She is quite an heiress, you know. She will have a lot of money waiting for her in trust.'

'Money means nothing to Mary now. She wanted Paul too much, Terry. It was an obsessive love and without that she has nothing.'

'You cared about him too, didn't you?'

'Yes, but in a different way. Besides, I had already said goodbye to him. He was going to marry her, not me.'

'But you still don't want to marry Matthew?'

'Not yet. It isn't just because of Paul. He was a part of it. He made me see myself differently – but there are other things.'

'You ought to see Matthew.'
'I shall ... Soon.'
'I told him to come to the house this evening,' my brother said. 'If you don't want the poor chap you should put him out of his misery.'
'Yes, perhaps you are right,' I agreed.
Matthew arrived as I was drinking tea with my mother. She offered to pour him a cup but he shook his head.
'I thought we might go out for a drink or something, Amy.'
'Yes, why not?' I stood up and smiled at him. 'We'll take a walk down to the river and see how we feel, shall we?'
We walked in silence for a few minutes, and then Matthew caught my arm, turning me to face him. His action was slightly rough and it sent a shiver of fear through me.
'Please let go of me,' I said. 'You're hurting my arm.'
'I'm sorry. I didn't mean to upset you.' He looked at my face. 'You're not frightened of me, Amy? You don't think I would do anything to hurt you?'
'No, of course not. It was just the way you grabbed me. I'm sorry, Matt. I know you wouldn't hurt me but ... I couldn't help myself reacting the way I did.'
'Has something happened to you?' He looked at me intently and I saw the pain in his eyes. 'Or is it that you can't bear me to

touch you because of Paul Ross? I know you were in love with him.'

'It wasn't that kind of love,' I said. 'And it isn't because of Paul – it's something else.'

'You've found someone else?'

'No, of course not! If I married anyone it would be you, Matt – but at the moment I don't want to get married.'

'Because of your job? I've thought it over, Amy. You're very young to have children. I wouldn't mind if you wanted to concentrate on your job for a while. I know I said I didn't want you to work after we got married, but being apart from you has made me realize that I can't bear to lose you. If work is important to you...'

'It is, but it still isn't the reason I can't marry you.'

'Can't marry me, or don't want to?'

'For the moment I can't...' I raised my head, meeting his eyes. He deserved the truth, even though it would shame me to tell him 'Something happened, Matt. Don't ask me for details, because I can't tell you, but a man tried to rape me.'

'Someone tried...' His face went white with shock as he stared at me. 'Oh my God, I'm so sorry, Amy. So very sorry. No wonder you can't bear me near you. Forgive me.'

'I don't blame you, Matt,' I said. 'It's not you, it's me. I feel ashamed – dirty.'

'But you're not! Of course you're not! Tell

me who the bastard is who hurt you like this and I'll thrash him.'

'He's dead,' I said. 'Only my father and mother know apart from you, Matt. Even Terry hasn't been told everything, though he may have guessed.'

'It was him, wasn't it? Mary Maitland's father?' He studied my face as I nodded. There was no point in trying to hide it when he knew. 'The wicked bastard. I wish he was still around so that I could kick the guts out of him.'

'Please don't say such things,' I begged. 'I didn't want him dead. I just want to forget ... to forget it ever happened. And to do that I need time, Matt.'

'If I'm patient,' he said hoarsely, 'if I promise not to ask again until you're ready, can I be your friend?'

'Yes, of course,' I said, tears slipping silently down my cheeks. 'I do care about you. I never stopped ... But for the moment I can't marry you.'

'Oh, Amy,' he said. 'I'd do anything if I could make it right.'

'I wish you could, but it haunts me,' I said. 'Perhaps one day it will go away but until then...'

'I'll wait,' he promised. 'I love you, Amy. I love you and I'll wait forever if need be.'

Twelve

'I just hope there won't be a strike,' Lainie said. 'Not in the middle of your show, Amy. After all your careful planning it would just be the end.'

'My show, as you call it, is weeks away,' I said and smiled at her. 'Don't worry so much. I'm sure all this talk of a general strike will blow over. After all, the miners have had strikes before.'

'But the mood is so bitter. Harold doesn't agree with you. He thinks we're in for a lot of trouble this time.'

'John thinks the same, actually. But he's promised he'll be out there driving buses or trams if need be.'

In the past year or so, John Fisher and I had become good friends. We had settled our differences at Lainie's wedding. Since then he had become a regular visitor. We went out together, sometimes as part of the crowd and sometimes as a couple.

John had introduced me to a lot of new friends, and my life could have been one social whirl if I hadn't been so busy with my work. I still saw Jane and Millie occasionally, and I'd made a lot of new friends of my own. Life was good for me, my time filled from morning till night. I suppose I was one of the Flappers, those bright young things that flitted through the twenties without a care. At least that was the image I seemed to have carved for myself.

'Is John driving you down to see Mary this weekend?'

'Yes. He offered to take me. He has been teaching me to drive and it will give me an opportunity to practise. Besides, he seems to like Mary. They spend a lot of time talking together and she always looks forward to his visits.'

'I do hope he isn't getting too interested in her.'

'He likes her as a friend. Mary has shown no sign of wanting to leave the nuns, Lainie. I don't think either of them has considered marriage, if that's what's worrying you.'

'It would worry me if I thought they had,' she admitted. 'I know you think I'm being unfair but she's still his daughter and with her family history – well, I would rather John wasn't too involved with her.'

'Don't you think it's time you forgot all that?'

'Have you?' She made a sound of disgust as I turned away to fiddle with a dress I had been displaying on a mannequin. 'No, don't try to put me off, Amy. Bridget was telling me that you're still refusing to even think of marriage. It's more than two and a half years since it happened.'

'Matthew doesn't mind waiting a bit longer.'

'But is it fair to him? You weren't raped, Amy. You just had an unpleasant experience. Believe me, what happened to you was nothing.'

'That's a bit harsh. You don't know how it made me feel. It was ages before I could get it out of mind. I felt so dirty.'

There had been other reasons for my state of mind, but I didn't remind Lainie. I believed my mother had told her that Mary had killed her own father, but Lainie had never mentioned it to me.

We were alone in the shop. Lainie had come up to town on one of her rare visits and we'd been discussing the small fashion show I had planned to put on in the shop at the end of May.

I wasn't important enough to put on a large show at a special venue as some of the top designers did, but I had a steady stream of customers wanting to buy my clothes and I'd planned a little show as a thank you to them. We had six girls in the workroom now. Margaret was head of the department. She and Terry had become engaged at Christmas but were not planning to marry for a year, which would give me plenty of time to replace her.

'Terry won't want me to work when we're married, and I'd like to have children fairly soon. But until then I want to continue helping build up the business,' she had confided shyly.

'Are you listening to me, Amy?' Lainie sounded impatient. 'Leave that dress and come into the office. I want to talk to you.'

I followed her inside. She took the bottle of good sherry we kept for special customers and poured us both a glass, drinking hers straight down.'

'Is something wrong, Lainie?'

'I've never told you all of my story. I've never told anyone but Bridget – and she told Joe when it became necessary. But I've decided you should know the whole truth. Perhaps I should have told you years ago.'

I sat down in silence. This had to be important.

'You knew that a man led me astray, and I expect you've realized that man was Philip Maitland. He promised me the Earth, Amy, and like a fool I believed him. I was promised to wed a good man but I wanted more than he could give me. I was going to work in a classy nightclub as a hostess and maybe become an actress. I had big dreams.'

'But he let you down and you had John. You told me you were bitter for a long time.'

'It wasn't because I had the baby.' Lainie took a deep breath then picked up the sherry glass I hadn't touched and drank the contents. 'Maitland seduced me but then he told me I had to pay for all the things he'd given me. I had to sleep with other men, men he owed favours to – rich old men who wanted a willing girl but not a prostitute.'

'Oh, Lainie! No!' I stared at her in dismay. I'd had no idea. 'What on earth did you do?'

'I refused. I was a fool but I wasn't a slut. He had me locked in a room and he set his apes on me. I was raped and beaten until I stopped trying to resist. After that there were so many men that I lost count. In the end one of them got careless and I escaped. I went back to Bridget and she took me in. I was pregnant and I'd lost my pride. I let myself go. I couldn't bear to be touched, even by my sister. I quarrelled with her and my mother. Ma died after our last row and I stole money from Bridget and ran away. I sank about as low as anyone can get.'

I sat in silence as Lainie finished, hardly able to think, let alone answer. To think that she had been through so much! It shocked me, filled me with pity.

'So you see, I do know how you felt after he tried to rape you. It was years before I could look myself in the face, but gradually I began to fight back. I found a good job and I went to night school to educate myself. I learned to speak properly and I learned to live again. I even learned to love.'

'You make me feel ashamed,' I said, my throat tight with emotion. 'I haven't suffered at all compared to what you went through. I don't know how you came back from all that. I think I should have wanted to just lie down and die.'

'I'm not saying it was easy,' Lainie said. 'I'm not saying that what Maitland did to you was nothing. I know it shocked and hurt you, but you have to put it behind you. Don't let what happened that night spoil your life, Amy. That way he wins.'

'I think I have,' I told her. 'It isn't just about what happened at Mary's house that night. There was Paul and the way I felt about him – and my work. I've been so wrapped up in my work I haven't had time to think about getting married.'

'But work isn't enough,' Lainie said. 'I know. I went down that road and it can be very lonely. My life has changed so much since I married Harold, and all for the better. I care for you, Amy. I just want you to be happy.'

'I am happy, but I suppose it is time I talked to Matt. We've fallen into a comfortable rut. We go out three or four times a month, and we talk on the telephone. He seems quite content with the way things are. I'm not even sure that he still wants to marry me.'

'Well, I've done what I can to make you see sense.' She shrugged her shoulders. 'Harold is waiting for me at the hotel. We're going to see Noel Coward's new play this evening. I'll leave you to finish your work.'

'Thank you for telling me your story, Lainie. I know it can't have been easy for you.'

'Bridget worries about you.' She smiled and kissed my cheek. 'Maybe we fuss too much. You're young, beautiful and becoming famous. Who are we to tell you how to live your life?'

'I shall talk to Matt when I see him. You know that he went up to Manchester for a couple of weeks?' She nodded. 'He wants to open a new branch of the business there and he was interviewing possible managers. I'm not the only one who works all the time. He has less time to spare than I do.'

'Has it occurred to you that Matthew works so hard because he is lonely? He loves you, Amy. If you don't want him you should let him go.'

I let my aunt out of the shop but I didn't answer her. I felt vaguely guilty about Matthew and I knew I should make up my mind one way or the other. I couldn't expect him to wait forever.

After Lainie had gone I finished my work then went upstairs to the flat, switching on the wireless. The news was not good. It sounded as though the strike might be happening soon. The TUC was talking about solidarity with the miners, which meant the country could soon be brought to a standstill.

Somehow the flat seemed empty that evening. I was aware of feeling lonely, of wishing that I had arranged to go out with friends. My plans had been to work on some sketches for a new range of afternoon dresses for the autumn, and an evening dress I had been asked for by a customer for a special occasion.

I did less of the embroidery myself these days. Sally's cousin had proved invaluable, bringing in other girls with the skills I needed.

Everything had gone so well, my list of clients expanding so rapidly, that I had thrown myself into my work. The past two and a half years had flown by and I'd thought I was happy enough, my nightmares coming less and less frequently. When I thought about it, I hadn't had one for months.

Lainie's story had shocked me, woken me out of complacency, and made me aware that I was luckier than I had realized.

I still cared for Matthew, but recently I had taken him for granted. He was there when I wanted him, a loving, caring friend who asked for nothing but a little of my time. That wasn't fair to him, and perhaps I ought to make a decision before it was too late.

I reached for the telephone, asking the operator for the number of the hotel where Matthew was staying.

'May I help you, madam?' the receptionist asked when I was put through.

'I should like to speak to Mr Matthew Corder please. His room number is one hundred and fifteen, I think.'

'Oh yes, I know Mr Corder. I'm sorry, madam I saw him go out a moment ago with his friend. I believe they mentioned the theatre.'

'His friend? Are you sure you are thinking of the right person?'

'Oh yes, I know Mr Corder well. He always has a nice smile and a friendly word, and he was with such a nice lady.'

'I see. Thank you.'

'Can I take a message for you?'

'No, thank you. It wasn't important.'

I replaced the receiver feeling cold all over. Matthew had gone to the theatre with a female friend. Perhaps I had already let things drift too long. Of course there was no reason why he shouldn't see other friends. I had a lot of friends that I saw without Matthew, so of course he must have too. I was foolish to feel so let down, so annoyed. He had every right to see other people. But I had thought we told each other things. I certainly told him whenever I'd been out with John or my other friends. He hadn't mentioned a lady in Manchester.

I walked into my bedroom and opened the wardrobe, lifting down the paint box that Paul had sent me as a parting gift. The fact that I'd received it the day after his death had given it extra significance and I had never been able to bring myself to use it. The paints were untouched, exactly as they were when he had sent it to me.

I stroked the top of the box with reverent fingers, then replaced it on the shelf. Paul was dead and life went on. My feelings of grief had long since dulled, leaving only a faint sadness when I thought of his wasted life.

My feelings for Paul were something I would never be able to explain – perhaps a part of finding myself, of discovering the woman who had been waiting to emerge. I had thrown myself into my work to forget all the pain and trauma of his death and what happened afterwards. Now I had to find the courage to move on.

John drove me down to see Mary that weekend. I took her some Fox's Glacier Mints, which were her favourite sweets, and some fruit. John took her a magazine and a box of Fry's chocolates. We went for a walk in the garden before tea, and they walked ahead of me most of the time, their arms linked. I thought Mary looked happy when we left her after tea.

On the way home I asked John if he had any thoughts of marrying her if she ever felt like leaving her refuge.

'I do love her,' he told me. 'She is so gentle and good, but marriage is out of the question. Mary wants to stay where she feels safe. She loves the nuns and they are so good to her, bringing her back almost to what she must have been before her illness. I think she may decide to become one of them one day.'

'Do you think she might? You didn't know her before she was ill, John. She is much softer now – nicer really. I know she seems very happy these days, but I thought it might be because of you.'

'No. We're friends, nothing more. Mary understands that.' He glanced at me and then back at the road, a little nerve flicking in his throat. 'You don't know, do you?'

'Know what?' I looked at him curiously.

John drew into a lay-by, stopped the car and turned to look at me.

'I haven't said anything because I didn't think you were interested, but you're the one I want to marry, Amy. I've been in love with you for ages. You probably don't know this, but I went into your room before we even met and I touched things on your dressing table – some little pots. The room smelled of you, and it was so gorgeous that I couldn't wait to meet you. I know you didn't like me at first, but we've become friends now, haven't we?'

'Oh, John. Of course we're friends,' I said, feeling tears sting my eyes. I had thought such dreadful things about him at the start. I was glad that he had never known. 'I'm so sorry. I had no idea how you felt.'

'I know. And I know you're not in love with me. It doesn't matter. I just want to be around you sometimes, to be your friend. I wouldn't have said anything, but you asked ... So now you know.'

'I'm not sure what to say.'

'Don't say anything. I know I'm not the one.'

He started the car again and edged out into the road, which was free of traffic. The country lanes were often like this and we sometimes didn't pass anything but a farm cart for miles. We wouldn't hit any real traffic until we went through a town.

I was silent as he drove on. His announcement had shocked me and made me feel guilty. Was I so wrapped up in my work that I had stopped noticing the people around me? I should have realized how John felt. I had been using him just as I used Matthew and it wasn't fair.

The first general strike in history was now official. A state of emergency had been called after talks broke down between the TUC and the government when printers at the *Daily Mail* refused to print a leading article entitled 'FOR KING AND COUNTRY'. The country had been divided into areas run by Civil Commissioners as talk of a long struggle threw fear into the hearts of many. In south Wales, Yorkshire and Scotland the troops were called out, and there was talk of violence being used to break the strike.

London was in turmoil. The buses, some trains and lorries carrying essential foodstuffs were kept going by concerned citizens who felt it their duty to keep the country from grinding to a halt. From the first, men and women had queued to sign up as special volunteers to move essential supplies. Undergraduates, stockbrokers and barristers took the places of the workers, driving steam trains and lorries, and usually thought it a jolly lark to be doing such a vastly different job from their own.

'It's all such fun,' Jane told me when she came into the shop a few days into the strike. 'We've got a canteen going for the heroes who are keeping us afloat, Amy. I've been organizing it all, ordering the food and getting people together. We could do with some volunteers to help out in the evenings. I don't suppose you would like to come and help?'

'Yes, I could do that,' I told her. 'My cousin John has been manning food lorries with some others from his office. I know he's working all hours, and he says that everyone is exhausted. The least I can do is serve at tables or something.'

'Oh, that's wonderful,' she said. 'A pretty face like yours always cheers people up ... But now to what I really came in for. I'm putting on weight and I need some of my dresses letting out at the waist. Do you think you could do that for me, Amy?'

'Yes, of course,' I said. 'Bring them in one or two at a time and Margaret will tell you if we can alter them successfully or not.'

She gave me a card with an address written on the back.

'Come at about seven if you can, Amy. Most of our volunteers want to leave before then, because they have to get home to their husbands and families. That's why I thought of you, because you don't absolutely *have* to do anything in the evenings, do you?'

'No. No, I don't,' I agreed ruefully, thinking of the designs I had planned to work on that evening. 'Nothing that can't keep for a while anyway.'

I was thoughtful during the day. First Lainie, and now Jane was telling me that my life was meaningless and empty. They were beginning to get to me, and I had been tempted to telephone Matthew again, but I was no longer sure that he would want to hear from me.

I dressed in a simple dark coat and dress that I thought suitable for serving at the canteen that evening. It was impossible to catch a bus and the taxis all had passengers, so I had to walk to the address Jane had given me, which fortunately took no more than half an hour.

She looked at me as I entered, glancing at her watch.

'You're a bit late, Amy.'

'I had to walk. I didn't realize the taxis were all so busy.'

'Well, of course. Your trouble is that you don't live in the real world. All you do is make those gorgeous dresses of yours and go to parties. I don't suppose you've realized how terribly busy we all are trying to keep London from grinding to a standstill.'

I thought it was a bit rich of Jane, who probably hadn't done a day's work in her life before this, but I didn't say anything, I merely listened to her instructions before I started to serve at tables. It was obvious that Jane was enjoying herself and liked her new sense of importance.

Some of the younger men joked with me as I served them their tea and hot food. One caught my hand and turned it up to look at the palms.

'It's a shame to spoil such lovely hands,' he said with a cheeky grin. 'Don't you let them make you help with the washing-up, sweet-heart.'

'I'll try to get out of that,' I said and smiled.

John came in at about half past eleven. He saw me at once and his face lit up.

'Amy, I didn't know you were here.'

'It's my first time. I've been here since about a quarter to eight. I'm due to leave in half an hour when we close. I don't think there's much left in the way of food – perhaps a cheese roll?'

'A cup of tea is all I need. I'll hang on and take you home when you've finished,' he said. 'I don't like you being out this late at night. We had a bit of trouble earlier in the evening. There was a fight and some of the men were hurt. I was at the hospital with one young lad, that's why I'm so late.'

'It's nice for me that you were. I had to walk here and I wasn't looking forward to the walk home.'

'I've got my car. I almost went straight home, but then I was passing and I thought I would call in and see how things were going. This place has been a godsend to the lads. Meeting up here helps to keep them going.'

I smiled and went to fetch John his tea and the last remaining cheese roll. He drank the tea but left the roll, which had become a little stale.

'I don't think I fancy that,' he said. 'I'll get something at home.'

'I could make you an omelette if you like. I'm not a very good cook, John, but I can make simple things.'

'That's more than I can,' he said. 'My landlady usually cooks supper for me but I told her not to bother this evening. But you won't want to go to all that trouble, Amy.'

'After what you've been doing?' I glanced at the empty tables. 'I'll just tell the others. I think we could close up now. I doubt we shall see any more customers this evening.'

John smiled and I went to get my coat as a sleepy woman emerged from the kitchen to lock the front door.

It felt pleasant when we went out, though the streets seemed quite eerie without the usual traffic and the lights were out in many of the shop windows because of the need to conserve energy.

'I'm glad I didn't have to walk home this evening.'

'Yes, it wouldn't have been nice for you,' John said. 'If you're going to work late again, Amy, I'll make it a habit to come and pick you up.'

'Then I insist that you let me make you some supper.'

'If you really don't mind. It's ages since I

ate anything.'

'I always mean what I say.'

John followed me into the kitchen as I went to make his omelette. I had just placed it on the table when the telephone rang. I was surprised, but went to answer it, my heart beating fast. I hoped it wasn't bad news. My father had seemed well the last time I visited, but why was someone calling me at this hour?

'Amy?' Matthew's voice came over the line. 'You're there now, then. I came round earlier and you weren't in, and I've rung you several times since. I was a bit worried. I know there has been some trouble on the streets.'

'Yes, John told me about it. He has been driving food lorries and he says there was a fight. He went to hospital with a young lad earlier.'

John called out something to me, and I answered him.

'I'm sorry. John asked me where to find the salt. I've just cooked him an omelette.

'Is he with you? At this hour?'

'Yes. He came into the canteen where I was working and brought me home. He hadn't eaten for ages so I made him something.'

'I see. It seems that I was worrying for nothing then. I won't keep you, since you have company, Amy – but perhaps I could see you one evening soon?'

'I'm going to be working for a few nights,

Matthew.'

'In that case, forget it.'

The receiver was hung up abruptly. I stared at it, surprised. I couldn't recall the last time Matthew had lost his temper with me. We had quarrelled often when we were courting, but since we'd decided to be friends he had never raised his voice to me in anger.

'Some bother?' John asked as I went back into the kitchen.

'No, nothing really. Matthew was in a bit of a mood.' John had finished his omelette and was about to put the plate in the washing-up bowl.

'Leave that,' I told him. 'You must be exhausted.'

'Perhaps Matthew didn't like the idea of my being here. I shouldn't have come.'

'Don't be silly. You're my cousin and my friend, and I decide what I do with my life, not Matthew.'

'He's very much in love with you.' John yawned. 'I'd better go. I've got to be on duty at six tomorrow.'

'Why don't you stay here? You can sleep in Lainie's room.'

'People would talk, Amy. It's not fair to you.'

'This is 1926, not the Victorian era. You look worn out. Besides, who is going to know? You will be gone before six.'

He was almost falling asleep on his feet. I took his arm and steered him towards the spare bedroom.

'If you're sure. I'll try not to wake you in the morning.'

'You won't. I'm up by soon after six most mornings. Goodnight, John.'

We parted and I went to my own room, falling asleep almost as soon as my head touched the pillow.

I worked every night for nearly a week at the canteen and John came to take me home in his car. I was grateful for the lift but after that first night he refused to come in.

'Someone might notice,' he said. 'I don't want you to lose your reputation for my sake. I'll get off home.'

Then, quite suddenly, the strike began to break down. The TUC had realized that solidarity with the miners was costing them dearly, and the government was determined that they would not be beaten on this issue. The union called its workers back, leaving the miners to struggle alone.

'I'm rather disappointed,' Jane said when she came into the shop to tell me that they were closing down the canteen. 'It was good fun. But we shan't need you this evening, Amy. I shall be writing to all our volunteers to thank them on behalf of the committee, but I wanted to tell you myself.'

I thanked her for calling in, knowing that she had also come to collect a dress that Margaret had finished altering for her. I was glad that the strike was over. Sally had told me that it was causing terrible hardship for the wives and mothers of the striking men.

'I can't imagine what them poor bloody miners' wives must be going through,' she said. 'It's all right for the men to dig their heels in, but the women 'ave to feed their kids just the same.'

Margaret agreed with her. 'We're having a bring and buy sale for the miners, Amy. It isn't that we agree with what they're doing, of course, but you can't let those little children go hungry.'

'I'll come, and I'll give you some things for the sale,' I promised. 'I'll go and fetch them now.'

I took Paul's painting box from my wardrobe and added it to the small pile of shoes, bags and bead jewellery that I had collected on the bed. It caused a tiny pang of regret to part with Paul's gift but I knew it was the right thing to do. I needed to move on and the money it fetched would help a good cause.

Margaret exclaimed over the box.

'This is far too good, Amy. It hasn't been used.'

'I want you to have it for the sale. I prefer to use my old one.'

'Well, if you're sure. We sometimes get quite good prices for our things, and I shan't let it go for nothing.'

I told her to sell it for whatever she could get and forgot about it. I had other things on my mind.

Matthew hadn't rung me since the evening I'd told him I would be busy for a few days. I had tried to telephone him but I'd had no answer.

I decided to telephone my mother that afternoon.

'Have you heard the news?' she asked. 'Thank goodness that dreadful strike is over, Amy.'

'Yes, it is good news.'

'I've been a bit worried about you working at that canteen every night.'

'It has been hard work and I'm tired. I think I shall have an early night. Then I really must get down to the last-minute details for my show.'

'Oh, yes, that's in ten days, isn't it?'

'Yes. Are you coming, Mum?'

'Of course I am. I wouldn't miss it for the world.' She hesitated, then said, 'Have you quarrelled with Matthew?'

'No. He was a bit moody last time he rang, but it wasn't a quarrel. I've been trying to reach him. Would you tell him I would like to see him, please, Mum?'

'Yes, of course I will, love. I'm glad you

haven't fallen out. He's such a help to your father. They're always planning something together these days. Are you coming to see us soon?'

'Perhaps this weekend. I've been too busy recently.'

'Good. I shan't keep you any longer then. Take care of yourself, Amy.'

I replaced the receiver and then went into the kitchen. Suddenly my usual supper of egg or cheese on toast wasn't very appealing, but I couldn't be bothered with anything more complicated just for me. I picked up an apple, munching it as I went through into the bathroom and turned on the taps.

An hour or so later I emerged from the warmth of the bath feeling refreshed. I pulled on a comfortable robe and wrapped a towel around my head. It was only then that I realized the doorbell was ringing. Groaning, I decided I had better answer it, since whoever was there seemed determined to keep on ringing until I did.

Running down the stairs, I fastened the chain my brother had insisted on installing for me before opening it a crack to see who was there.

'Matthew!' I cried in surprise. 'I'm sorry I was so long. I was in the bath.'

'Sorry. Bridget said you wanted to see me.'

'I did – I do.' I unfastened the chain. 'Come upstairs. You can wait in the sitting room while I get dressed. It won't take a minute.'

'I should've telephoned first.'

'It doesn't matter. You're not going to take advantage just because I'm improperly dressed, are you?'

Matthew didn't answer, his mouth set in a grim line. I hurried on ahead of him, towelling my hair and running a comb through it afterwards. I slipped on some pretty silk underwear and a simple dress. I was fastening the buttons at the front when I went back to join him.

'I haven't bothered with make-up and my hair must look a mess.'

'You always look lovely to me. These days I never see you unless you're dressed up like something from a fashion magazine.'

'I have to look smart. My customers expect it.'

'Oh, yes, keep the customers happy. They are the important ones. It doesn't matter what I think.'

'Matthew! Are you trying to quarrel with me?'

'I might be. Sometimes I feel like strangling you, Amy.'

'Matthew!' I was startled. 'What's wrong with you this evening? Is it because I cooked supper for John the other night?'

'Was that all it was – supper? His car was here all night. I saw it at five thirty in the morning when I passed by.' His eyes smouldered with resentment as he looked at me.

'He was exhausted. He slept in Lainie's room. There was nothing between us. There never could be. John is just a friend.'

'The way I'm just a friend?' he asked bitterly. 'Do you like to keep us dangling like bloody fools? Does it amuse you to see men suffer? Anyone can see that the poor devil is besotted with you.'

'John is fond of me, but he knows I feel only friendship for him and that is all he wants.'

'If you believe that you are blind or mad. John is in love with you. He hangs on in the hope that one day you will care enough about him to marry him.'

'Then I'm sorry, but I didn't ask him to fall in love with me. I can't help the way he feels. Besides, I don't see what John's feelings have to do with you, Matt.'

'Don't you? Then it's about time you started to look about you and take notice of what other people think and feel, instead of being wrapped up in yourself all the time. I'm tired of running every time you snap your fingers.'

'I don't snap my fingers!'

'I ask you if we can meet and you say you're too busy. Then you ring your mother and leave a message that you want to see me

– what else am I to think? You've got time on your hands so you send for me to amuse you, as if I'm a puppy dog.'

'That's not fair. It wasn't like that. I've tried to telephone you several times and there's never an answer. I thought that perhaps you were out with your new friend.'

'What new friend?' His eyes glinted with anger. 'I've no idea what you mean, Amy.'

'You went to the theatre with a lady when you were in Manchester.'

'Nonsense! You're the one who is always out. I do nothing but work.'

'The hotel receptionist told me she knew you and that you were talking about a visit to the theatre with a very nice lady.'

'She made a mistake...' He stared at me for a moment and then gave a harsh laugh. 'No, I did go somewhere with a friend, but it wasn't the theatre.'

'It doesn't much matter where you went. You weren't there when I phoned, and you've been out every time I've rung this past week.'

'John wasn't the only one to do voluntary work, Amy. I've been helping on the buses every night for a week and I'm tired.'

'Perhaps that's why you lost your temper with me.'

'No, I don't think so. It's time we sorted things out between us, Amy. I'm not prepared to go on like this any longer.'

'What do you mean?' My heart was beating so fast that I could scarcely breathe, and I did not dare to look at him.

'I mean I don't want to be your friend. It isn't enough. Either you want me or you don't. I've been patient. God knows it's been hard, but I've kept quiet because I knew you were hurt and I wanted to give you time to heal, but it's over. You have to let the past go and move on.'

'I have, Matt.' I moved away from him, turning away because I couldn't bear to face him. 'I did grieve for Paul but that's over now. I'm not sure what I felt for him but whatever it was it has gone.'

'And the other business ... with Maitland?'

I found the courage to turn and look at him. 'I've realized that I must just forget that night. In a way I was lucky. Nothing very terrible happened to me. But it was all mixed up with Paul, and what Mary did, and the nightmares.' A shudder ran through me. 'It took a long time to get it out of my mind, and at first the only way I could do that was to work. I worked all the time because I couldn't bear to think – and it just became a habit.'

'And you've been successful,' Matthew said. 'Everyone says you're going to keep rising in the fashion business. Don't think I want you to give all that up. I know you're not like Margaret. You wouldn't be happy just being a wife and mother. I know you need a career. I understand, but I have to know if I mean anything to you. I can't take this friendship stuff any more. I want you, Amy. I want to make love to you.'

'Oh, Matt...' I stared at him and then I began to cry. Not silent tears but noisy sobs that shook my whole body. 'Oh, Matt, I'm so sorry. I can't...'

'That's it then? That's my answer? You don't want me.'

He turned and walked out of the room. I was so stunned that I couldn't move immediately. By the time I managed to make myself function he was walking down the stairs, at the bottom before I'd even reached the top.

'Matt! Don't go!' I cried and took a hasty step forward, missing the top stair and stepping into air. I screamed and went tumbling forward. Matt came rushing towards me, catching me and breaking my fall, but as he fought to steady us both, my foot twisted underneath me and I screamed with pain.

'What's wrong?' He looked at my face, which I knew must be white with pain. 'Have you damaged yourself?'

'I think it's my ankle.'

'You silly little idiot! What did you think you were doing?'

'I wanted to stop you.'

'You could have broken your neck.'

'Stop quarrelling with me and help me back upstairs. I don't think I can make it alone.'

He glared at me, then stooped to pick me up, carrying me back to the sitting room and depositing me gently on the settee.

'I'd better have a look. If you've broken a bone you'll need to go to hospital.'

'I think it's just a sprain.' I touched his hand as he knelt down and began to examine my ankle very carefully. 'Don't be angry, Matt. I'm sorry I've been so awful to you.'

He stood up. 'I'll get some cold water and bathe it. I think it is just a nasty sprain.'

The cold water eased the worst of the stinging pain. I caught his hand again as he was about to gather up the bowl and cloths he had used.

'Please don't go, Matt.'

'I thought you wanted me to.' He frowned. 'You said you were sorry but you couldn't love me...'

'No! I was trying to apologize for being so selfish. It wasn't easy and you didn't give me a chance to finish.'

'No, I suppose I didn't.' He looked rueful. 'I've always been a bit impatient where you're concerned, and I was sure you were telling me you didn't love me. I've been dreading this for ages, but I had to know the truth, Amy. I love you so very much.'

'Oh, Matt...' I said shakily. 'I was trying to tell you that I do love you. I've always loved you, but I was too young when we were together the first time. Working for my aunt, meeting Mary and Paul – it made me realize that if I married too soon I would be missing so much that I needed to know about life and myself. But I never stopped loving you. Even when I felt so muddled and confused, I knew that I needed you in my life.'

'You haven't shown it much lately. And loving someone isn't the same as being in love.'

'Yes, of course, I know that,' I said, reaching for his hand and holding it tightly as he sat beside me on the edge of the settee. 'I am in love with you, Matt. There has never been anyone else for me in that way.'

'You were in love with Paul Ross.' His eyes were hard with accusation.'

'No. No, it wasn't like that. It might have been if he had been different – but he was such a sad person, Matt. I think it was sympathy I felt for him, and understanding. He was haunted by his fear of madness and he had lost what was most important to him in life. Something in me responded to his need – but even then I knew you were the one I wanted to marry one day.'

'You might have let me in on the secret, Amy.'

'After what happened at Mary's house ...

For a long time I felt dirty, Matt. I felt that I wasn't good enough for you, that I had spoiled what we had – made it shabby.'

'How could you have thought that? You knew I loved you.'

'I wasn't thinking at all for a long time,' I said. 'And then I wasn't sure that you cared any more. I thought that perhaps there might be someone else.'

'If you mean the lady in Manchester...' Matt chuckled softly. 'Beatrice is the wife of a good friend of mine. Her husband was taken ill that day, and they had rushed him straight to theatre to have an operation. I was taking her to the hospital to see him.'

'Oh, Matt!' I smiled at him in relief. 'What an idiot you must think me. Believing that you ... And then falling down the stairs...'

'It's good to know you're not the sophisticated, super-efficient woman I thought you had become,' he said with a wry grin. 'You always seem to be talking about your rich clients, and you fly over to Paris at the drop of a hat. I thought I wasn't exciting enough for you any more.'

'Oh, Matt! Now you're being an idiot. I've been to Paris twice. Besides, flying to Paris is about work – and clients are work, even if some of them do ask me to their parties. What I need is a life of my own – a husband and children to love me.'

'Won't children get in the way of your work?'

'I shan't be able to do as much, but I've been delegating most of the embroidery and fitting to the girls for a while now, and I've decided to look for someone to take my place in the shop. I would rather concentrate on my designing, which I can do just as well from home.'

'Are you sure that's what you want?' Matt looked at me anxiously. 'Don't do it for me, Amy.'

'I'm not going to give up entirely, but it has been in my mind for a while. I've had several enquiries from large stores that would like to use my designs in their ready to wear collections, and I may decide to go down that road.'

'What does Lainie think to all this?'

'I haven't told her yet,' I said. 'But why are we talking about work? I thought you said you wanted to make love to me...'

He smiled ruefully. 'I think that has to wait a little, don't you? I can hardly seduce you when you've just sprained your ankle, can I?'

'You could try,' I said, and smiled as he bent down to kiss me on the lips. 'Don't be such a gentleman, Matt. I want you to make love to me tonight.'

'I'm afraid you can't always have what you want, Amy. I've waited a long time for this and when it finally happens it's going to be perfect.' He frowned as I moved towards him impatiently and winced at the pain. 'See what I mean? There's no way I'm going to take you to bed when you're in such pain.'

'Then carry me there, and lie beside me,' I said. 'At least you can hold me and kiss me, the way you used to...'

'Yes, I could do that,' he said. 'And I think perhaps I'd better spend the night here. By morning that ankle may be so swollen that you won't be able to go down and open the shop.'

'People will talk, Matt,' I teased.

'Let them,' he said. 'If I have my way it won't be too long before I make an honest woman of you, Amy Robinson. Besides, there's no way I'm going to leave you alone when you're in pain.'

'Have I ever mentioned that you are incredibly bossy, Matthew Corder?'

'I think you may have done, but not for a long time.' He smiled as he bent down to lift me gently in his arms. 'I've missed you, Amy. Welcome back, my darling. It's good to have the girl I fell in love with back again.'

'She never really went away,' I said, putting my arms about his neck and kissing his ear. 'You may remember I used to be rather fond of getting my own way. And this is what I want.'

Thirteen

'It makes me wish I was getting married all over again,' Jane said as she congratulated me after my show. 'That wedding dress you ended the show with is divine, Amy. Will you be wearing it yourself?'

'No. Mine is much simpler. I designed it a long time ago, and Margaret is making it for me.'

'What shall we do when you hand over to the new people?' Millie asked plaintively. 'I'm going to miss you so much, Amy. It won't be the same without you.'

'It was Lainie's decision, not mine,' I said. 'Apparently she'd had an offer for the business on the table for months, but put off making her decision until I made up my mind to get married. But you'll still be able to buy my designs, Millie. I'm going to be working from home for one of the largest fashion designers in London, though I can't tell you any details just yet because we haven't finalized the contract. And I might come up with something personal for my favourite customers.'

'I do hope that means us,' Jane said instantly. 'I'm putting on so much weight these days, and the only person who knows how to disguise that is you, Amy.'

'Well, it will only be for special occasions,' I said. 'But I don't want to completely lose touch with my friends.'

Millie looked at me oddly. 'You still visit Mary, don't you?'

'Yes, at least once a month. She is very much better now, but I don't think she'll ever leave that place. The last time I saw her she was thinking of joining the religious order.'

'She must have changed so much,' Jane said. 'It doesn't sound like the Mary I knew at all.'

'She isn't the same, she never could be,' I said.

Neither Jane nor Millie could ever understand what had happened to Mary, and the reasons for the huge change in her. They knew about Paul, of course, but the rest of it would always remain a secret.

'Well, I must be leaving,' Jane said and looked round. 'Goodness, we're almost the last. Come along, Millie. I'm sure Amy wants to close the shop and clear up the mess we've all made.'

I saw them to the door, then put the bolt on and went upstairs to join my mother and Lainie, who had insisted on washing the last of the glasses.

'Have they all gone?' my mother asked. 'I thought those two would take root, so I did. Don't they have homes to go to?'

'They were telling me how much they would miss me.'

'You're not going to change your mind?' Lainie looked at me in alarm. 'Only I'm just about ready to sign the lease over to the new people.'

'Of course I shan't change my mind,' I said. 'It's my wedding next week. Everything is arranged.'

'Of course she won't change her mind,' my mother said. 'I think Matthew would have something to say about that.'

'Yes, and he can be very forceful,' I said, laughing at the memory of our last meeting. 'He's taking me out this evening to celebrate, and so if you don't mind...'

'She's telling us to go,' Lainie said and pulled a face at my mother.

'Yes, I think she is.'

'We'll let ourselves out,' Lainie said. 'I'm glad the show was such a success, Amy, and I'm sorry in a way that you've decided to give up just when everything was going so well – but I'm glad you're going to marry Matthew.'

'So am I,' I said. 'Don't forget, I shall be doing what I always wanted to do – concentrating on the designing. I might even have another show one day, but that won't be until my children are old enough to go to school.'

'What children?' My mother gave me an old-fashioned look.

'The children we're going to have when we're married,' I said. 'If you don't go I shan't be ready when Matt comes to pick me up.'

'We're on our way,' Lainie said and, taking my mother's arm, steered her to the stairs. I could hear them arguing good-naturedly as they left together.

I went to have a bath as soon as they'd gone. The show had overrun by more than an hour and if I didn't hurry I was going to be late. I was only just emerging from the bathroom in my comfortable old robe when I heard Matthew run up the stairs. He had his own key now, and came in carrying a bottle of champagne and a huge bunch of red roses.

'I thought you would be ready,' he said. 'But I suppose they all wanted to talk afterwards.'

'Something like that,' I said as I took the roses from him. 'Pop the champagne in the ice bucket, Matt, and we'll open it when we come back from dinner. I'll just put these in water and then I'll get dressed.'

He came to the kitchen to watch as I placed the roses in a crystal vase, then as I turned to leave he reached out and drew me into his arms, drawing me close and kissing me hungrily.

'Have I ever told you that you're beautiful?'

'Like this?'

'Especially like this,' he murmured huskily. 'I seem to recall that you gave me an invitation a few days ago, one I was forced to decline because your ankle was hurting. It looks fully recovered to me...'

'It is, perfectly,' I said as I slipped my arms up about his neck, tangling my fingers in the hair at the nape of his neck. 'I thought we were going out?'

'Later,' he said huskily. 'I've waited so long. I don't think I can wait for the wedding, Amy.'

'That's the nicest thing anyone has said to me today.' I lifted my face for his kiss. 'I wasn't very hungry anyway.'

Later, a long, long time later, when I lay nestled in his arms, content and pleased with the world, I sighed and Matt looked down at my face.

'Not regretting anything?'

'Do you need to ask?' I teased, trailing my fingers over his naked chest and down his navel. 'I think any doubts you might have had about my feelings for you should now be finally put to rest.'

'Yes, I think we can agree on that,' he said

and kissed my shoulder. 'So how does it feel to be an almost-married woman, Amy?'

'Quite nice,' I said. 'But it will be even better when we can do this every night.'

'You always were very demanding, Amy.' He smiled as he bent his head to kiss me lingeringly once more. 'I'm not sure about every single night...'

He laughed as I nipped his ear with my teeth.

'I'm hungry,' he announced, throwing back the covers. 'Get up and make my supper, woman – or, on second thoughts, stay there and I'll make something for you.'

'We'll do it together,' I said and got out of bed. 'That's the way it's going to be in future, Matt. Whatever we do, we'll do it together.'

A smile started deep down inside him, lighting up his eyes.

'I like the sound of that,' he said.